Life
After
Theft

APRILYNNE PIKE

Life After Theft

HARPER TEEN
An Imprint of HarperCollinsPublishers

HarperTeen is an imprint of HarperCollins Publishers.

Life After Theft
Copyright © 2013 by Aprilynne Pike
All rights reserved. Printed in the United States of America.
No part of this book may be used or reproduced in any manner
whatsoever without written permission except in the case of brief
quotations embodied in critical articles and reviews.
For information address HarperCollins Children's Books,
a division of HarperCollins Publishers,
10 East 53rd Street, New York, NY 10022.
www.epicreads.com
Library of Congress Cataloging-in-Publication Data is available.
ISBN 978-0-06-199900-0
Typography by Alicia Mikles
13 14 15 16 17 CG/RRDH 10 9 8 7 6 5 4 3 2 1

First Edition

To Miss Snark, who loved it first;

to Kara, who bugged me for two years to finish,

and to Bill Bernhardt, who showed me how.

One

I HATE THIS SCHOOL.

I tugged at the lame plaid tie that was about three millimeters away from suffocating me, and revised. *I hate this tie.* The whole uniform get-up—tie, buttoned shirt, slacks, *sweater-vest,* I kid you not—was worlds away from the baggy cargoes and T-shirt I'd worn to my old high school just last week.

I caught sight of the name tag the chubby advisor with too much lipstick had slapped onto my chest—*HI! MY NAME IS JEFF*—and changed my mind again. *I hate the name tag the most, the tie second, and I still hate this school.*

What started out as an idea my dad had six months ago to move us all from Phoenix to Cali had morphed into an exciting but unlikely adventure three months later, and then a nightmare when I literally came home from school and the *SOLD* sign was up on our house. Yeah, I agreed to it in the beginning, but how many of Dad's ideas *ever* came to fruition?

The big ones, I guess. Maybe I should have known better.

I tried to make the case that it was the middle of the school year and transferring credits was going to be a nightmare, but apparently private schools are more interested in bank-account numbers than GPAs.

I looked down at the piece of paper in my hand and then up at the rows of lockers. I was pretty sure my assigned locker was on this floor, but I must have taken a wrong turn out of the office. I backtracked, trying to stay out of the way of the stream of students, and finally found the right corner.

The first thing I saw was the pink bubble gum, four feet lower than it should have been, inches above the ground, framed by a set of perfectly painted lips.

It was one of those huge bubbles you just know is going to pop and cover the girl's face, and she'll shriek and yell and whine that her makeup is ruined, blah, blah, blah. But the bubble didn't pop—she did that thing where you suck all the air back into your mouth, and the bubble deflated into a little pink heap.

The girl and her bubble were lying on the floor.

In the middle of the hallway.

I tilted my head to get a better look at her legs. Maybe this school wasn't *all* bad.

A guy came tearing around the corner clutching a bright pink backpack that I had a sneaking suspicion was

2

not his. He pushed a few people out of his way, veering to the side and clipping me with his shoulder before I could move away.

"Watch it, jerk!" I muttered, not quite loud enough for anyone to hear.

Then I realized he was running straight at the girl on the floor. He was looking back over his shoulder, so there was no chance he would see her before he ran right over the top of her.

"Hey!" I yelled, pushing past a guy in front of me. I had to warn her. Or stop him.

But she just rolled her eyes and pulled her arm out of the way an instant before his Eckos pounded down right beside her head. "Look out, asshole," she said without flinching.

Jerk didn't even glance back.

I rushed forward. "You okay?"

She looked up at me with wide, surprised eyes. "Are you talking to me?"

Right. Any girl who could look that hot in a black skirt and plaid vest and had the guts to lie in the middle of the hallway was not going to tolerate being talked to by some brand-new nobody like me. "Forget it," I said, and turned to look for my assigned locker. Again.

"Wait!"

I stopped walking but didn't turn around.

"Were you talking to *me*?"

I turned and gave her my best I-don't-care-that-you're-rich-popular-and-gorgeous look. I admit: I haven't had much practice with it. "Yeah. And?"

She sat up. "You can see me?"

So *that* was a pretty weird conversation starter. Still, a hot girl was talking to me; I'm not one to question these things. "I sure can."

"What color is my skirt?"

What? "Black," I replied hesitantly, trying to figure out where she was going with this.

She sighed. "Stupid uniforms. What color are my eyes?"

I looked. She fluttered her lashes dramatically. Was this some kind of trick? "Blue?"

"Is that a question?"

"Your eyes are blue, okay?"

She stared at me for a long time in a way that made me want to look over my shoulder. She was ... impressed. And that certainly didn't make any sense. I had to be missing something. "You really can see me, can't you?" she said, sounding—of all stupid things—*awestruck*.

Our conversation had sailed straight past run-of-the-mill weird and docked in crazytown. Hot or not, I was ready to get away from this girl. "Yeeeeah, well," I said, looking down at my schedule, "it's been fun and all, but I have to—"

"Nobody else can see me," she said. The seriousness in

4

her voice was kind of freaking me out. "No one in this entire school, except you."

"Sorry, I didn't notice your invisibility cloak," I said, edging away. Was everyone in California this nuts? I could feel the crowd around me staring as they walked by, and despite the crazy coming out of her mouth, I had a feeling they weren't staring at Blond Girl. Fabulous. My chance to make a decent first impression in this school was swiftly and surely melting away.

"How many?" the girl said, holding up two fingers like rabbit ears, then changing her mind and switching to four.

"This is ridiculous." I was still trying to look cool—or, barring that, casual—but I was on the verge of exploding at her.

"Answer the question, freak."

Just my luck—it had taken a whole five minutes for the school nut job to latch on to me. Don't judge a book by its cover, I guess. Or a girl by her hotness. "*I'm* a freak? You're lying in the middle of the floor pretending to be invisible, and *I'm* a freak?"

She gasped. "It's really true! You *can* see me. This is the best day of my . . . well, more than a year, anyway. I thought this would never happen. But now you're here. You're here . . . um . . ." She glanced at my loser label. "Jeff." She scrunched up her nose. "Jeff? Ew." When I rolled my eyes she raised her hands in surrender. "I take it back. Jeff's fine. But can I call you Jeffrey at least? That is your whole name, right?"

"No."

"Can I call you that anyway?"

"No." *I gotta get out of here.* People were starting to seriously gawk.

"Fine, we'll work on the name later. We have so much to *do!*" And then, I kid you not, she started bouncing up and down on her toes.

"Stop!" *No, really, for the love of all that is holy, stop.* I held up both hands. "Who *are* you?"

I'm not sure what made me ask—a name to put on the restraining order, maybe?—but she gestured to herself like she was a celebrity I should recognize instantly. Maybe she was—this was Santa Monica, after all. "Kimberlee Schaffer? *The* Kimberlee Schaffer?"

I shrugged.

She sighed dramatically. "Come with me." I followed her down a hallway and into the main foyer, where she backed up against a wall and gave me a cheesy, toothy grimace—more sarcasm than smile. She gestured grandly to her left at an eleven-by-fourteen framed picture of herself.

"So . . . your parents paid for the school?" I asked. Maybe it was the only way they'd let this psycho in.

She rolled her eyes and pointed a long, fake fingernail at a small bronze plaque beneath the portrait.

I glanced at her, then back at the photo. "That's really funny." I made myself look her in the eyes, my best fake smile plastered into place. "You almost had me. Ha-ha. Joke on the new guy. That's really good. Now if you're finished, I have to go to class." *Preferably before everyone starts staring again.*

"Can I come?" she asked all chipper, like she hadn't just pulled the world's lamest joke on me. Pretending to be a dead girl—that was seriously messed up. And stupid.

I'm such a moron.

"No, it's *school*. You go to your class; I'll go to mine." I knew I should feel flattered that a hot girl wanted anything to do with me, but there's a saying about what you don't do with crazy people.

Ever.

She jumped in front of me. "Listen, *Jeff.*" She said my name like it was a bad word. "You don't get it. I'm dead. Ask anyone. I've been stuck for a year and a half and no one has been able to see or hear me except you."

"Look, your little trick worked, Kim. Isn't that—"

"Kimberlee."

"What?"

"Kimberlee. With two *e*'s. *No one* calls me Kim."

Unbelievable. "Forget it. Just leave me alone, okay?" I stepped around her and continued walking. Maybe I could blend in with the other sweater-vests all over the place and get away. Sadly, this wasn't my old, overcrowded public high school, and disappearing would take more work than I was used to despite the matching uniforms.

"Wait. Please?"

I didn't.

She trotted alongside me. "What class do you have?"

"Like I'm going to tell you."

"I'll help you find it."

"You'd like that, wouldn't you?" I stopped and turned to her. "Then you could get me totally lost and ditch me. A special welcome for the new guy. Just leave me alone!"

A tall brunette edged away from me like a first-grader who had just learned about boy cooties. "What a dork," she said, loud enough for everyone within ten feet to hear her.

"Really, Jeff," Kimberlee said, far too calmly. "You should stop yelling at me. People are going to think you're schizo."

I looked down at my schedule and pretended Kimberlee wasn't there.

"You gotta go upstairs for Bleekman's classroom."

I gritted my teeth, and hurried up the stairs hoping I could lose her. In the hallway I slowed down and counted off room numbers.

204.

205.

206.

Damn. She was standing outside room 207.

"Clever boy. You found it all by yourself."

There must be an elevator . . . somewhere. I let my eyes slide by her and walked into the half-full classroom, hurrying to plant myself in the last seat on the back row.

"I wouldn't sit there if I were you. That's Langdon's spot," Kimberlee said, sounding almost bored.

Ignore, ignore, ignore.

"Fine, but don't say I didn't warn you."

I kept my head down and pulled out a notebook as more students filed in, quickly filling the remaining seats.

"Dude. If you're not out of my desk by the time I count to two, I personally guarantee your life will end before lunch hour."

I looked up at what appeared to be a non-green version of the Incredible Hulk.

"One. One and a half . . ."

I jumped up from the desk so fast I cracked my knee against one of the legs and had to bite off a yelp. "Sorry," I mumbled. "Didn't know."

"Liar!" Kimberlee yelled from across the room, where she was lounging on a windowsill.

Shut up! I glared at her and looked for another seat.

The only one left that wasn't in the front row was over by Kimberlee's windowsill.

I sat in the front row.

The bell rang and Mr. Bleekman rose from his desk. He was a perfect caricature of every English teacher on TV: tall, painfully thin, with a comb-over sprayed crispy, and thick glasses. Finally, some normalcy. He stood in front of my desk and studied my name tag. "Mr. Clayson, I presume?"

"Yes."

"Yes, *sir*," Mr. Bleekman and Kimberlee corrected in stereo.

I refused to even look at her. "Yes, *sir*," I repeated.

"Take notes for now, but stay after and I'll give you the material you'll need to catch up."

I nodded as Kimberlee walked over and plunked herself down on top of my notebook. "I've taken this class already. I'll help you."

I raised my hand.

"Yes, Mr. Clayson?"

"Could you please tell *Kim* to get off my desk, sir?"

"Excuse me?" Bleekman asked, looking right past Kimberlee and staring at me like I'd sprouted an extra head.

I glanced at Kimberlee for just a second. Something was seriously wrong. There was no way *this* teacher was part of the joke. "Oh, shit," I said, the words slipping out before my brain caught up enough to stop me.

Bleekman's eyes widened. "Mr. Clayson. I will let you off with a warning because this is your first day. But in the future, *any* use of profanity at Whitestone Academy will result in detention. Do you understand?"

I gaped at Kimberlee, unwilling to believe she could possibly be telling the truth.

"I told you," she said, studying her fake nails. "No one can see or hear me but you." Her eyes flicked to Mr. Bleekman. "You'd better say 'yes, sir,' before Bleeker has a coronary."

"Yes, sir," I said quickly, snapping my gaze back to the front of the room.

Bleekman stared at me for a few seconds as the rest of the class snickered. He finally looked away and started droning on about Victor Hugo.

I waited a few minutes for everyone to turn their attention away from me. "You're not joking anymore, are you?" I hissed at Kimberlee through clenched teeth.

"Never was," she said at full volume.

No one even glanced in our direction.

"What do I have to do to get you to stop acting like the freak you are?" She paused. "You want me to walk through a wall?"

I glared at her but refused to snap at the bait. *This can't be real.*

She slid off my desk. "No, I mean it. If I walk through that

11

wall, will you believe I'm dead?"

I rolled my eyes. But I nodded.

She stuck her nose in the air and lifted an eyebrow. Her eyes never left me as she walked to the wall and, without slowing, slid right through it.

TWO

"I'M HOME," I YELLED. I wasn't sure I'd ever been so happy to see my own house. After Bleekman's class—and seeing Kimberlee walk through the wall—my head basically exploded. I still couldn't digest what I'd seen, or figure out how it could be real. I didn't believe in ghosts! Somehow, for some reason, I was hallucinating; Kimberlee was a figment of my imagination—and that meant ignoring her for the rest of the day.

Easier said than done. She followed me everywhere and got louder and louder. By the time I dropped my schedule card full of signatures in the basket at the front office I had a pounding headache *and* a ghostly companion.

"Jeff, there you are." My mom sniffed as she came into the room. Her eyes were red and wet.

"What's wrong?"

"Wrong?" She looked at me cluelessly. "Oh, the tears?" She laughed. "I'm just rehearsing, sweetie. I have a funeral scene tomorrow."

My mom's an actress. Always has been. Community theaters and stuff. But part of moving to California was so she could pursue an acting career for real, in Hollywood. And apparently she's good because even without an agent or anything, she went out the first day and came home with a walk-on part in CBS's latest cop thriller. Now she's got a couple gigs lined up, dramedies or something. It's all very surreal.

I reached into the fridge and pulled out a Coke. "That's great, Mom," I said absently. "What show's it for?"

She shook her finger at me and clicked her tongue. "Ah, ah, ah. If I told you that you'd know someone was dying next season." She reached her hand out and ruffled my hair. "Trade secret."

My mom's only thirty-three. I was thirteen when I first realized that I was born while she was in high school. She always wanted to be an actress; she'd been the lead in every high-school play and musical until the year she was pregnant with me. Somehow, her theater director just couldn't handle an eight-months-pregnant Ado Annie belting "I Cain't Say No." Go figure.

The nice thing about having me when she was so young is that now she's just the right age to start a new career in Hollywood as a "mature woman." Which means she plays twenty-five-year-olds.

She's married to my dad. Like, my biological dad. They got married the night they graduated high school; I was one. My dad is supersmart and he always told my mom he'd make up for getting her life off track. So when he was offered a small ownership stake in a startup venture—social networking on the internet; everyone said it would never last, *right*—he took it and ran with it. The company survived the "Dot Bomb," but for a while there Dad was drawing stock more often than a paycheck. Fortunately, it was a risk that paid off. After twelve years of accumulating ownership, he cashed out, bought us three new BMWs for Christmas, sold our house in Phoenix, and moved us to Santa Monica so Mom could chase her dream.

And now, instead of an inner-city school with a 62 percent graduation rate, I get to go to a spoiled-brat private school that feeds more or less straight into Yale. Lucky me.

I really should be grateful—the lockers stay closed at Whitestone and I suspect their PE equipment is less than fifty years old, but despite the advantages, I missed my friends. Even after just a week, it was obvious I wasn't cut out for the long-distance friendship thing. I figured I'd make new friends, but, well, these Whitestone kids weren't really my type.

"So how was your first day?"

Ummmm. "It was fine."

"Fine? Is that all?"

I took a breath and smiled. "I think it's going to be a good school for me," I lied. Well, sort of lied. It really was a great school, academics-wise. Apparently not so good if you want to keep your sanity intact.

"I hope so," she said, putting on her special-moment face. "You deserve to go to a great college. You have so much potential."

"Thanks, Mom." I don't know why she has to be so *mushy* about stuff sometimes. Maybe it's an actress thing. Still, I wasn't above taking advantage of her good mood.

I wasn't sure quite how to start—maybe there *wasn't* a good way—so I just dived right in. "Hey, I was thinking . . ." I paused. "Is there any history of . . . craziness in our family?"

She looked at me with one eyebrow cocked, a smirk ticking at the corner of her mouth. "You mean before you at this moment?"

"I'm serious," I said. She had no idea just how serious I was. "Do I have any crazy old uncles or anything? Murderers, public nudity"—I hesitated—"schizos?"

Mom thought about it for a second. "Well, my granddad had dementia pretty bad for the last two years before he died. And I think your dad's uncle Fred—you know, the one with the yogurt-carton collection?—I'm pretty sure he doesn't play with a full deck. Why the sudden interest?"

"Uh . . . we had a discussion about mental health in . . ."

Oh, great. I wasn't in any classes that this particular subject fit into. "Lit-er-a-ture," I finished, dragging the word out syllable by syllable.

"Literature?"

"Yeah, you know, *Les Mis*." Whatever that meant. "I'm gonna go play some games," I said, making my escape before Mom could ask any more probing questions.

I went upstairs to my sitting room—no lie, I have a sitting room—and turned on the TV, lying back on my humongous beanbag. This whole Kimberlee thing had to be my imagination. Stress of the first day in a new school and all that. Or maybe I'd wake up tomorrow and realize this was just a long, very vivid dream and that I was about to start my *real* first day of school.

"Okay, don't freak, but we seriously need to talk."

I sprang to my feet and spun to find Kimberlee standing right in the middle of my room.

"Listen, I know you're wigging out, but the fact is, I have no one else to turn to, so I'm not going away."

I closed my eyes and counted to ten before opening them and turning my head. There she was, looking far too real to be a figment of my imagination.

"You're not real and you need to leave me alone," I said slowly, carefully.

She rolled her eyes. "Look, I'm trying to make nice here,

and trust me, I understand where you're coming from. You know how long it took me to convince *myself* I was real? Ages."

You'd think that if my head was going to make someone up it would give me someone nice. I was feeling officially betrayed. "Not real, not real, not real," I whispered under my breath.

"This'll be a really long year if you're going to walk around muttering that all the time. I *am* real; it's just that no one else can see me."

"How convenient!" I laughed. "Give me one logical reason for *that*." *Why am I still talking to it? Her. No, me. I'm talking to myself; it is not real.*

She crossed her arms over her chest and raised an eyebrow. "Beats the hell out of me. I've been screaming at every student in that school—new kids included—for ages. Apparently, you won the medium's lottery. Wait," she said, stepping forward. "Maybe that's why. Do you see other ghosts?"

I backed away from her as though she had some kind of contagious disease. A *not-real* contagious disease. "No! I don't see anything. Technically I don't see you; you're not real."

"Oh," she said, her mouth drooping. "Well, whatever. You *can* see me and that's all that matters. I need your help."

"No! No help. No nothing. Not for fake people."

She shot me a nasty look and put her hands on her hips. "Fine, I'll prove it. Get out your computer, now!"

There is something irrationally terrifying about being ordered around by a hallucination.

I pulled my laptop out of my backpack and set it on my messy desk. Couldn't hurt. If nothing else, I could catch up on XKCD while she spouted her nonsense.

"Go to Google."

At least my alter ego knew what Google was.

"Type in my name."

I had gotten to the first of the double *ee*'s when I stopped. "Wait a second," I said. "If I Google your name, all that proves is that there is some dead girl out there named Kimberlee Schaffer. You tell me about yourself first and *then* I'll Google and see if you're right." *Oh yes, outwitting my own brain. Sweet.*

But Kimberlee shrugged nonchalantly. "Fine. What do you want to know?"

"How'd you die?"

"Drowned."

Drowned? That's the best my subconscious could come up with? "You drowned? Like, you didn't know how to swim?"

"Of course I know how to swim, moron; I live . . . lived on a private beach. The same one I drowned at, actually." A touch of something resembling real emotion clouded Kimberlee's eyes for an instant before she ran her fingers through her hair; whatever it was I'd seen was erased by that casual gesture. "I got caught in a riptide," she said softly. "It happens."

"But why—?"

"Dude, riptide. Move on!" Kimberlee snapped, scowling.

"Fine. Uh, what color of flowers did you have at your funeral?"

She bit her bottom lip. "I don't know," she admitted. *Score one for me.* "I didn't go. I was so busy trying to figure out what the hell was going on that I didn't really start going anywhere until about two weeks after the funeral."

"Convenient," I scoffed.

"What else do you want?" she said. "I drowned in a riptide, I went to Whitestone, I was seventeen, my dad's a judge, my mom's a CFO, I'm an only child. Good enough?"

"I guess," I muttered, turning back to the screen and typing the rest of her name.

"*S-c,*" Kimberlee corrected from behind me.

"Get over there!" I said, pointing to the opposite side of the room. "You are not allowed to see this!"

"Fine!" she said, sulking away.

I pressed *Enter,* fully prepared to bask in the proof of my own brilliance.

But the first page of more than 4,000 results popped up on my screen.

Teen Dies in Tragic Accident. Local Judge Mourns the Death of His Only Child. Prominent Prep School Suffers Tragic Loss. Teen's

Body Found on Private Beach. Missing Seventeen-Year-Old Confirmed Dead.

I skimmed the articles, my jaw dropping as the details swirled in front of my face, complete with a number of photographs that were unmistakably Kimberlee. Not the least of which was one of her in her freaking coffin.

"I—I could have read this last year," I said, scrambling for an excuse—totally not ready to accept this.

"Eventually you're going to have to stop trying to talk yourself out of this and believe me. Besides," she said, turning to face me now. "Who *tries* to convince themselves they're insane instead of accepting the fairly rational explanation of someone being a ghost? Maybe you really *are* a nut job. Like a hypochondriac, but for craziness."

I'm agnostic, but that moment was the first time in memory I wished I did believe in a god. Then I would have someone to beg to deliver me from this demented undead. "Whatever," I mumbled, clicking through website after website, skimming each for mere seconds before scrolling to the next one. It *was* possible, wasn't it? That my brain had unconsciously stored the details of something I'd read and "forgotten," then used that info to spit out a made-up person? Now I was really starting to sound crazy. About being crazy. I was *double* crazy.

"Your email," I said, coming up with one last test. "You have a Yahoo or Gmail account or something?"

"I did," Kimberlee said, clearly not following my stream of logic.

"Okay, tell me your username and password. There's no way I could know that, so if it works it would prove that you're not some figment of my imagination." *Cool, calm, logical. I can do this.*

"Not a chance," Kimberlee said.

"Why not?"

"I don't want you cyberspying on me!"

"It's not cyberspying—it's proving your story."

"My email is private. Don't go there."

I hesitated. "Facebook?"

She snorted. "That's hardly better." After a moment of hesitation: "How about my MySpace page? I didn't use it for, like, years before I died, but it's still there and definitely mine."

I nodded. "That'll work. What is it?"

After a few moments' thought she rattled off her MySpace username and I found the page. Not surprisingly, it was pink and seizure-inducingly sparkly.

And covered with pictures of a definitely alive Kimberlee from junior high school. She looked a little different but it was definitely her. I squinted at a couple of group shots and recognized Langdon, the guy who had almost squished me to a pulp today. "Hey!" I said, pointing. "That's Langdon."

Kimberlee rolled her eyes. "So?"

I turned back to the computer and took a deep breath. "Okay," I said, "this is definitely Kimberlee Schaffer's MySpace page. What's the password? And none of this guessing stuff. You nail it the first try, or I ignore you for the rest of my life."

"Fine," Kimberlee said, leaning forward with a predatory look in her eye, "but I get a part in this deal, too. If the password works you believe me, one hundred percent. No more made-up-person stuff. Deal?"

I swallowed hard. "Deal."

Three

"UMMM," I SAID SLOWLY AS I stared at the screen.

"What?" Kimberlee said, tension spiking her voice about two octaves. "It didn't work? You typed it wrong, then—do it again!"

"You have over three thousand new messages."

"Oh," Kimberlee said. Then she straightened casually, as though she hadn't been on the verge of hysteria an instant ago. "Well, dying makes you popular."

I stared at Kimberlee as if seeing her for the first time. All the ghosts in movies were see-through and white and did that glowing thing. And they floated. Kimberlee looked solid and walked right on the ground like anyone else. The lights made her hair shine a little, but she definitely wasn't glowing. "Can I touch you?" I asked curiously.

She put her hands on her hips and pushed her chest out. "I admit, I haven't gotten any action in a while."

"Not like that," I protested, mortified. "I mean in terms of, uh, physics. Can I touch your arm, or will I go right through?"

Kimberlee studied her arm quizzically. "Everyone else goes right through. Course, none of them can see or hear me either. You can try." She held out her arm.

I lifted my hand for a second before wussing out and turning back to my computer. "I don't want to."

"Come on," she said. "If you don't, I will."

I felt something cold pass through my shoulder and a massive chill shot down my spine. "Okay," I said when I could talk again. "That was the creepiest thing that's ever happened to me. And after today, that's really saying something."

But when I turned to her, she looked disappointed.

"What?"

She gave me a one-shouldered shrug. "I—I hoped you'd be different, that's all."

"Sorry," I muttered. Not that I could help it. "So," I said, feeling suddenly very awkward. "You're a ghost, huh?"

"Nothing gets past you, does it?" she said, rolling her eyes. "Are you going to help me now, or what?"

"Uh . . ."

Her perfectly plucked eyebrows furrowed. "Look," she began hesitantly, "you can see me. And hear me. So you're the only one who can help me. You *have* to say yes."

I sighed. "What do you need help with?"

"My unfinished business."

"Your what?"

"In books and movies people become ghosts when they have unfinished business. That must be why I'm still here."

"Did someone tell you that? Did you have some, I don't know, *angel*, I guess, tell you what you need to do?"

She shook her head. "Uh-uh. I just woke up in the middle of the school and I was dead. I'm guessing on the rest."

"What's your unfinished business?"

She twisted a ring around on her finger. "I kind of stole some stuff when I was alive and I think I need to return it."

"That's it? No unrequited love? Revenge unrealized?"

"Nope."

"And you want me to return it so you can be on your merry way?"

"That's the plan. It's the only thing I can think of. I had a great life. Pretty much everyone loved me—except the people who wanted to *be* me—and I had everything I ever wanted."

"Which forced you into a life of crime?" I have never understood rich people stealing.

"Whatever. Will you help me?"

I laid my arms on the desk and let my head rest against them. "I return a couple a things for you and you leave me alone?" I asked, more to the carpet than her.

"Yes."

"Forever?"

26

"I promise." She laughed. "I'd pinky swear, but, you know."

I did know—and I didn't want to do that again.

I was kinda starting to miss just being crazy.

"Jeff?"

I looked over at her. Her smirk was gone. So was her pout.

"Please?" she asked, her tone completely genuine.

I'm such a pushover. "Fine. I'll do it."

She squealed and clasped her hands together. "Thank you thank you thank you!" and then in the same breath, "We gotta go to the cave."

"The cave?"

"It's where the stuff is."

"You're in Santa Monica and you hid stuff in a *cave?*"

"It's on my parents' private beach. I found it when I was, like, ten. It's been my secret place ever since."

"Okay," I said. "We can go tomorrow."

"Why can't we go today?"

I dug around in my backpack and held up a copy of *Les Misérables*, and *not* the abridged version. "Because I have a hundred pages of this to read tonight. Not to mention calculus homework and a history outline everyone else has already been working on for a week." The thought of all the homework I'd had heaped on me today was almost enough to make my ghost problem seem small.

Almost.

"Unlike some people, I still have a life," I muttered.

Kimberlee's lips pressed into a straight line and before I could apologize, she spun on her heel and disappeared through my bedroom door.

When Kimberlee popped up silently beside my locker the next morning, I tried to apologize for my harsh comment. "I was stressed," I said quietly, hoping no one was close enough to catch me talking to myself. Again. "I should have kept my mouth shut."

"Whatever," she said, not meeting my eyes as I slammed my locker shut. "I just want to get this over with."

I had almost reached the stairs that would take me up to Bleekman's room when a flash of red grabbed my eye. I tuned Kimberlee out and my eyes tracked the redhead.

Finally, something good about Whitestone.

Fingers snapped in front of my face. "Hello? Focus!"

Kimberlee. It was a testament to the sheer hotness of the other girl that I had, for ten seconds, managed to forget Kimberlee entirely.

Hot Girl was standing less than twenty feet away, digging through her locker with her back to me. I was trying to figure out a nonlame way to approach her when she stopped and turned. I glanced away, afraid she'd been able to sense my eyes burning a hole in her back. Maybe a few inches *below* her back.

After what I hoped was a safe amount of time, I glanced in her direction again. It took me a few seconds to find her.

Hugging a guy in a letter jacket.

I couldn't tear my eyes away from the two of them. It was like a car wreck—you don't really want to see the guy all mangled inside, but you can't look away. And it wasn't some third-string nobody—this guy was majorly ripped and could probably break my neck with two fingers. Maybe one. It took me a second to realize that he wasn't very tall—but what's a little height when you've got shoulders like steel girders? The redhead leaned against the lockers next to him and smiled.

I knew that kind of smile. It was a special smile reserved for special people. Like, boyfriend people.

Damn.

But really, why *wouldn't* she be taken? She was totally gorgeous and—considering she was at Whitestone—almost certainly rich. Girls like that don't just wander around single.

"Enjoy your little trip down fantasy lane, loverboy?" Kimberlee was leaning against my locker looking totally bored.

Oh yeah.

But I couldn't help glancing back at the hot girl again.

"Trust me; leave that one alone," Kimberlee said, following my gaze. "She was this total slut as a freshman, but she doesn't really date now. Probably not even into guys anymore."

29

I looked over at Kimberlee with my best *duh* face and flicked my head in her direction. "Human tractor over there?"

"Wait, wait," she said, laughing. "Him? Mikhail?"

She *would* think this was funny.

"You're barking up the wrong tree. Mikhail is—" Her mouth snapped shut and her eyes took on this funny look. She sighed melodramatically. "I must be wrong. After all, just because he was dating someone a few months ago doesn't mean they're still together. I'm *so* out of the loop." She sighed again.

Was she being sarcastic? I felt like I'd missed something, but couldn't imagine what.

"You really better stay away from her now," Kimberlee continued. "Mikhail could break you in half without even trying."

"Just tell me her name," I whispered.

"Why?" Kimberlee shot back. "So I can help you keep 'having a life'?" So much for her *whatever*.

"I'm helping you," I reminded her.

"Fine," she said, sounding way more pissy than I thought my request could possibly justify. "It's Serafina. Serafina Hewitt. I'll meet you outside of Keller's class at three fifteen sharp so we can go to the cave. Back out and you'll be sorry." She shot a finger gun at me and walked through the wall of lockers.

Four

AS SHE'D PROMISED, Kimberlee was waiting for me after school, just inside the front doors. "Finally," she muttered.

I pushed open the door and instinctively held it a few seconds to let Kimberlee out. She snickered as she walked by. "Holding the door for your imaginary friend?"

"That's only an insult to yourself."

She tossed her hair. "Whatever. Where's your car?" she asked.

I grinned. I couldn't help it. A black BMW Z4 convertible was my mom's idea of a good, sensible car. Something about them lasting forever? I turned to Kimberlee. "This way."

I headed to the farthest end of the lot, where almost no one parked. The spaces on both sides of my Z4 were empty. That was worth the walk.

Kimberlee stroked her fingers along the black hood as though she could actually feel something. "I saw this yesterday when I followed you home," she said, as if following people home was completely normal. "Daddy's?"

I put my shades on as I pressed the unlock button on my keychain. "Nope. She's all mine. Kimberlee, meet Halle."

"Halle?"

It's not that I'm embarrassed that I named my car, but, well, it's kind of personal.

Kimberlee stood outside the door. After almost thirty seconds I rolled down the window. "You coming?"

"I thought you were going to open the door for me."

"I thought I wasn't supposed to do stuff like that for my *imaginary friend*."

She rolled her eyes. "Fine." She slipped through the door and settled in the seat.

I stared at her, everything I'd learned in physics screaming that this made no sense. "Why don't you fall through the bottom of the car?" I finally asked.

"I don't know," she said testily. "Why don't you?"

I shook my head and put the key in the ignition.

"Should I put on my seat belt?"

"Can you?"

That shut her up.

"Come on, why Halle?"

Okay, not completely. "*Not* telling you."

"Spill!"

I didn't have the stamina for another battle of wills with Kimberlee. "I named her after Halle Berry. She played

Storm in the X-Men movies."

"You're such a nerd. Why her?"

I could feel my face getting hot. "Well, you know ... 'cause she's hot. And black. And my car is hot, and black."

Kimberlee smirked. "So you want to ride her all over town?"

"*What?* No, it's a compliment! Like naming a boat! I just—it's just a stupid ... Forget I said anything. Can we just drop it now?"

"Whatever you say, Grand Wizard."

I shook my head and started the car. She was just baiting me. Again. How did I keep walking into her traps?

"You drive like my grandma," Kimberlee said after a few minutes of inching along.

"You think that's an insult? Try harder." I knew what this car could do. The first week I got it I took a trip to Vegas and made it from Phoenix to the Hoover Dam in just over two hours. My car is *fast*. And I admit, I roared into school moving pretty quick yesterday, but then I realized the kids here all drive like they're on crack. Seriously. So after a near miss with a red Miata, I'd decided that slower was better.

At least until I got out of the parking lot.

Kimberlee pointed me down several streets, each wider and more stately than the last, until I pulled up in front of a huge white mansion.

"Whoa, sweet." Our house was supernice, but this was the

kind of house you see on the home-design shows my mom watches. The *feature* homes.

"Turn down that little road over there. It'll take you to the beach," Kimberlee said, clearly not impressed.

"Are you sure nobody's going to arrest me for being here?" Because I was most definitely *not* sure.

"Nah. There's a gate. I'll tell you the code."

I pulled onto the drive on the right side of the house and stopped next to a keypad.

"Eight-six-four-two-two, star."

I punched in the numbers, then my finger hovered over the star. I closed my eyes and pushed, expecting flashing lights and cops with their guns drawn. I could almost hear the megaphone. *Step out of your car with your hands up!* But all I actually heard was the quiet whir of the gate sliding open. *So far, so good.*

The road sloped sharply before ending in a ten-space parking lot in front of a gorgeous white beach, surrounded on both sides by tall cliffs. "Whoa!" I said as I climbed out of my car, feeling more like I was on a movie set than what was essentially someone's backyard.

Kimberlee glared at the foamy green waves. "You'll excuse me if I don't share your enthusiasm."

"Why? 'Cause you died here?"

"Let's just get to the cave."

"You're reading my mind."

She stayed a few feet ahead of me as we trekked across the sand.

She didn't leave footprints.

"This whole ghost thing is still freaking me out," I said, my eyes fixed on her feet.

"Yeah," she said without looking back. "Took me about a month to really get a handle on it, too."

Great.

When we reached what looked like the face of a mini-cliff, she took two running steps and jumped, then basically floated into the cave.

I was stuck ten feet below. "You suck," I shouted.

"Wimp. There are handholds all the way up. That's how I did it when I was alive."

I found a ledge for my foot and stepped up to reach for one with my arms. In a few seconds I had four limbs on little ledges and was sure I looked like a bug clinging to the wall for dear life—all of three feet above a sandy beach. I looked up to Kimberlee for help. She was staring out at the sea. A gust of wind made her skirt flutter suddenly, giving me an eyeful. I froze, lost my balance, and slid down the rock. Or, more accurately, fell sprawling into the sand.

"Perv," Kimberlee said with a sinister laugh that made me remember that wind couldn't touch her clothes. Only

Kimberlee had any effect on Kimberlee's clothes.

"Don't do that again," I said darkly. *At least not while I'm clinging to the side of a cliff.* Without looking at Kimberlee I started to climb again, more carefully this time. It took me about three tries and at least ten minutes, but I made it. I peered back down at the beach. The climb looked a lot shorter from up top. "Okay," I said as I scrambled to my feet. "Where's the stuff?"

She tilted her head to the back of the cave. I turned and blinked, letting my eyes adjust to the darkness. When they finally did, my jaw dropped.

There must have been a hundred boxes stacked in the back of the cave, which was way deeper than I'd expected. "A few things? A *few* things! Are you insane?" My voice echoed through the cave, repeating my words back to me.

"Jeff . . ." Her voice was uncharacteristically quiet.

"This is ridiculous. You lied to me."

"I did not."

"No one in their right mind would *ever* classify this as 'a few things.' You lied to get me up here and hoped you could just flutter your eyes and it would be all better. Well, it's not." I backed away from the massive pile of boxes. "I'm not doing this."

"Jeff . . ."

"I should call the cops," I said as I backed away. No way

could I return all this stuff on my own, not in any reasonable amount of time. "I'll bet they could—"

"No!" Kimberlee shouted, running after me. "They'd just confiscate it all. Then I'd be stuck here forever! Jeff, please."

"No. I'm leaving," I said, as much to myself as to Kimberlee, "and I am *not* coming back." I looked over the edge and tried to find the handholds I had used climbing up. *It's only ten feet. Just jump!* I let myself down as far as I could while holding on to the ledge, then tried to fall slowly. My feet hit the sand a moment before my ass did. My tailbone stung, but at least I was out of the klepto cave. I looked over at my car and forced myself to walk calmly instead of running—which would probably make me fall and look like an idiot.

Again.

Kimberlee was right beside me. "They're organized," she pleaded. "It'll be easy. A bag for each person. The boxes are sorted by category. A couple of trips and we'll be done."

By category? "A couple of trips? A *couple* of trips? Maybe if I had a semi. That," I said pointing up at the cave, "is a lot of stuff, Kimberlee. You have a problem."

"Had."

"What?"

She shrugged. "Can't do it anymore, can I?" She laughed shakily for a few seconds before falling silent.

"Real funny," I scoffed. I ducked into my car and slammed

the door before she could say anything else. As I drove I stared at Kimberlee in the rearview mirror until the road curved and cut her out of sight. As soon as I got out of her cul-de-sac, I stomped my foot on the gas and drove home as fast as I dared.

How the hell was I going to get out of this?

When I got to the house, Mom was gone, but Tina—our housekeeper—was washing down countertops and a good smell was coming from the oven.

"Ah, Jeff, there you are," Tina said. "Your mother is at a taping and your father is on a conference call. You know, the ones your mother keeps telling him to stop taking. I have to take off as soon as I pull the muffins out of the oven. Healthy ones—don't tell your father. Tell him they are cupcakes and he will eat them." Tina had only been with us for two weeks, but she was already determined to make my dad into a health-food junkie—clandestinely, of course, though her methods were hardly James Bond.

I slumped down on the counter and let my backpack slip to the floor.

"You look awful."

Thanks, Tina.

"Bad day?"

Actually, Tina, it was swell. I saw this girl—of course, she's totally untouchable, for me, anyway. Oh, and there's this other girl—she's

38

untouchable, too, for everyone! But she's all mine, whether I want her or not.

"Just long," I said with a shrug. "Lots of homework."

She reached up and patted my head in a way that was comforting in spite of the awkward grandmotherliness of it. "You'll get it all done. You're a smart boy."

"Thanks," I said, smiling a little. "I better go upstairs and get to work."

But rather than start on my homework, I fired up my Xbox. After what I'd just seen, I deserved to chill out a little. I played GTA for about an hour and imagined everything my car ran into was Kimberlee, or one of her boxes of stolen stuff. I kept looking over my shoulder, expecting to see her or hear one of her smart-ass comments, but all I heard was the cathartic symphony of gunfire and people screaming.

Why was this whole ghost thing happening to *me*? Kimberlee said I was the first person to see her—ever. Nothing in my life was all that special. *I* certainly wasn't special.

Maybe it was something about Santa Monica. In the three weeks since we'd moved here my life had turned upside down. My mom was on TV, my dad was a retired workaholic who couldn't keep his fingers out of the old business, and I had a ghost. And a housekeeper. A year ago, any of those things would have sounded like a joke. Getting them all at once—well, who could blame me if I needed some time to adjust? But last time I checked, seeing ghosts wasn't a symptom of homesickness or stress.

I did have to give Santa Monica points for the redhead I'd spotted at school, though. *Serafina*, Kimberlee had said. Man, she was gorgeous. But I couldn't even think about her for more than a few seconds before coming back to the same humongous problem that suddenly overshadowed every aspect of my life.

Kimberlee.

I wondered if Santa Monica had any good exorcists.

Five

"JEFF? JEFF?"

"I'm up, Mom."

"Open your eyes, Jeff."

I rubbed my face with my hands and squinted with one eye.

"Holy hell!" I shouted as Kimberlee came into focus. I jerked away from her and pulled my blankets around me. "Get out of my room!"

"Why?" she asked, noting the death grip I had on my bedding. "Naked under there?"

"Yes. Now leave!"

She scrunched up her nose. "Ew, gross. I was totally kidding."

I rolled my eyes. "I'm not naked. But I'm just in my boxers."

Kimberlee shrugged. "Nothing I haven't seen before." She grabbed for the end of my comforter.

I gripped the blanket tighter and tried to scoot out of

reach. When her hand passed right through the comforter and my face went white, she laughed like it was the most hilarious thing in the world.

"You're such a freak," she said, studying me with her arms crossed over her chest.

"*You* wanted to see my underwear."

"I showed you mine. It's your turn."

"Turn around so I can put some jeans on."

She spun with her arms over her head like a ballerina.

"Ready?" she asked as soon as I jerked my zipper up.

"Yeah, sure."

She turned back and looked me up and down. "Sexy. A little skinny, though."

"Like it matters to you."

"Hey, I like a little eye candy as much as the next undead."

"Are you here to beg and plead with me to help you again?" I walked into my bathroom and grabbed my toothbrush. "'Cause if you are, you can forget about it."

She laughed mirthlessly; a laugh that embodied the word *sinister*. It made my skin crawl. "Beg and plead? Who do you think I am? I don't beg and plead; I threaten. After today, you agree to help me, or I'll do some real haunting."

I spat and tried to sound braver than that laugh made me feel. "What, yell 'Boo!' in my face? That'll convince me."

"That stuff's for amateurs. I'll just sit and watch you in the shower."

"I could get used to that," I said. *Eventually.*

She chuckled, making the hairs on my neck stand on end. "I wasn't finished. I'll sit my ass in the middle of your lunch at school—*bon appétit,* accompany you on dates and freak out whoever is with you, and then yell and scream all night until you go insane from sleep deprivation. It's easy."

Crap. "That's not fair."

Her eyes narrowed. "Do you think it's fair that I sit here all day, every day with no one to talk to and no way to help myself?" she shouted. "To be stuck in a world I don't belong to and where I can't do anything?" Her face stayed angry for a few seconds, then crumpled into despair.

There's a reason girls always win arguments with me. Tears are like Kryptonite. "Don't cry, Kimberlee," I said with a sigh.

"You would cry, t-t-too," she wailed, "if you only had one person in the whole world who you could talk to."

I could feel my will crumbling as I walked over and slumped down onto my bed.

Kimberlee stayed by my bathroom doorway.

I cleared my throat and patted the spot beside me. "Okay," I said as she slowly sat. "If I help you, and I do mean *if,* there've got to be a few rules."

She sniffed but nodded.

"Rule number the first is, no coming into my room until I'm dressed. Got it?"

She took a deep breath and swiped her sleeve across her face, wiping away her sad expression along with any traces of tears. "Fine. What else?"

There was only one other person I'd seen turn tears off that quickly. Like an *on/off* switch. My mom. The *actress*. "None of that . . . other stuff you talked about," I said, starting to feel like a total sucker.

Kimberlee just shrugged. "No problem. Any other demands?"

"I'll . . . make up more rules as we go along." Now I was just pissed at her fake breakdown.

"'Kay," she said, suddenly very businesslike. "Go shower or you'll be late."

"All right, but you stay out here. No peeking, no popping through the shower wall, no nothing."

"Like I'd want to," she muttered.

I hurried into the bathroom and showered as fast as I could. It was true that I didn't want to be late, but the main reason was so Kimberlee wouldn't change her mind and decide to come play a little peek-a-boo. I got out and jumped into my uniform half-wet; at least I was covered. I pulled out my electric razor and turned it on.

44

"Stop! *Stop!*" Kimberlee melted through the wall with her hands over her eyes. "Put the razor down. Do you really shave?" she asked, peeking through her fingers.

I pointed to the razor with my best *duh* look.

"No, I mean do you *have* to shave? You get stubble and everything?"

"Yeah."

"Lemme see." She leaned close and studied the fringe of hair on my chin and around my mouth. "That's sexy; you can't get rid of that."

"But the dress code says no facial hair."

"Oh, please. They won't bust you for stubble."

"Why would I want stubble?"

"Girls love stubble. If you can grow it, it shows you're more virile."

I rolled my eyes. "Do you even know what that word means?"

"Capable of performing sexually as a male," she said proudly. "I looked it up."

I looked at my chin in the mirror and my thoughts flashed to Serafina. That wrestler guy yesterday probably had a little stubble, too. "Virile. You know, I'm feeling virile."

"Whatever—do your hair."

I took a comb and parted my hair, then brushed it back with my fingers.

"You're kidding me."

"What? It's the messy look."

"I know the messy look, Jeff, and that is not it. Do you have any gel?"

Last straw. "Listen, I am not changing my hair. If you want me to help you, you take me the way I am or no deal."

Kimberlee folded her arms across her chest. "Whatever," she said. "But if no girl will touch you, don't say I didn't try."

It took fifteen minutes of coaching before Kimberlee was satisfied. I wasn't convinced. I had poky spears on one side with a flattened patch on the other, and bits of crunchy bangs were hanging down over one eye. "I look like an idiot."

"No, you look hot!"

"I don't know, Kim, maybe—"

"Kimberlee."

"*Kimberlee.* Maybe this really isn't the look for me."

"Trust me. You've never looked better."

Trust Kimberlee? Every instinct rebelled against that thought, but what choice did I really have? Kimberlee was born and raised in Santa Monica, and based on what I'd skimmed from her internet presence—yes, I did more Googling—she apparently was the queen of Whitestone for almost three years before the riptide cut her reign short. I had nothing.

Besides, I'd spent so long on my hair I only had ten

minutes to get to school. No time to start over.

I poked my head in the kitchen. Just my luck: Mom, Dad, *and* Tina. As big an audience as our kitchen ever got this time of morning. I tried to appear confident as I rushed through the kitchen, attempting to not be seen.

"Jeff! Look at you!" my mom gushed. "You look like Ryan Seacrest."

Was that a compliment?

My dad didn't even look up from his paper. I was okay with that.

I grabbed my breakfast burrito to go, said my good-byes, and slipped out to my car before anyone could make any more comments.

"Loosen your tie," Kimberlee said, popping suddenly into the front seat.

That I could handle.

"Much better. Now you look like someone I can stand to have working for me."

My mouth dropped. "I. Don't. Work. For. You," I said, each word hard and clipped. "I am doing you the biggest favor in the world and—"

"And I just made you look like the kind of guy someone in this school might actually make out with. And considering you have to wear a uniform just like everyone else, that's some pretty mad skills. I would think you would be grateful."

"I was fine the way I was. All you did was make my hair weird and convince me not to shave. I would hardly call that 'mad skills.' I don't need your help."

"If you say so," she said casually.

I fumed the entire drive to school and considered tightening my tie out of spite. Between the fact that my car has a hair-trigger gas pedal and being pissed at Kimberlee, I made it to school five minutes before first bell. *Perfect.*

Kimberlee slid through the car door and was gone so quickly I couldn't even tell where she went. Not that I cared.

I managed to park near the entrance closest to Serafina's locker and started searching for her as soon as I opened the door. She was there, unloading her backpack. As I watched, she stood on her toes and reached up to put a book on the top shelf, lifting her skirt an inch or two. Her legs were very, very nice, but that wasn't the only reason I stared.

They were totally ripped.

Her calves had that big bump that you see on girls who do weights. Not veiny, I-shoot-horse-testosterone legs, but perfect, fitness-model legs that could probably squeeze me like a python if they ever got me in a scissors hold.

Scissors hold. Hoo, boy.

I turned to my locker and grabbed my books, wishing I had more time before the three-minute bell.

More time talk to her. Or, at the very least, more time

to work up my nerve.

She closed her locker and started my way. Just as she was about to pass me I gritted my teeth and forced myself to turn around. "Hey," I said. *Brilliant.*

She turned, surprised, as if she couldn't quite tell who had spoken to her in the crowded hallway.

"H-how's it going?" I said, stepping a little closer and hoping she didn't notice the little stutter.

"Good," she said, smiling uncertainly.

I stood there for a few seconds, just staring. That was it. I had nothing more to say. "Oh, I'm Jeff. I just moved here from Phoenix," I said, extending a hand. "Arizona," I added. *Stupid, stupid, stupid!*

She reached out to shake my hand. It was only after our joined hands started moving up and down that I realized how lame the whole shaking hands thing was. "Sera," she said quickly, pulling her hand back after about three shakes.

Sera. One of my favorite names. Starting now.

I looked up sharply as the bell rang.

"Well, it's time," Sera said, edging away.

"See you around," I said, giving her my best grin.

I don't think she noticed.

Still, that wasn't so bad. First contact made and all. She knew my name now, at least. That was step one. There were about twenty-four more steps that involved her discovering

I'm the love of her life and ditching her jock boyfriend, but what's that quote about every journey beginning with a single step? That was my single step.

"Nice," Kimberlee said, pulling me out of my daydream. "Now instead of being an unknown nobody, you're the loser who told her what state Phoenix is in. Well done."

Everyone's a critic.

Six

FIRST THING I RAN INTO in Bleekman's class was Langdon's back. Literally.

"Heeeeeeey, Jeff, right?" Langdon said, pushing a meaty arm around my shoulder. That was one heavy arm.

"Yeah?" I said tentatively, a little afraid I was about to get beat up on front of everyone.

"Whatcha doing Saturday night, buddy?" *Buddy?*

"Uh . . ." There were a couple of people gathered around now. Not all humongous meatheads like Langdon, but definitely some of the Whitestone elite—you know, the ones everyone else makes way for in the hallways. There's just an . . . an air of intimidation, I guess. Some kind of international language of superiority.

I noticed most of them had spiky hair, too, and every single one had their collar unbuttoned under their loosened ties, just like me. Never thought of hair and clothing as camouflage before, but maybe they figured I was one of them now.

Or maybe Kimberlee haunted them into this. Could she do that?

"We're having a kegger up on Harrison Hill," Langdon continued. "It's gonna be wild. You're the new guy and I'm thinking you need a bona fide Whitestone welcome."

This is the difference between jocks at Whitestone and jocks in public school. At Whitestone they know words like *bona fide*. "Oh yeah?" I said hesitantly.

"Dude, everyone'll be there," one of the more preppy-looking guys said. "We have parties up there a couple times a year and it is *the* place to be."

"You should come," Langdon said, the look in his eyes making me feel like a feeder fish—the ones in the store that have no purpose in life whatsoever except to be eaten by bigger, fancier fish. "Seriously, bro," he said, extending one enormous fist out to me, "you'll be my special guest."

Kimberlee breezed in while I was walking to my seat. She looked down at me with one eyebrow raised. "What's with the sappy grin? You look like a moron."

Got invited to a party, I wrote in my notebook.

Kimberlee graced me with a deadpan look. "Fantastic; a D&D rave."

I rolled my eyes and fixed her with a glare that I managed to wipe off my face about a second after I realized Bleekman would think I was looking at *him* like that.

I don't even play D&D.

And it's true. I haven't played D&D in years. At least *a* year.

It's a kegger on Harris Hill.

"Harrison Hill? Seriously?" Kimberlee asked. Squealed is probably a better word. "I *love* the Harrison Hill parties!"

I admit I was relieved to hear that. Now I knew the party was legit. Probably.

"Wait," Kimberlee said, her voice deadly serious. "Did you get an invite?" She put a fist on her hips and held up one finger like she was scolding a five-year-old child instead of a sixteen-year-old . . . uh . . . me. "Don't you dare show your face at Harrison Hill without an invite."

I looked up at her and nodded slightly.

"From who? You can't get some loser invite and think you're actually in because a nerd managed to get info."

For some reason, after our run-in on the first day, I didn't want to admit to Kimberlee that it had been Langdon. Besides, that preppy guy had chimed in, too. That was good enough, right? Since it was a little hard to describe a guy who was dressed just like everyone else—you never realize how much you use clothes to describe people until you go to a uniformed school where everyone is a freaking clone— I drew a quick diagram to point out the preppy guy who'd piped up.

Kimberlee glanced back at him. "Neil?" She raised her eyebrows, considering. Even looking a little bit impressed. "Okay, you're in." She grinned now. "Awesome. See? It's totally the hair."

Sad thing is, she was probably right.

When the lunch bell rang a couple hours later, I froze as I was zipping up my backpack. I'd been so focused on Kimberlee yesterday that I hadn't bothered with the whole lunch ritual. Halle and me and an old bag of chips I found under the seat made for a cozy luncheon.

Now, unless I wanted to be that guy who sat by himself every day, I had to find an actual table.

And hope I hadn't already blown my shot by being Mr. Nonsocial yesterday. This is serious stuff! Which is why Kimberlee found me standing in the middle of the cafeteria holding a full lunch tray, suffering an acute case of analysis paralysis.

"What are you doing, loser?" she asked.

"Ummmmmm . . ." I answered honestly.

She paused for a moment, then sighed. "I really should just leave you alone and let you make a fool out of yourself, but seriously, Jeff, what kind of impression do you think you're going to make standing here while your lunch gets cold? Go sit the hell down!"

She did have a point.

I was about to head to a half-full table and attempt to make small talk with total strangers when Sera breezed through the doorway.

With the big dude wearing the letterman's jacket.

Crap.

I looked down at my tray and decided my mashed potatoes were in dire need of some extra pepper. I turned around and headed back to the condiment station, futzing with the small pepper shaker way longer than I could rationally justify, but most likely, no one was watching me.

Probably.

Sera made it to the end of the line and turned. She met my eyes almost immediately; probably something to do with the heat that was building up on the back of her head where I'd been staring for the last two minutes. She looked down almost nervously and tucked a strand of hair behind her ear. I figured that would be it, but after a second, she looked up and smiled shyly. I wondered how soon my life would end at wrestler-guy's hands if I smiled back.

I took the risk.

After a second she looked away and started walking toward the opposite end of the condiment station. Still, I'd take what little victories I could.

To my surprise, Mikhail didn't follow her; he went and sat at a table with a group of guys as muscular as he was. Well, *almost* as muscular. Sera headed toward a rapidly filling table on the other side of the room.

She was about ten feet away—and I was about ready to admit defeat and sit alone—when she paused and looked back at me.

"Hey, it's Jeff, right?"

Seriously? "Uh, yeah," I said with great bucketloads of suave.

"You look . . . lost."

Lost?

"You want to come sit with me and some friends—for today, anyway?"

A half-assed invitation; I'll take it. I grinned—probably sappily—and muttered something affirmative before falling into step behind her.

"Don't forget the boyfriend and all the bones in your body that he can breee-aaaaaak," Kimberlee called in a sing-song voice as I walked away from her. I resisted the urge to flip her off.

As we sat down I noticed that Sera caught Mikhail's eye across the room and smiled.

One problem at a time, I reminded myself. I was already just glad she was more than an incredibly pretty face. I mean, she'd asked me—a new nobody—to come sit with her. At the very least that meant she was nice.

"Hey, who's your friend, Sera?" a girl with brown hair and glittery eye shadow asked, eyeing me a little like I was a piece of meat.

It was very strange.

"Oh, this is Jeff, guys. He's new." Then she set her tray down and started pointing around the table and rattled off about a dozen names. There was a Hampton and a Jasmine, some guy named Wilson, and I think there were two Jewels. Glitter-girl was named Brynley—or Breelee? Something like that. What was wrong with the parents in this city? Hadn't anyone ever heard of naming their kids Kevin or Amber or anything even remotely mainstream?

"So," one of the Jewels said when Sera was done. "Where're you from?"

"Me?" *Duh.* "Phoenix."

"Ooh, do you have rattlesnakes there?"

"Out in the desert, yeah. But I lived in the city." *In the ghetto, I almost added. Well, not exactly the ghetto, but compared to here? Ghetto.*

"Oh." She sounded disappointed.

"What do you play?" a guy asked. Wilson?

"Uh, Xbox?" I said with a nervous laugh.

"No, I mean, you're pretty tall—you a baller or what?"

"Kinda," I said. Blatant lie. People always assume I play basketball because I'm tall. I'd like to ask people if they play miniature golf because they're short, but I had a feeling breaking that one out right now wasn't going to endear me to anyone. "I hear our team is pretty good," I tacked on. More lies.

"Yeah, you should come to a game," the guy said. "Sera and Jasmine cheer."

"You're a cheerleader?" Now I understood the ripped legs.

"Junior co-captain of the squad," she said. I didn't know what that meant, but it sounded important.

"So are you the girl they always, like, throw in the air?" I asked.

Her chin rose just a little. "Sometimes, but usually I'm the one tumbling in the front."

The thought of Sera jumping around in a cheer skirt stoked a sudden passion for hoops within me. *Why, of course I love basketball. Go team!* And, note to self, find out what our team is. Probably the Fighting Preppies or something like that.

"Cool," I said, wondering if I should be glad I found the nice cheerleader, or even more convinced that she was out of my league. Her profile was perfect. She had long eyelashes that were probably red or blond under her mascara. All I knew for sure was I could stare into her eyes all day.

Another ten minutes of small talk flowed around me. It wasn't that they talked about things that weren't interesting—local indie concerts, who was hooking up or breaking up, which teachers were the lamest—it's just that I didn't know enough about anything to join in.

When there was a lull, I worked up the nerve to turn to Sera and ask, "So, you heard about the party this weekend?"

She looked over at me, but said nothing.

"Harrison Hill?" I added nervously, hoping Kimberlee— not to mention Langdon and his friends—hadn't fed me a total line about it being the place to be.

"Yeeeeaaaah," she said, drawing out the word. "I did hear something about that."

"I was kinda thinking maybe I'd see you there."

"I don't do keggers," she said, her smile tightening. "Not my thing."

"You're not going?" I did *not* have a backup plan for that.

"Sera doesn't do the partying scene," Wilson piped in "helpfully."

"How come?" I asked.

Sera shrugged. "I'm in the middle of competition season for cheer. The last thing I need is to get wasted on the weekends."

"You don't *have* to drink." *You could, say, make out with me instead.* But I had a feeling it wasn't in my best interest to say that out loud.

"Trust me, the parties are only fun if you're drunk," she said.

I laughed but she didn't look amused.

"I'm going," Brynley said, looking up at me.

"Me too," Hampton added.

I pulled out one more piece of ammunition. "I'm going with Langdon," I said, hoping he actually was as cool as Kimberlee made him sound.

"Langdon?" Sera said, though not in quite the same tone of voice I had said it.

"And Neil," I added, not so confident in my invite anymore.

She looked like she wanted to say something, and then changed her mind and took a bite instead. "Maybe I *should* drop by," she said after swallowing.

"Nice job, bro," Wilson said softly, nudging my shoulder. "She hasn't gone to one of these things since freshman year." He whispered *freshman year* like it was a secret. As though being a freshman was some kind of embarrassing option.

The guys around me chuckled nervously, but I was lost.

After a few seconds Sera smiled awkwardly and grabbed the edges of her tray. "I better—"

"Are you going to bring your boyfriend?" I asked, totally cutting her off. Yes, I am a desperate loser.

Everyone at the table fell silent.

"Do you have news for us?" the *other* Jewel said, leaning forward on her elbows with her eyes glinting.

"No," Sera said flatly.

No?

No!

"What about that Mikhail guy?" I hedged.

Sera raised an eyebrow and looked at me in confusion. "Khail?"

"Yeah, the, uh . . . wrestler?" Everyone was looking at *me* now, and I wanted to disappear—melt right through the floor like Kimberlee could. Then, almost as one, they started laughing. Not social, polite laughing; serious you-got-*Punk'd* laughing.

And I had no clue why.

I must have started to look pitiful because Sera finally let me off the hook. "Khail's my brother. We're very close. But not *that* close," she added sarcastically.

My candle of hope instantly relit. No, "candle" is far too tame; this was a torch, a bonfire, a shock-and-awe *explosion* of hope.

Kimberlee was dead meat.

Seven

KIMBERLEE DIDN'T SHOW UP again until after
school, when she fell into step with me in the hallway—as if
nothing had happened. "Are we going now?"

"You are in so much trouble," I said quietly.

"What are you talking about?" she asked at full volume. I
think she enjoyed being able to talk loud when I couldn't.

I burst through the front doors into the crisp January
air. A little chilly, but mostly a perfect, sunny day. Like pretty
much every day in Santa Monica. I stayed silent until I let
myself into my car and Kimberlee slid into the passenger seat.

"Open the top," Kimberlee said. "It's, like, sacrilege to keep
the top up on a day like this."

"Not till I'm finished," I said.

"What's your problem?"

"Sera and Mikhail?"

"What about them?"

She had so much nerve. "Sera and Mikhail *Hewitt*. I'll give you a hint. They're not married."

She at least had the courtesy to look slightly abashed. *Very slightly.* "So?"

I glared at her.

"Okay, fine, I should have told you. Big deal."

The glaring continued.

"What do you want me to do?" Kimberlee said, not apologetic in the least. "Are you gonna pop the top or what?"

"Not today," I grumbled.

Kimberlee rolled her eyes. "Gimme a break. I just forgot."

"You really expect me to believe you just *forgot* he was Sera's brother?"

"Fine, I didn't forget. But come on, it was *funny*! You should have seen the look on your face. Priceless."

"You don't understand. I like this girl, Kimberlee." Like, a lot. Weirdly a lot.

"All the more reason for me to warn you off her. Really, Jeff, she's totally untouchable."

"What the hell does that mean? First you say she's a slut, then you let me think she's dating her brother, now she's *untouchable*?"

"You may be ready to hand her your heart on a silver platter, but she won't give it back. She's cold."

"Even if that did make any sense, why should I believe you? You lie as often as you tell the truth. More often, really,"

I added, realizing the truth of it even as I said it.

"Well, believe me this time. She's not the innocent angel she appears to be."

"And you *are?*"

"You're not getting involved with me, are you?" She raised her eyebrows. "Though you seem like the kind of guy who would try, if he could."

I swear she had one more button done up last time I looked over.

"I'm at least as hot as she is. And my boobs are way bigger." Another button was mysteriously gone.

I focused on the road and didn't look again. "And fake, probably."

"Hey, they don't feel fake when you got 'em in your hands."

I almost swerved off the road. "Are you serious?" My eyes involuntarily returned to her chest; they didn't *look* fake.

Kimberlee smiled victoriously and rebuttoned her blouse.

I turned to face the road again, feeling like a total schmuck. She knew just how to play me and I fell right into it. Kimberlee, one—Jeff, zero.

Even though this was my second trip to the cave, I still felt like a trespasser. But at least I climbed the wall faster.

Sadly, the scenery hadn't changed.

If not for the rough, rocky walls and floor, it could have been an office storage room. Lidded file-sized boxes were lined up in rows with one wide aisle down the middle and an odd code of numbers and letters I didn't understand written in black Sharpie on each box. Off to the side was a stack of still-flat boxes in plastic wrapping, and I could imagine alive-Kimberlee buying—or, more likely, stealing—them in anticipation of more pilfered items.

It was kind of sick, really.

"I don't get you," I admitted as we sorted through boxes. Well, *I* sorted and she directed. Unfortunate drawback to working with ghosts: Only one of you can actually work. Luckily, Kimberlee was happily interpreting her weird code on the boxes, and the bags inside were neatly labeled with names and dates.

"Jeez, it's not that hard," Kimberlee said. "This number means—"

"Not your code," I said, pulling another box down. "*You*. I've seen your house—you're obviously super-rich. And I get that whole thrill-seeking thing behind shoplifting, but *this?*" I asked, beckoning at the mass of boxes. "This is something else. Why?"

Kimberlee shook her head, looking down at the floor of the cave. "I don't know," she said sheepishly. "I just . . . couldn't help myself."

"But you have everything you stole just hidden in here. You didn't use any of this stuff."

"That wasn't the point," Kimberlee said, her tone brittle. "Besides, that kind of stuff gets you caught. I'm not stupid."

"I didn't say you were." I totally didn't *say* it. "So . . . you never got caught? Even after all of this?"

"There were a couple of close calls."

"And people just—what?—didn't notice?"

Now a sly smile crossed her face. "Oh, they noticed, all right."

That did not sound good. "What does that mean?"

"There was a . . . *bit* . . . of a theft scandal at Whitestone for, um, several months before I died," Kimberlee said, avoiding my eyes. "Things . . . things were pretty bad, and I was taking a lot of stuff."

Great. Just great.

"Principal Hennigan got complaints from students, teachers, parents, you name it. He was obsessed with catching the culprit. He kept trying to get the cops to come out and, like, send someone undercover—he is so lame—but obviously things eventually stopped disappearing and everyone moved on with their lives."

"And no one realized the stuff stopped going missing when you *died*?" I asked skeptically.

"People never see what they don't want to see," Kimberlee said, looking out at the ocean. Anywhere but at me.

"But when this stuff starts coming back people are going to realize it's the stuff that got stolen before, right?" Just when I thought things couldn't get any worse.

"Maybe," Kimberlee said quietly.

"Maybe? I don't think there's any *maybe* about it, unless the entire school is much less intelligent than the brochures say. Returning this stuff wasn't supposed to draw attention— it was supposed to be subtle." I had no idea when I agreed to this that it was so . . . big.

"It *can* be subtle," Kimberlee said, clearly attempting to sound optimistic.

"I have serious doubts," I said dryly. "Especially considering we've got three boxes of stuff just from the teachers."

"I'm trying to make amends," Kimberlee said, irritation creeping into her voice. "My entire future—whatever that consists of—is resting on this. What do you want me to do?"

And as I stood there looking over box after box of stolen stuff, I realized I had no idea how to answer that question.

"So," Kimberlee said, sounding strangely detached. "Do you want to give stuff back to people first or take stuff back to stores?"

I closed my eyes and sighed. I must have been insane when I agreed to this. "Let's try people first."

"Okay. Box numero uno. Miss *Serafina*," she said, batting her eyelashes.

Ah yes, Sera, I thought and smiled, remembering all over again that she was single. Until I realized that if Kimberlee had a bag for Sera, there was something in there she'd stolen. "What did you take from her?" I demanded.

She rolled her eyes. "Go look."

67

I grumbled under my breath as I looked through the bags until I found the ones marked with Sera's name. A cheer skirt and shoes. They looked brand-new, but Kimberlee had been dead for over a year. "When did you take these?"

Silence.

"Kimberlee?"

"The date's on the bag, okay?"

Of course it was. How could I expect anything different from Miss OCD Klepto? "When she was a freshman?" I said, counting backward.

Kimberlee poked her head out from the boxes. The *middle* of the boxes. I was never going to get used to that. "She was the first freshman at Whitestone to make the varsity squad."

"So you thought you'd take some of her excitement away? That's real nice."

"Shut up. I didn't ask for commentary." I couldn't tell if she sounded angry or hurt.

"Well, she's a really awesome girl." *And hot. So very, very hot.*

"Says who? You've known her for what, a day?"

"Yeah, but she was nice to me without even knowing who I was. Nicer than anyone else I've met here so far," I added in a grumble.

"Hey, I *totally* talked to you," Kimberlee argued.

"I said *nice*." I stuffed the cheer gear into my backpack. "I have room for some more; who else?"

I managed to gather bags for half a dozen of the kids Sera

had introduced me to at lunch before my backpack started to look like that blueberry girl in *Charlie and the Chocolate Factory*. The pile of boxes didn't look any smaller. If anything, it looked *bigger*.

"Day one," I muttered.

My mom was constantly telling me that getting started on any project is the hardest part. I hoped she was right and that the worst was now behind me. On both the Kimberlee front *and* the Sera front.

When did my life become a soap opera?

I got the idea when I spotted a printing shop as I was driving home, trying to ignore Kimberlee belting rather off-tune to the radio beside me.

"What are you doing here?" Kimberlee asked, looking up at the nondescript shop.

"We."

"Huh?"

"What are *we* doing here. You have to help."

"Help what?"

"You'll see."

I pushed open the poster-laden front door and something chimed the first few notes of "Raindrops Keep Fallin' on My Head." A man in a button-up sweater poked his head out a doorway at the back of the store. "I'll be right with you," he chirped.

"No hurry," I called as I turned to a display of stickers and labels.

Kimberlee huffed beside me—and not too quietly. "Shh," I hissed at her.

"Why? It's not like Mr. Rogers back there can hear me."

I rolled my eyes and turned back to the stickers.

After I had browsed for a few minutes, the clerk took his place at the register. "What can I do for you?" he asked, sliding his order pad in front of him.

"You do all these custom, right?"

"Of course."

"When could you have them ready for me?"

"If you use one of our designs and just add words, I can print them for you in about an hour. Send-out takes five business days."

"Your designs'll work. Can you just give me this white oval?" I pointed to a strip of plain white stickers.

The man scratched on his order pad. "What would you like them to say?"

"I'm sorry, comma, Kimberlee. That's K-I—"

"Are you kidding me?" Kimberlee shrieked. "You can't just blab to the world that I'm suddenly giving a bunch of stuff back a year after I'm dead!"

I shot her a nasty look, but she didn't even notice.

"I forbid you to put my name on there! If you want to put

someone's name on there, put your own." Her voice was grating on my eardrums and it seemed like it just got louder with each word.

I cringed as the salesman asked, "M next? Right?"

Kimberlee screamed again, a sound that probably would have shattered the windows if she'd been alive—and I forced myself not to cover my ears. "You know what? I have a better idea; give me these instead." I pointed to the same round stickers, but just a little bit bigger with a pretty red flower and some decorative leaves printed along the bottom. "Leave off the name. Just print 'I'm sorry' on them with the flower." I shot a very pointed glare at Kimberlee.

The sales guy glanced at me worriedly but said nothing as he scratched out the order and started writing again.

"This is ridiculous," Kimberlee said. "But at least it's better than the name thing."

I rolled my eyes and turned back to the man. "How many?" he asked.

It was depressing to even think about. I looked up at the display. There was a bulk discount at a thousand. And that should definitely cover it.

I hoped.

"A thousand," I said, digging into my back pocket for my wallet.

The guy looked over the rims of his glasses at me for an

instant, probably wondering just how sorry I was for whatever I had done. "All right. About an hour."

Kimberlee didn't even bother waiting until we had left the store before starting up again. "Why are you doing this?"

"It's the principle," I said as I slid into my car. "If you're stuck here till you make amends, you should do more than just return the stuff. You *should* be sorry."

"And if I'm not?" she huffed, with her arms folded over her chest.

"By the time we're done, I bet you will be. But if you start trying to apologize then, it'll be too late. Start now." I slid into my seat and pulled on my seat belt. "If I have to do this, I'm going to make sure it gets done right. You don't get a choice on this one."

Kimberlee rolled her eyes. "You are the lamest thing that ever happened to me." Then she turned and walked away.

Eight

THERE'S SOMETHING ABOUT having a fight with a ghost that makes you paranoid in the morning. I kept checking over my shoulder in the shower, and I peeked out of my bathroom door before darting to my closet for the shirt I'd forgotten to bring in with me.

But in the end Kimberlee popped up beside me at my locker, two minutes before the bell, acting as if we hadn't argued at all.

I think that was the moment I understood how desperate she was. She could get mad and rage and ignore me all night, but in the end, she needed me. It made me feel really powerful for a few seconds before the guilt sank in. Of course I was powerful. She was a helpless ghost. Pain in the ass or not.

Okay, there was no reason to even end that sentence with "or not."

Nonetheless, when we put our plan into action a few hours later, I was glad she was there.

"Is anyone coming?" I asked.

"No, but hurry."

Kimberlee watched the doors as I ran across the cafeteria to the table where I saw Sera sitting yesterday and opened my backpack. I threw six gallon-sized plastic bags into a pile in the middle of the long rectangle and ran back as my heart sped up to about three hundred beats per minute.

"All clear," Kimberlee said, her eyes still scanning the halls. "Just look cool and keep your bathroom pass where the teachers can see it."

I haven't used a bathroom pass since I was in, like, third grade—and *never* one the size of a dinner plate. But at Whitestone they insisted such a nonconcealable pass cut down on the number of students who wandered the halls. Personally, I thought it was a good reason to hold it until lunchtime.

"Why can't we just look everyone up in the phone book and drop stuff off on their porch?" I muttered.

"Oh please," Kimberlee said. "People who can afford to send their kids to Whitestone are *not* listed in the phone book. And even if they were, do you know all these kids' parents' names? I sure as hell don't, and I've been going to school with them since kindergarten."

I glanced back down at the pass. "Fine."

It was ten minutes until lunch when I returned the

enormous pass to its spot and started on the assignment that would now be homework, since I didn't get to work on it the whole class period. Great.

Everything was quiet—so quiet that when the bell rang, I gasped and knocked my book on the floor. I should never apply for the FBI. For everyone's sake.

I entered the cafeteria hesitantly, and not just because the stuff I'd returned was there. Sera hadn't actually *said* that I was invited back, but the guys seemed to think I was cool enough, and she was coming to see me at the party. So . . . that meant I could sit with her again, right?

Sera was nowhere to be seen, but I wasn't going to make the mistake of standing like a dork with a tray full of food again, so I headed toward the table and hoped my invitation didn't have an expiration date.

"Ah, man," Wilson said just as I came into earshot, "someone left a bunch of crap on our table." He raised an arm to sweep it onto the floor.

Stop! Don't! my mind screamed. If this stuff got trashed Kimberlee was going to haunt me *forever.*

"Wait a sec." Hampton edged in and plucked one of the bags from the table. He pulled out a small day planner covered with Sharpie doodles. "This is mine." He stared at the planner in confusion, then flipped through it, pausing at some of the pages. "I lost this when I was in seventh

75

grade. It had a hundred bucks in it." He dug into a small pocket on the back page and pulled out a Benjamin. "No way. Sweet!"

Brynley pulled a pink T-shirt from another bag. "This was my favorite shirt freshman year. Someone stole it out of my gym locker."

I forced myself not to shoot Kimberlee a nasty look, but I heard her clear her throat behind me.

Brynley looked back at the bag. "What's this?" she asked, poking at the sticker.

I proceeded to get very interested in the wall to my left.

"'I'm sorry'? That's weird." But she tossed the empty bag into the garbage without another word and stowed her shirt in her backpack with a smile.

I caught sight of Sera making her way toward the table and subtly stepped back so I wasn't blocking the seat beside my tray. Because I'm supersmooth like that . . .

A few other people pulled things from the pile as she walked up—one from two years ago and one from just a few weeks before Kimberlee drowned. It was exciting to watch all the happy faces around me, and I tried not to be too obvious as I turned to watch Sera find her bag.

She sat staring at her skirt and shoes for a long time with no expression on her face at all while everyone else started digging into their food. Finally, when the din at the table settled, Sera said, "This is too creepy."

"Why?" I tried to ask casually. "Someone's conscience got to 'em."

Sera shook her head. "No. I know who stole these and she didn't have a conscience at all." She addressed the whole table again. "You all remember Kimberlee." It wasn't a question.

Wilson snorted. "Who could forget *that* beyotch?"

I stared straight ahead, not daring to look at Kimberlee. She told me she hadn't gotten caught, so how did Sera know?

"*She* stole these," Sera said. "I saw her do it. But she never would 'fess."

I tried to look as clueless as possible. "Kimberlee who?"

"Schaffer," she said with a dismissive wave. "Before your time."

"So, she reformed and gave you your stuff back?" I hoped it sounded like a natural—and uninformed—theory.

"Dude, she's dead," Wilson said.

"And good riddance," Sera muttered into her pasta.

I stared at Sera in shock. This was *not* the reaction I'd expected. Sure, she could be annoying as hell, but I figured it was just because *I* wasn't one of her friends. Hadn't Kimberlee told me how wonderful her life was? How popular she was? Open dislike was hardly the way someone as popular as Kimberlee claimed to be should be treated.

Especially a dead someone.

I chanced a look around. Kimberlee was nowhere to be seen.

She didn't show up again until I got into my car after school. And even then she slid silently into her place.

"Hey."

"Let's just go to the cave," she replied shortly.

We made it to the beach, and I filled my backpack with bags for Monday and started packing two boxes to set me up for the rest of the week before she spoke again. "I probably shouldn't have taken all this stuff," she said, her admission echoing in the cave.

I paused for a moment, then resumed yanking on my backpack zipper. "It's not really a 'probably' thing. You said you had *everything*. Why wasn't that enough?"

She sat on a box and stared at the ground. "I tried not to, but I couldn't stop. You don't know what it's like. What if I asked you to stop breathing, or eating—could you?"

"But it's not breathing or eating, Kimberlee. It's *stealing*."

"Don't you think I know that?" she snapped. "Don't you think that every time I came up here with more stuff to file away I hated myself for it?"

"Could have fooled me," I said, gesturing to the masses of boxes surrounding us.

She looked at me for a long time; not glaring, just studying me until I started to feel uncomfortable. "You think being a klepto means I *like* to steal stuff? I don't. I hate stealing. I hate stealing more than anything in the entire world."

"Then why didn't you *stop?*"

"I couldn't. I know you don't believe that, but it's true. I tried so hard. I went, like, four months one time. Then one day, I was walking behind this lady at the mall, and she had this stupid little fluffy keychain on the strap of her purse. And I wanted it so badly I couldn't think about anything else. I walked away. I went and sat on the water fountain and tried to think of anything except the keychain. And I started to shake. My whole body was, like, having convulsions. I was seriously afraid I was going to die if I didn't find that woman and take her keychain." She stared down at the ground, something that looked eerily like shame filling her face.

"So what happened?" I asked quietly.

"I found her and took the keychain," she said as if it was the most obvious thing in the world. "And I've never felt so good and so bad at the same time. I got this amazing high like I could conquer the world. But that was the moment that I knew I would never, ever conquer stealing." She shrugged dejectedly. "I kinda gave up after that. There didn't seem to be any point. I guess dying was the only way to stop."

"I'm sorry." But it felt like a stupid thing to say.

She shrugged. "My own fault for swimming out into that riptide."

"We all make mistakes."

"We don't all die from them."

"No, but some of us end up being miserable for the rest of our lives." I paused for a moment, considering that. "Maybe that's worse."

"As opposed to being miserable for the rest of your afterlife?"

Something in her voice made me feel sorry for her, and it wasn't a feeling I wanted to have. I needed to stay rational and in control here. Kimberlee was a veritable emotional steamroller and I was constantly in danger of getting myself flattened. I sat down beside her, but not close enough to touch. The cold, creepy feeling still freaked me out. "But it might not last too much longer. You return everything and apologize and you'll be out of here . . . to . . . wherever."

"It'll be a good place, won't it?" Kimberlee said, starting to smile now.

A little.

But I was so the wrong person to ask.

When in doubt, lie. "Absolutely," I said, without meeting her eyes.

Nine

"WAKE UP, LAZY ASS!" Kimberlee shouted at about two-hours-before-rational-time o'clock the next morning. "It's Harrison Hill day!"

"Sure," I said, grabbing a pillow and dropping it on top of my head. "And in case you didn't hear right, I'm going at ten o'clock *p.m.*"

"Duh. We have to go shopping now and get you something decent to wear."

That cheered me up like a kick to the head. "Shopping? Uh, no."

"Dude, I've seen what's in your closet. Old tees and faded jeans. And Converse? Please!"

"Vintage," I corrected her, defending my eclectic collection of shirts I'd very carefully selected from some of Phoenix's finest thrift stores.

"Whatever. Not good enough for Harrison Hill. When you go to a school with uniforms, you make the most of any chance to actually show off your taste. This party will be a full-on fashion show and your clothes will totes stick out. And not in the good way."

"I never stood out in Phoenix," I grumbled, smooshing my face back into the pillow.

"This is not Phoenix."

I mumbled something incoherent into my pillow.

She sat down on the bed, almost touching me, and I cringed. "This is your first chance to make a real impression on the social scene. You want to do it right."

Sometimes Kimberlee does have a point. "Fine," I said. "But nothing too wild. I don't want to look like some kind of weird freak show, fashionable or not."

"Absolutely," Kimberlee promised. "We'll go chic and elegant instead of cheap and flashy."

Chic. Elegant. That sounded good. Good enough to drag myself out of bed and into a nice, hot shower.

I admit, I didn't hurry. I lingered over the coffee and donuts that my dad had declared a new Saturday-morning tradition—I think it was his own little rebellion against Tina's health-food espionage—and I really *needed* to see the end of some news show that was on. Current events, right? By the time I finally grabbed my keys, Kimberlee had been pacing and throwing me dirty looks for fifteen minutes.

"Finally," she grumbled as I clicked into my seat belt.

"Where's the mall?" I asked, as I turned on my signal and headed out of our neighborhood.

"You're kidding, right? People like us do not shop at the mall. Not for a Harrison Hill outfit."

Well, my chances of picking out something quick and easy at Macy's just went out the window. "Where, then?"

"Oh please; Montana Avenue, duh."

"Huh?"

Her mouth dropped open and she gave me her best *you are an idiot* stare. "You don't know Montana Avenue? *Everyone* knows about Montana Avenue. It's the hottest place to shop." She settled back in her seat. "We'll find something fabulous there."

The light was still red, but it was going to turn any second. "Which way?" I asked, ignoring her lecture.

"I can't believe you don't know this."

"Get over it. Which way?"

The light changed and the Mercedes behind me honked.

"Which way?" I asked, gripping the steering wheel.

Kimberlee looked at me like I was a particularly gross bug, and the Mercedes honked again.

"Straight it is," I muttered, peeling out.

"You should have gone left," Kimberlee said with no change of expression.

I gritted my teeth and reined in my temper as I casually,

slowly, thoughtfully cut off about six cars, flipping a U-turn that left an arc of black tire marks across three lanes of traffic.

I was going to have to apologize to Halle later.

Kimberlee shrieked and attempted to grab hold of something, but she ended up sprawled across my lap. Well, sprawled *inside* my lap, since she sank right through my thighs. I gasped as ice shot up my spine and I was wracked with a bone-grinding chill that almost made me let go of the wheel. After that, she quietly directed me down the Santa Monica 10 to Lincoln Boulevard. My nerves were somewhat recovered by the time we reached the outdoor strip-mallish street that looked about two miles long.

At least Kimberlee was excited. She got out of the car, straightened her shoulders, and took a deep breath. "Let's go," she said cheerfully, as if nothing had happened.

I shuffled after her.

I have to admit, Montana Avenue was impressive, though I tried to act all nonchalant. Every kind of store you could imagine lined the streets, their displays so bright it was almost hard to look at. Hundreds of people milled around, most of them looking either like dazzled tourists or runway models.

Guess which category I fit into.

We passed a store with tailored suits and colorful dress shirts hanging in the window. "Let's go in here," I whispered to Kimberlee. This was classic and chic, wasn't it? Girls go for that metro look. I think.

But Kimberlee just wrinkled her nose. "SEAN? Oh please. What are you? A future MBA? No, don't answer that; I don't even want to know. Come on." I took one last glance at the window before trudging after her.

"Here," she said, surveying the front of a funkily decorated store, her hands on her hips. "This looks promising."

I looked up at the sign. Citron. My eyes went down to the window display. I wasn't even completely sure it was clothing. I mean, there was fabric on mannequins, but it was all drapey and covered with strange designs. Lots of snakes, flowers, and . . . Buddhas?

"Are you sure?" I asked.

"In, in!" she ordered.

Someone help me. Pushing open the door sounded a very soft tinkle in the back and a tall, thin woman with dark brown lipstick came walking up to me with a huge smile on her face. "Welcome to Citron. Can I help you find something?"

"Tell her you're just looking right now," Kimberlee said, already studying the racks of clothing.

"Just looking, thanks," I mumbled. "So what now?" I asked, flipping through the rack Kimberlee was eyeing.

She snorted. "I suggest you start by going to a stand with *men's* clothing on it."

"How can you tell?"

She rolled her eyes and strode to the other end of the store. I looked around, comparing the two sides. I guess there was a difference. The male side looked a little more brown. I squinted. Yeah, definitely more brown. I sighed and went over to stand next to Kimberlee.

"Hold this up," she said, pointing to a hideous yellow button-up shirt with brownish swirls all over it.

"You're kidding, right?"

She sent me a look full of fire and I yanked the monstrosity up to my chest. "Nope," Kimberlee said. "Put it back."

Thank you, universe.

She had me hold up several more shirts—some were a little less hideous and some a little more, but none were anywhere near the range I'd have considered wearable. I held up a semisheer, long-sleeved black thing with an intricate silver design on it, and Kimberlee paused. Then she walked all around me and continued to stand in front of me and stare. I was starting to get uncomfortable when she nodded.

"Get that one."

I looked around me. "This one?"

"Yeah."

"You don't want me to try it on or anything?"

She laughed like that was the silliest idea in the world. "I know what size you wear. Just go buy it."

"Fine," I huffed.

I took the shirt to the register without looking at it again, and the saleswoman gushed that it was the newest thing from some spring lineup, or something, and then took about ten minutes folding it into an oversized paper bag with tissue paper and everything.

"Here you are," she said with that fake smile. "That'll be eighty-four ninety-nine."

I turned and shot a wide-eyed look at where Kimberlee had been about two seconds before, but she had conveniently disappeared. I dug out my credit card, glad my mom had mentioned just yesterday that I should get some new clothes. Maybe she'd understand.

I was afraid of where Kimberlee might take me next, but relief washed over me as she lead me into a store called Blue Jeans Bar. This couldn't be too bad.

And it wasn't—until she made me buy a glittering silver belt.

"It matches the shirt," she protested when I refused to even pick up the spangled accessory.

"So? The shirt sucks!"

"The shirt is awesome. Trust me."

"Trust you?"

"Maybe that was the wrong phrase to use." She paused, thinking. "Believe in my innate fashion sense that has never been wrong."

My shoulders slumped. She *was* the one who had been to all the Harrison Hill parties before.

I picked up the belt.

"I knew you had good judgment," she said, flouncing off toward a huge display of baggy, torn jeans.

I tried to argue about the faded and patched jeans that looked just like the ones I had at home, and even more strongly against the jean jacket she paired them with. But when it came to fashion among Santa Monica's elite, I had nothing to go on, and though I'd never seen Kimberlee in anything but her uniform, I kind of assumed she must have been fashionable.

I refused to even look at the amount when the cashier rang me up. I could decide if it was worth it after the party.

"One more stop," Kimberlee said, heading back up the street.

"No, no, no, no, no!" I insisted as quietly as possible. "I am not getting shoes," I said, cutting her off.

"What?"

"I'm not getting shoes." I pointed at the bags I was holding. "This is enough."

"Who said anything about shoes?"

Well, that was comforting.

I followed her a few more steps into a store and stood there for several seconds before I realized I was surrounded by lingerie of every shape, size, and color I could have possibly imagined.

And several my imagination had never come up with.

The ten or so women in the store were all staring at me.

I froze for a few seconds before muttering, "Excuse me," and fleeing the store. As soon as I was safely on the sidewalk I looked up at the sign. Lisa Normal Lingerie. Perfect. Kimberlee strikes again.

Kimberlee walked out of the store with that wide-eyed expression of innocence I was becoming sickeningly familiar with. "You won't come in and just browse with me?" she asked. "I can't exactly move the hangers myself."

"You think this is about me being afraid to touch underwear?" I sputtered. Remembering that no one could see Kimberlee but me, I lowered my voice and slipped around the corner of the store. "This isn't about the underwear. You keep doing this! Putting me in stupid or embarrassing situations and then acting like you have no idea how it happened. Well I am *not* going to go in and do you a favor after you pull that kind of crap on me. No!"

"Whatever. You just don't want to be in a lingerie store."

"I am not afraid of bras!" I said, knowing, even as the words escaped my mouth, that I sounded like a total moron.

Kimberlee sighed dramatically. "Fine. I'll have to hope I get lucky with one of the other browsers."

"And I'm not going to wait out here on the sidewalk for you."

"Whatever," she said, and strolled into the store without looking back. I just grabbed my bags and walked back toward my car. She could find her own way home.

Ten

AT NINE THIRTY THAT NIGHT I stood in front of the full-length mirror on my closet door in an outfit that no one in their right mind would *ever* refer to as either chic or elegant.

"I look ridiculous," I whispered to Kimberlee who had, as I suspected, made her way back just in time to direct—as she called it—my transformation.

"Please," Kimberlee lectured. "I *led* the fashion revolution around here. When I was alive, I didn't just wear fashions, I made them. What you 'look' is fabulous. Stop complaining."

I watched my eyebrow raise in the mirror.

"This outfit accentuates your form," Kimberlee insisted, her hand doing this funky silhouette thing. I thought it just made me look skinny.

For starters, the pants were too big; the only thing keeping them from sliding down to my ankles was that appalling sparkly belt balanced on my hip bones. The shirt was covered with the jean jacket, which was too small. It only just reached my waistline and was too slim to zip up in the front.

"It's not for warmth," Kimberlee protested when I pointed that out. "It's decor."

At least she let me wear my old scuffed Doc Martens. "They're practically vintage," she said, using the same word that hadn't been good enough for my jeans and tees this morning.

I didn't care what she called them as long as she let me wear them.

"Okay," Kimberlee said after scrutinizing me from head to toe. "Let's go." She paused. "Unless you want to do some guy-liner—just a little?"

My eyes widened. *Oh hell no.*

"I didn't think so," she said, heading toward the door. "Come on, then; I'll show you the shortcut."

This was the hard part. "Uh, Kimberlee?"

"Yeah," she said distractedly.

"Can I go by myself?"

She paused and turned to look at me. "Yourself?"

I nodded.

"Why?"

I shrugged. "I'd just be more comfortable."

She still stared at me.

I was going to have to tell her. "I'm meeting Sera there."
Sort of.

Kimberlee stiffened. "She doesn't go to the parties."

"Well, she's coming to this one. Listen," I said before Kimberlee could speak. "I know you don't like her. So I think we'd both be better off if you just didn't hang around when I'm with her."

She laughed, a short, condescending bark. "You think that's going to happen very often?"

"Maybe, maybe not. But it's going to happen tonight and I want a little privacy."

She said nothing.

"Kim," I said, as gently as I could.

"Kimberlee," she corrected, but she sounded more hurt than mad.

"I don't think it's too much to ask for a night on my own."

"Fine," she grumbled. "Go." She plopped down on my bed.

"Kimberlee?" I said tentatively. "You want me to . . . turn on the TV for you or something?"

"Just go," she said, turning away.

I opened my mouth to explain further, but after the hell she'd put me through, I decided I should take the opportunity to leave and hope she wouldn't change her mind. I put my hand on the door and was about to turn the knob when Kimberlee said, very softly, "Wait."

I looked over at her and she seemed a little surprised that she had spoken at all. "What?" I said, not bothering to hide my exasperation.

She lowered her eyebrows for a second then said, "Be careful."

"Yes, Mom," I muttered under my breath.

"And stay away from Langdon," she added in a rush.

"Langdon?" I asked, my hand tightening on the doorknob. I still hadn't told her it was Langdon who'd actually invited me. "I thought you two were tight."

"We were," Kimberlee said, making me think there was much more to *this* story. "That's how I know he's a mean drunk." The concern vanished from her face as she flipped her hair back. "Just stay out of his way."

I wasn't totally confident Kimberlee hadn't dressed me up like a freak for revenge, so when I arrived at the bonfire I slipped very slowly out of my car and walked with my shoulders hunched forward. But to my surprise, most of the guys looked pretty much like clones of me—a few even had sparkles on their belts. By the time someone dropped a big red plastic cup of beer into my hand, I was feeling pretty confident. I looked down at the foamy amber liquid that almost reached the brim of my very large cup, and sniffed it tentatively.

Now, it's not that I hadn't had alcohol before. I always

got some champagne at Christmas and an occasional glass of wine at dinner. But I'd never had beer. Back in Phoenix, my friends and I had been planning a big party once school was out, so it was in my future, but none of us had gotten brave enough to acquire any on our own yet.

It didn't smell much like wine. But everyone here was gulping it down like it was liquid crack, so it couldn't be that bad. Right?

Right.

I took a deep breath and a big mouthful. Bleh. *Swallow, just swallow.* I finally got it down and looked around at all the partiers with new eyes. *What the hell are they thinking? This is disgusting.* Maybe the second taste wouldn't be so bad; I knew what to expect now and I hadn't liked wine on the first taste, either. I sipped this time instead of gulping. *Hmmm, not much better. But maybe a little.* I sipped again. It needed something. *Sugar?* I tried a bit more. *Salt,* I decided, but doubted I'd find any of that here. I'd have to just sip and walk and sip and walk while waiting for Sera to show.

As I walked around I saw familiar faces everywhere. In hindsight, maybe I should have brought a big duffel of bags from Kimberlee's klepto-cave. I could have handed twenty bags back to people who were too drunk to remember who gave it to them the next day.

Though somehow I couldn't see Kimberlee being very

happy about *that* plan. Oh well.

I eventually finished my beer and managed to grab some more fresh from the keg. I took a sip and made a very important note to myself—beer is better cold. Who had handed me a warm beer in the first place? I couldn't remember. But cold was much better.

Better is relative, of course; it was still gross.

"Heeey, man," someone slurred as a meaty arm found its way across my shoulders.

I looked up into Langdon's grinning face. I'd almost forgotten about him.

"I was hoping you'd come," he said.

"Hey . . . Lang," I said, smiling back.

He lifted his cup toward me, and I touched the side of my cup to his. Cheers.

"That your first?" Langdon asked.

"Second."

"We gotta fix that," Langdon said with a laugh, herding me off. Away from the direction of the keg. I resisted a little, not completely sure I wanted to leave the safety of the masses. And, well, I wanted to watch for Sera. But Langdon's arm was really heavy.

Luckily, we didn't leave the crowd, just kinda moved to the edge.

"You got 'em?" Langdon said to a guy who was handing

out shots from a box where a bunch of bottles were semi-concealed.

"Course," the guy muttered, and lifted out a cooler full of little plastic containers of Jell-O.

Well, not Jell-O *per se*. Jell-O shots in little condiment cups. I knew what they were, though I'd never actually had one before. I looked down at my beer and then over at the colorful display of Jell-O shooters. I wasn't the world's biggest fan of Jell-O, but anything was better than the beer.

I spent the next hour listening to Langdon and his friends make lame jokes while nursing my beer till the taste got to be too much, and switching to the Jell-O shots—Langdon always had a new one ready for me—to chase the taste away. Then, because drinking beer seemed like the "right" thing to do at a kegger, I'd grimace and start on it again. After going back and forth a few times, the beer didn't taste so bad. In fact, it was starting to taste pretty good. And Langdon's jokes were even getting funny.

I lost track of the time and jumped when Sera walked up beside me and touched my arm. "He-e-e-e-y-y-y-y," I slurred.

Those gorgeous green eyes looked up at me, then rolled. "You're so toasted."

Damn. "Yeah," I said with a sloppy grin. "But that's okay, 'cause you can have this." I handed her the rest of my beer.

"Thanks," she said dryly, and poured it on the ground.

"You want some Jell-O?"

"That's . . . okay," she said. Then she looked up at Langdon and I swear, the temperature dropped. "Langdon, I wouldn't say it's a pleasure to see you, but hello."

Smooth.

Landon's ego seemed to deflate for a second, but he recovered quickly. "Sera, my favorite cheerleader. Come to join the festivities for once?"

"I think you know better than to even ask," Sera said coolly. She grabbed a shooter, jiggling it slightly. "Jell-O shots? Really? That's what you've moved on to?"

"Dude, they're *awesome*," I said.

"Yeah," she said, holding the little cup between two fingers for a second before returning it to the table and turning her back to Langdon. "How many of these have you had?"

How many *had* I had? I tried to count, but suddenly I wasn't quite sure. Four? Five? Twenty-eight? I had no freakin' clue.

"That's what I thought," she replied to my silence. "You ready to go?"

"Go? Where?"

"You're wasted. I should take you home."

"No," I said, trying to sound suave. "I should take *you* home." And I tapped my finger on the tip of her nose. Or I meant to. I'm just glad I didn't poke her in the eye.

She smiled condescendingly. "Yeah, I don't think tonight's a good night for that. Come on."

"Hey, he doesn't want to leave." I felt that heavy arm around my shoulders again. "He wants to party. Don't you, bro?"

"Shut the hell up, Langdon," Sera snapped. "Jeff, where are your keys?"

"Not a chance, Barbie," Langdon said, and suddenly he didn't look quite so drunk anymore. Or so happy. "You think you can just waltz in here and ruin our fun? Crawl back under your rock."

That edge in his voice brought Kimberlee's words back into my brain with a jolt. *Mean drunk.* I was seeing it now.

"You know, when I heard you'd invited Jeff, I hoped it was just a casual invite—that you'd outgrown this stupidity. But we both know where this is going and I'll be damned if I'm going to leave him here with you."

"And you think I'm just going to step aside?" Langdon asked, straightening so he towered over her.

Sera didn't even flinch. "See this?" she said, holding up something black and . . . sparkly? *Oh, cell phone! Shiny.* "I'm one button from calling Khail if you don't let go of Jeff right this second. I am not taking any of your shit tonight."

I didn't know why that was such a threat, but after a second Langdon's arm slid off my shoulders. He looked mad as hell, but he didn't try to stop Sera as she grabbed my hand and pulled me away.

I turned and waved good-bye, but Langdon just glared at me with a level of hatred that didn't match the grinning guy who'd been handing me shooters for the last hour. And I was way too drunk for any of it to make sense.

"Gimme your keys," Sera said as she dragged me out to the dusty lot where all the cars were parked. "I caught a ride with Brynley and she won't want to leave yet."

"Oh no," I said, covering my pocket with my hand. "No one drives Halle but me."

She looked at me for a long moment before she smiled and said, "Well, maybe I can change your mind."

I liked the sound of that.

She curled her fingers through mine and pulled me closer. "You like me, don't you, Jeff?"

"Course."

"You don't mind if I do this, do you?" She slid her hand along the sides of my hips.

"Nooo . . ." *Oh, please don't let this end.*

"You could put your arms around me."

I was so in heaven. My hands worked their way around her waist and went right to her ass. *Oh yeah.*

"Ahem."

I looked at her with what I hoped was a convincing blank look.

"A little higher, or you can *walk* home," she said with a tight grin.

I moved my hands up a few inches.

"Much better."

Her hand was doing something on my hip, but I was too busy trying to look her in the eye. If only she'd stay in one place! "You're so beautiful."

"Oh yeah?"

"Yeah. I've wanted to kiss you from the first time I saw you."

"Really?"

"Uh-huh." If I didn't take this chance it might not come around again. I moved my face closer and she didn't pull away. I was almost there and let my eyes start to slide shut when she stepped back and something sparkly and loud jangled in front of my face.

Hey, keys!

Oh—my keys.

"Okay," she said. "Let's go."

I am such a loser.

Eleven

I DIDN'T SAY ANOTHER WORD until we were both safely inside my car. "You sure you know how to drive a stick?" I asked as she pushed in the clutch and turned the key.

She barely glanced at me as she smoothly eased the car out of its parking spot. "I think I can handle it," she said, accelerating and shifting gracefully from first right to third. Without taking her eyes from the road she changed the radio station, turned down the bass, and flicked off her brights as an oncoming car approached—like she knew every single button in my car.

"You've done this before," I said, not managing to form a more coherent sentence.

She laughed. "My dad has one of these. I drive it all the time."

So much for my special car.

As we wound around curves on the drive back to Santa Monica, I started to feel a little sick. I'm not sure now how I had expected to get home. I guess I just didn't plan on having more than one beer. It really was a good thing Sera came to rescue me.

I tilted my seat back and turned my head just enough to stare at her. The streetlights slanted across her face as she drove, giving her the look of being not quite real. Or maybe more than real. She had gone over and above for me tonight. Either she actually liked me or was amazingly nice. Maybe some of both.

We went around a few more curves and I realized that my stomach was starting to really get angry with me. I must have started to look sick because soon Sera stopped the car in front of some kind of park. "Come on," she said, opening her door and walking toward a small playground.

I felt a lot better in the cool air.

We walked over to the swings and while Sera swung high, I kinda pretended to swing low. The initial relief from the fresh air was slowly yielding to simmering nausea. After about ten minutes, I had to grind my feet into the sand to keep the swing from moving at all. Every motion made me feel worse.

Sera looked down at me then flew off her swing and landed soundlessly what looked like a hundred feet away.

"Wow," I said, before clapping a hand over my mouth.

"Come on," Sera said, tugging on my arm. "You'll feel better after you hurl and the kids who play here will feel better if you don't do so all over their swings."

I couldn't open my mouth to argue.

She pulled me over to a large garbage barrel and was kind enough to step quite a ways away as I puked up what felt like an ocean of beer.

I definitely did not drink that much.

Or eat that much Jell-O . . .

. . . did I?

When I finally stood up straight again, my physical relief gave way to embarrassment. *Extreme* embarrassment. Here I was, puking my guts out in front of one of the most beautiful girls I'd ever met. All I needed now was for Kimberlee to pop up and start pointing and laughing.

Finally I turned to Sera. "Sorry about that," I mumbled.

"It's okay," she said. "The real test will be if you go get plastered again the next time Langdon sponsors a party."

I grimaced and shook my head back and forth. "No thank you."

Sera dug in her purse for a few seconds. "Here," she said, offering a packet of tissues and a travel-sized bottle of Listerine mouthwash. "I packed this for you earlier."

I stared at them for a long time, feeling suddenly very sober. "You knew I was going to be an idiot," I muttered.

"Well, I didn't *know*. I try to give everyone the benefit of the doubt. But pretty much everybody falls for the lure of being Langdon's *special guest*," she said, then shrugged. "I did."

"Really?"

She smiled tightly and nodded. "End of football season my freshman year—the party to celebrate the last game." She turned and started walking up a grassy hill. I swished and spit some of the sharp mouthwash before following her. I stayed a few paces behind her as she walked up the hill, swishing all the way. By the time we reached the top, the bottle was empty, my mouth felt clean, and my stomach was getting back to normal. The air was fresh and crisp again and I felt a second chance coming on.

"Langdon invited me personally. I felt really cool. He kept giving me shots of Jägermeister till I lost count. And I know I kept going a long time after that." She reached the top of the hill and sat on the grass.

"Jägermeister?"

"Yeeahhh, trust me, Jell-O shots are much more . . . gentle. But I was a freshman and I wanted to be cool, so I choked it down till it started tasting better."

That sounds familiar. I sat down beside her, just close enough that our thighs touched. "So you got drunk and puked everywhere, too?"

She coughed out a sharp laugh. "I wish it were that simple. Yes, I got drunk, and yes, I eventually puked all over. But Khail had found out Langdon's plan from someone. They were going to get me plastered enough that they could make a fool of me in front of everyone. I imagine pictures would have been involved."

"What happened?" I whispered, almost afraid to hear.

But she smiled. "Khail rescued me."

"Like you rescued me?" I said with a grin.

"No, I just intervened tonight. Khail seriously had to *rescue* me. By the time he found me it was obvious I was in a really bad place. He dragged me away and put me in his car. I was half passed-out but they told me later he . . . he messed Langdon up pretty good. Broke his nose, loosened a tooth or two. He had two black eyes when he came to school on Monday."

"Sounds like he deserved it."

"Oh, he did," she said seriously. "But if Langdon hadn't been too scared to say anything, he could have made some real trouble for Khail. That's the kind of stuff no one wants on their record. My brother risked a lot for me when he taught Langdon a lesson."

I nodded somberly. "But it turned out okay."

"It did. Langdon has hardly said a word to me since and . . ." She hesitated and then seemed to change her mind. "Let's just say everyone got what they deserved."

She smiled up at me, but her smile was tight. "It's a Harrison Hill tradition now. Someone gets to be the butt of everyone's drunk humor. It's . . . not pretty. And I've never found out who it was going to be early enough to help. I'm glad I did tonight," she said, looking up at the sky.

My stomach felt sour again. No wonder she had suddenly paid attention when I said Langdon had invited me.

I had wanted her to think I was cool. She'd known better all along.

She turned toward me and the moon illuminated her pale skin. She had freckles that she probably hated—seems like all girls do—but I liked them. "I'm glad you're all right. I'm glad Khail was there."

"So am I," she said quietly.

The moment felt serious and I considered going in for a kiss, but it seemed too soon after—well, puking up my pride along with the beer and Jell-O. I rubbed my hands through my hair instead, feeling some of the crisply gelled spikes give way to the kind of fuzzy disarray I was used to.

Sera looked up and me and grinned. "You missed a spot," she said softly. Then she reached up and rubbed my hair, loosening more of the crispy strands. "There," she said after a few moments. "Much better."

"*Better* like this?" I asked.

She nodded and laughed as she plucked at my jean jacket. "And don't even get me started on your outfit."

"You don't like it?" Cue sound effect of my remaining

confidence shattering into about seventy billion pieces.

"It's okay," she said with a shrug, "I just don't think it's *you*. I mean, when I first saw you, you looked . . . relaxed. Nobody in Santa Monica is relaxed. You were wearing Converse and you looked about as comfortable as you can get in our stupid uniforms. Then something happened—maybe the preppies at Whitestone got to you—but you totally changed. The funky hair, the metro getup."

"Wait," I said, and my mind was trying to make a connection I was still just a little too drunk to get at easily. "You noticed me my first day? Like, before I did this to my hair," I added, pointing at my "ruined" hair.

Sera looked down at her lap, and even in the darkness I saw her cheeks flush. "I'm a front-office TA," she said evasively. "I notice all the new students."

Sure she did. "Okay, no more weird," I said with a smile. "That I can do."

She ran her fingers across my chin. "This I like, though."

The stubble. Score!

"It makes you seem more . . ."

"Virile?" I suggested.

"I was thinking more along the lines of *laid-back*," Sera said, laughing.

I hesitated, but figured I had nothing to lose by being honest. "I just wanted to impress you tonight."

She raised an eyebrow.

"No really, I saw you that first time and—"

"The day you thought I was Khail's girlfriend?" she teased.

I sighed. "I figured you were a popular cheerleader and you'd be into this kind of guy," I said, gesturing to my outfit.

Sera laughed again and shook her head. "I'm not exactly your typical cheerleader. I don't even like the actual cheering that much. But it gives me a chance to perform and compete with gymnastics."

"Can't you just do that in . . . uh . . . gymnastics?"

She looked away. "It's kind of complicated. I . . . I *was* in gymnastics. I was training to be a national competitor, but I took a couple years off right when training is the most crucial. So, basically I got left behind. Catching up isn't easy; trust me. I have a private coach now, but I don't compete or anything." She shrugged and smiled sadly. "Someday I might be good enough to be on a college team, but right now I'm not that great, and it feels weird competing against thirteen-year-olds. So I cheer instead."

"How come you took that time off if it's so important?"

Sera waved the question away. "I just did." We were quiet for a few minutes before I leaned over and bumped her shoulder with mine.

"So you're really not into the whole trendy-guy thing?" I said.

She shook her head. "Nope."

I mussed up my hair a little more. "That's a relief."

She grinned and looked up at me. "What would you have worn tonight if you hadn't been trying to impress me?"

"My Luckys. One of my vintage tees. A hoodie. It's what I usually wear."

"That's exactly how I pictured you."

My head was still spinning, and though I suspected it wasn't just from the company, I said it anyway—I might never get another chance. "Honestly? I probably wouldn't have gone to the party at all if you hadn't agreed to show up."

"Oh yeah?"

"Th-there's just something about you; something different," I stuttered. "I've wanted to get to know you since the first time I saw you in the hall."

I lifted a hand and let my finger trace down her face. I don't know how I mustered up the courage, but my hand slipped behind her neck and I let my head drop forward until our foreheads touched.

"Um," Sera said hesitantly, "are you seriously trying to make a move on me after you puked in the garbage can fifteen minutes ago?"

I froze. "No?"

She grinned now. "Yeah, I believe *that*." She reached out and squeezed my arm even as she pulled her head away from mine. "Maybe another time," she said softly.

Close enough.

We watched the six or seven stars that struggled to shine through the smog and the Santa Monica lights, and laughed when one of the "stars" flew away. We chatted idly about nothing until Sera groaned and pulled her hand out of her pocket. A soft blue glow from her Rolex brought us back down to earth. "It's almost one. That's my curfew on weekends." She looked over at me. "I don't think you're quite ready to get behind the wheel yet. I'll drive you home and have Khail come get me."

I shook my head ruefully. "I would have been fine if it weren't for all those Jell-O shots."

"How many did you have?"

I grinned at her self-consciously. "After a couple it's so hard to remember."

She laughed and poked my stomach. "You really are a lightweight."

"And you're not?" I retorted, elbowing her ribs gently.

She rolled her eyes. I stood and reached down to help her up. "Thank you," I said. "For . . . for everything."

She hesitated. "Jeff?"

"Yeah?"

"Next time there's a big party, will you come hang with me instead?"

"Really?"

She shrugged one shoulder. "You're nice. Different," she said, looking sidelong at me, "but nice."

"Of course I will," I promised. "This was way better than any party could have been."

And with a smile like hers, I didn't need beer to feel drunk.

Twelve

"WHERE THE HELL WERE YOU?"

The voice reverberated painfully in my skull as I attempted to open my eyes. The instant they met the glaring, early morning light I screwed them shut again.

"Well?"

This was definitely not the way my mom usually talked to me—even when I was in trouble. I held my hands up to my eyes and squinted through my fingers. *Yep, Kimberlee.* "What do you care?" I mumbled and squished my face into my pillow.

"I got bored and went to the party—I wasn't following you; I went to see other people. And you were *gone*! I had no clue what might have happened to you. Dead on the highway, taken off and gang-raped by the chess club—I don't know!"

I raised my head for a few seconds, not even having the energy to get mad at her for breaking her promise. "Aww, you care. That's sweet. Would you shut up now?" I flopped back onto my pillow. My head was throbbing and every word she said echoed through it like a racquetball.

She kept pacing and yelling, but I didn't hear much after that. I pulled my pillow over my head and in the relative quiet managed to slip back off to sleep.

When I woke up again, she was gone.

Thank goodness.

My stomach rumbled and I glanced at the clock: one p.m. *Damn.*

I staggered out of bed, stumbled down the stairs, and tunnel-visioned in on the coffeepot—which luckily still had a few cups in it. That was exactly what I needed this morning. Afternoon. Whatever.

As my hand touched the pot handle my mom said, "Nuh-uh, Jeff. Coffee'll only dehydrate you."

I spun around and about dropped my mug as the kitchen lights made streaks across my vision.

My mom's tinkling laugh went through my ears like a sledgehammer through a window. "Sorry, didn't mean to scare you." She gestured to the chair across from her. "Sit."

I did as commanded and laid my cheek against the cool tabletop. I was halfway back to sleep when my mom patted my shoulder.

"Trust me, this will be better."

I raised my head and looked down at a large cup of tomato juice, a bagel with strawberry cream cheese, a smaller glass of

114

orange juice, and two white pills. I pointed at the pills and muttered, "Huh?"

"For your headache."

Man, I was in so much trouble.

The bagel looked at least edible. I nibbled on one side to avoid thinking about the enormous tomato juice.

"Be sure you drink both glasses—you need fluids and electrolytes."

I nodded as though we were discussing the weather instead of my very underage night of binge drinking. Or, uh, Jell-O shootering. I picked up the huge glass of tomato juice and forced down two swallows.

By the time I'd finished the bagel and both glasses of juice, I didn't feel like I was standing at death's door anymore . . . more like waiting at the end of the driveway. Mom schmeared me another bagel and brought a glass of water with it. "So," she began, "you want to tell me about last night?"

I groaned and let my head sink into my hands. "I don't even want to *think* about last night. It was awful."

"How much did you drink?"

"About half as much as I puked."

She laughed.

I cringed.

"Sorry."

"My own fault." Fun fact: I have gotten out of more

115

trouble with these three words than you can possibly imagine.

"Yes, it is."

"How did you know?"

"I went in to grab your laundry while you were sleeping and it reeked of smoke and beer; that was my first clue. But mostly it was because I tried to poke you awake and you didn't even move." She looked amused. "There was a lot of snoring and drool, though."

There wasn't much I could say to that.

She put on her Mom face. The Jeff's-in-trouble face. "How did you get home? Your car is here; I hope you weren't driving drunk. There are serious consequences for that. And I don't mean with the law."

"A friend drove me home."

"In *your* car?"

I laid my cheek down on the cool table again. "Uh-huh."

"Was this friend drunk at the time?"

"No, she doesn't drink."

Mom leaned forward on her elbows. "She? A girl?"

I'm never going to hear the end of this. I nodded.

"A special girl?"

"Maybe."

Mom nodded slowly. "Okay. You're off the hook for drunk driving. So what did you think of getting drunk?"

"It sucked."

"How much?"

"A lot. But not as bad as the hangover. I'm dying, Mom."

"I'd say that's a pretty good consequence right there, wouldn't you?"

I nodded.

"You're not off the hook," Mom warned. "There are still consequences in your future after I talk to your father, but for now I think you're punishing yourself pretty well."

"Thanks," I mumbled.

"Don't thank me yet. Part of your punishment is definitely going to be telling me more about this girl who took pity on you."

I sighed in defeat and threw my hands over my eyes.

"I hope you had a good time last night," Kimberlee said from across the room as I was attempting to pull on my socks.

I fell off the bed in surprise.

I hate hangovers.

More than ties. More than name tags. Maybe even more than mean, kleptomanic ghosts.

"So?"

"So what?"

"How was it?"

"The party sucked ass and I don't know what anyone sees in beer."

Kimberlee scoffed. "Sera shut you down, didn't she?"

I grinned. "Nope. She saved me from the beer."

My cell phone rang and I desperately rummaged through my jeans for it. I wanted nothing more than for the ear-splitting noise to stop. I finally found it and jabbed the talk button.

"Hello?"

"Jeff?"

Sera! My hangover seemed to melt away. Well, half of it anyway. Maybe a quarter. "Hey, how's it going?"

"Good," Sera responded. "I just wanted to check that you were okay."

"Better now."

Kimberlee pointed her finger down her throat and walked into my closet. Through the door, of course.

"How'd you get my cell number?"

"Told you—I'm a front-office TA."

I laughed. "You *stole* it?"

"I am a master thief." I wished Sera could have guessed at even a fraction of the irony in those words.

It took me a few seconds to realize that since there was no school today, she must have gotten my number *before* the party. Nice.

I was sure there had to be a great, snappy comeback to that, but all I could come up with was, "Yeah." *Idiot.*

"You're really feeling okay?"

"Better than I was an hour ago."

"Good enough to do something tonight?"

"Depends what you had in mind," I teased, knowing full well that I was game for anything other than maybe poking our eyes out with red-hot needles.

And even then, if there was making out involved, I'd probably think about it.

"I didn't really have anything planned, but there are a couple of good movies showing. And I'm one of those girls who actually eats, so when I say I'll buy the popcorn if you buy the tickets, it's an even split."

Split? I was *so* not letting this girl pay for *anything*. "Yeah, that would be cool," I said. My head started spinning so I sprawled onto my comforter with the sad realization that I wasn't going anywhere in the immediate future. I glanced at the clock. 1:48. "How about at like seven?"

"So what *exactly* happened last night?" Kimberlee asked, reappearing the instant I hung up. "You said the party sucked and now you're traipsing off on a date with the girl who is known for *not* attending the parties. Did you even go?" She asked in the kind of tone my mother would ask about skipping out on dinner with my grandparents. "Because if you got an invite from Neil and skipped you are *never* getting an invite again. I worked really hard to get you ready and you—as usual—were totally ungrateful and I should have known you'd blow the whole thing off for this stupid girl like the—"

"Stop!" I finally managed to say, ending her barrage of words. "I went to the party, okay?"

"Then what happened?"

I let myself fall back onto my bed, closing my eyes again. "I went, Langdon got me drunk, Sera rescued me."

"Langdon? What about Neil? I told you to stay away from Langdon."

"Neil didn't invite me—Langdon did," I replied, still not opening my eyes.

"You lied to me?"

I didn't even have the energy to dignify that question with a response.

"Why didn't you tell me?" she demanded, her voice getting shriller.

"Two words," I said, groping blindly for the edge of my blanket to pull it over my head. "Special. Guest."

That got her. Well, for a few seconds. "Langdon invited you as his special guest?" she said quietly.

"Yep," I said from underneath the comforter. "Thanks for the warning."

She was silent for a good thirty seconds. I wasn't convinced I had ever been in her presence for a silent thirty seconds. I hoped she was feeling bad.

"I'm stuck with the loser who got brought out to Harrison Hill to be Langdon's special guest. I *am* in hell!"

My eyes popped open and I peeked out at her. "Seriously?" I croaked. "I almost got burned at the social stake and you're concerned about your reputation? Which, by the way, doesn't matter because you're *dead*?" Maybe we were *both* in hell.

"Oh sure," Kimberlee said. "Play the dead card. That's fair."

"I'm not trying to play *cards*. All I'm saying is that you could have warned me that Langdon's an asshat and told me to stay away from him *always*, not just when he's drunk."

"Hey, Langdon's a nice guy."

"No, Kimberlee, he's not! He's a sociopath. Anyone who would purposely get someone drunk just to make fun of them is a worthless jerk. Period. End of story."

Kimberlee snapped her mouth shut and clenched her jaw. For one terrifying moment I thought she was going to start yelling again. Then, for some reason, she burst into tears and left.

I will never understand girls.

Thirteen

WHEN I ARRIVED AT SERA'S, all I could do was sit in my car and stare. This was not a *house*. It was like a cross between a mansion and a castle. A mastle. Even Kimberlee's house wasn't this big.

At the top of a winding walkway I was almost surprised to find double wooden doors instead of a drawbridge. I tried to decide if it was more appropriate to knock or ring the bell and briefly wondered if there would be a butler.

Finally I decided that unless there *was* a butler standing within about three feet of the door, no one was ever going to hear me knock. I sucked in a breath and touched the glowing white button to the right of the door. Honestly, I expected to hear something like a big gong from inside, but what I actually heard was nothing. I was just starting to wonder if the bell was broken, or if I hadn't pushed it hard enough, when the doorknob turned.

I was pretty sure it wasn't a butler, but seeing as how the

person who opened the door was a man in a suit—tie and all—I think my momentary confusion was justifiable. We stared at each other for about five seconds before the man raised an eyebrow and asked, "Can I help you?"

And since I'm always cool under pressure I gracefully responded, "Yeah, um, Sera and . . . Is Sera . . . I mean, can I . . ." Finally I thrust out my hand and said with a stupid grin, "I'm Jeff."

He looked at my hand for a beat before shaking it with a less-than-confident grip. And I don't mean *self*-confidence.

"I'm here to pick up Sera," I said, still smiling like a dork and trying to figure out just who this guy was. Dad? Creepy uncle? And I still hadn't *entirely* ruled out the butler thing.

"Oh," he said, his eyes narrowing. That definitely swung the votes in favor of *dad*. I irrationally wished I'd worn a tie.

"I'm here!" Sera called from the top of the stairs, hurrying down. Right before her dad's eyes swung to her, she mouthed *I'm sorry* to me.

We managed to make it out of the house without too much drama, although Sera's mom did peer around one of the many doorways to remind Sera to be home by ten. Or at least she said the words "Sera, remember, home by ten," but the whole time she was staring straight at me.

Once the front door was shut and we were far enough that I was *fairly* sure that they couldn't hear us, I asked, "Man, how is it that parents manage to be the scariest creatures on the face of the earth?"

"You're telling me," Sera grumbled.

I looked sidelong at her. "They're scary to you, too?"

"They rule my life."

I guess she was right, but I never thought about *my* parents that way. They were cool; always had been. Note to self: I am lucky.

We got into the car and I eased Halle away from the curb. I had a sneaking suspicion Sera's parents wouldn't be overly impressed by my peeling out of their pristine cobblestone driveway. "You can, uh, pick whatever you want to listen to," I said, pointing at the radio.

Without a word she flipped the station to something rock, but not hard, then turned the sound down to an obvious talking level. *Excellent.*

"So, where do you want to go?" I asked.

"Well, I did say something about a movie earlier today," she said helpfully.

I fidgeted. "Yeah, but . . . I was hoping we could talk. Last night"—I laughed as I ran my fingers through my hair—"I was in bad shape." I wondered if it was a stupid move to even remind her. "I just . . . I want to spend some time with you when we're both on even ground."

She smiled. "Sooooo," Sera said, dragging out the word,

"did you have any suggestions?"

"Um, are you hungry?"

"Like any proper girl going on a date of unknown destination, I am *halfway* hungry."

"Uh . . . what?"

"It's when you eat a little bit before you go out so that you're hungry enough to eat something if the guy takes you for food, and full enough that you won't be starving the whole time if he doesn't."

Sera always has a plan. And probably a backup plan.

I never do.

"How about dessert?" I asked.

"Dessert?"

"Yeah, since you're all halfway hungry, you know?" *Wait*— I framed the question carefully. "Do you . . . eat dessert?" I mean, you never know with girls.

She gave me a full-out grin on that one and I about melted. "I love dessert."

I pulled into the first restaurant I saw and a few minutes later we were tucked into a booth with a peanut-butter milkshake and a brownie-fudge sundae in front of us as well as a Diet Coke. I always think it's weird to see people who order a dessert . . . and a Diet Coke.

"I like the way it tastes," Sera said, defending herself when I pointed it out.

"Suuure," I slurred, spooning the whipped cream off the top of my milkshake.

We polished off our desserts in the first fifteen minutes or so, then sat and talked idly. She told me about Whitestone; I told her about Phoenix. And I had to ask her what it was like living in such an enormous house.

"I'd be lying if I said I didn't like it," she admitted. "We have a gym and a theater room; I have my own bathroom, that kind of thing. But . . . I don't know, when I think of my 'family' I don't think of my parents. I think of Khail. Just him. I guess I wish I had a real family and a smaller house."

I grinned and told her about my parents and their rather inauspicious beginning. "I have a few memories of living in an apartment where my 'room' was the couch," I said, and she shook her head.

"Seems like everyone wants what they don't have," she said, then looked up at me. "But you kinda have everything you want now, don't you?"

I shrugged. "I'm lucky, I guess." Or would be, if I could get rid of psycho ghost girl and keep things moving along with Sera.

Another hour passed in good but oddly awkwardness-free small talk until the waitress's glares became a little too obvious to ignore.

"Not exactly your 'linger over coffee' kind of restaurant,

I guess," Sera said with a giggle as we headed into the parking lot. I wondered if it would be too weird to take her hand. After all, we were only twenty feet from my car.

But it also seemed weird to not do anything. Finally, when we were only about ten feet away, I placed my hand at the small of her back. She didn't react; I wasn't sure if that was good or bad. When we reached the car she turned and looked up at me as she leaned against the door.

"So, what now?" she asked with a coy grin.

I found myself smiling back. "I don't know."

She looked down at her watch. "Well, I have to be back in twenty minutes, but that gives us about ten before we have to actually get going."

Was she trying to say something? I couldn't be sure.

I finally decided that at the very least, she was saying *something*, so I carefully placed my hands on either side of her waist, making sure I wasn't putting them anywhere near her ass. No repeating my lame mistakes from last night.

She smiled up at me like she was indulging me, but she didn't pull away. "I'm not really like the guys you usually date, am I?" I asked. May as well know.

She laughed, and shook her head. "Maybe not."

"Then . . . why did you say yes?" Part of me didn't want to know, but hey, after embarrassing myself so badly last night, a simple question could hardly be a deal breaker.

"Well," she said, looking thoughtful for a few seconds. "I haven't had a boyfriend in a while—"

Great. I'm the rebound guy. I braced myself.

"But when I was dating a lot it was always jocks or the really popular guys and they all turned out to be jerks." She shrugged. "You seem nice. *Actually* nice—not just nice to get in my pants."

Well . . .

"And I guess I'm trying to follow my instincts this time instead of my social compass."

Was that a compliment or not? Screw it—I didn't care.

So I kissed her.

Her mouth was so soft and warm I could hardly believe it was real. But when I got nervous and pulled away, her fingers pressed tight against my back and she ran her other arm up around my neck, pulling my face back down to hers. My hands, still at her waist, pulled her toward me, our hips snug. I could taste the restaurant's complimentary mint on her breath. Her hands gripped my shoulders, almost like she needed help balancing. Foreheads still touching, I reluctantly ended our kiss.

And when she smiled I started another one.

I did manage to get her home on time. Barely.

Fourteen

"SO WHEN DO WE DO IT?" Kimberlee asked just before getting out of the car the next morning. It wasn't a *great* plan, but it would work.

"Not during Bleekman's class. Or Wilkinson's. I left his class on Friday. He'll get suspicious."

"Okay, how about second hour? That'll give me enough time to get the combos. You can tell Mrs. Campbell you have to pee."

My shoulders slumped at the thought of carrying around the piss-pass again. "Fine," I said. "You do your job and I'll do mine."

"Whatevs," she said, flipping her hair over her shoulder and strolling off. She looked so normal and solid until someone walked too close and an arm or a shoulder passed through her. I shuddered involuntarily at the thought.

Luckily, I had something much more pleasant to look forward to. "Hey!" I said, smiling as I approached Sera at her locker.

She turned and smiled back and I tried to move in for a kiss and she turned it into a hug.

Yeeeeah.

"Sorry," Sera said, sounding very genuine and impulsively grabbing for my hand instead. "I swear, I don't know how to do this anymore. I'll be honest: I haven't had a boyfriend in a while. Like, over a year. I'm . . . rusty." Her face flushed and I was stunned to realize that she wasn't having second thoughts about *me*; she really was just out of practice.

I could work with that.

"Sera," I said, and I waited until she looked up at me. "It's okay, things are kinda new. But I had a great weekend with you, and I don't want that to go away." I grinned now and leaned my face a little closer. "And if you just want to use me as your get-back-in-the-game fling, well—I've done worse."

She totally cracked a smile.

The bell rang, a loud clang in my ears that made me grit my teeth, but at least the air was cleared. "So . . . see you at lunch?" I asked, shifting my backpack.

"Yeah."

I didn't try for a kiss again—just squeezed her hand. I really liked her and I wasn't going to mess things up by being impatient. I could wait.

For a while.

Besides, I had work to do today. I didn't hear a word in

Bleekman's class—just kept wondering if Kimberlee was going to come through for me. I mean, it was her salvation and all, but I never could tell with her.

But just before English ended, Kimberlee slipped in—through the wall—and started whispering numbers in my ear. I wrote them down in my notebook vertically, hoping that if someone looked over my shoulder they wouldn't be able to figure out what they were.

And maybe because it made me feel all secret-agentish.

Kimberlee followed me to second hour and hovered over my desk in the most nerve-racking way possible. Of course.

Class started and, without so much as a hello, Mrs. Campbell stepped up to the board and began lecturing. My class in Phoenix hadn't been quite as far along as this one, so I really couldn't afford to space. I attempted to tune out Kimberlee asking, "Is it time yet?" about every three minutes and waited until halfway through the class, then sheepishly raised my hand.

Mrs. Campbell looked at me skeptically when I picked up my backpack on the way out the door, but she didn't stop me. After all, I was carrying the oversized pass and I'd left my book on my desk. Not really an ideal combination for ditching.

As soon as the door closed, Kimberlee led me to the closest locker. I was glad, for once, that she was there. I'd have spent my full bathroom-plausible ten minutes just looking for it. As the combination lock clicked open I looked surreptitiously down both halls, certain someone was going to burst in at any moment.

"Go!" Kimberlee prompted.

I unzipped my backpack, double-checked the name on the bag, tossed it in, and slammed the door shut. It had been less than ten seconds. My heart beat madly as Kimberlee hurried toward the next locker and pure adrenaline flowed through my shaky limbs.

We repeated the process twice more before Kimberlee looked at my watch. "Good time," she said. "Now hurry back."

Now I was so terrified I really did have to pee. Unfortunately, despite the enormous pass in my hand, I no longer had time.

I walked back into class and slid into my seat, sure everyone's eyes were on me. But I heard nothing but the scratch of pencils on paper surrounding me. After another ten minutes passed, I allowed myself to breathe normally.

Every day that week Kimberlee and I skipped out of a different class and hit three or four more lockers. If that sounds like a lot of progress, let me break it down for you: It wasn't. It was like trying to empty a bathtub with a teaspoon.

But at least we were doing *something*.

Kimberlee tended to disappear for most of the morning—

far longer than should have been necessary to get the combinations to our target lockers. That was fine with me, though; the less she was in my life, the better.

Thanks to Sera, I had started to think of lunch as the most wonderful time of the day. Things were getting a little less weird with her friends, though I still didn't participate in the conversations very much. But I was starting to realize that Sera didn't either. Not that she was standoffish, just quiet. Maybe even a little shy. It was like she wore cheerleader camouflage to fit in, but she wasn't really one of them, in a lot of ways.

On Friday we slipped away from the lunch table fifteen minutes before fourth hour. Sera was talking about some assignment for her Trig class as she was getting books out of her locker, and I was sort of listening, but I admit she was wearing one of her shorter skirts and I was taking full advantage of the fact that her back was to me. Besides, I was in AP calc—if she asked me a question, I could *probably* come up with a decent answer fast enough to avoid getting caught.

Sera pushed her locker closed with a clang and turned to me with a smile. "You're such a good listener," she said appreciatively.

I shrugged in a faux-modest way. *Just don't ask me what you were talking about.*

"Other guys I dated wanted to talk about their games

and their latest session in the weight room and . . . well, about themselves, pretty much all the time."

"That's the advantage of dating a nerd," I said. "Guys are pretty much all the same. We like to talk about how awesome we are and all the coolest stuff we've ever done. For jocks it's their big goal in football—"

"Touchdown," Sera corrected with a grin.

See, I'm funny, I thought, laughing inwardly at my little joke. "Yeah, that," I said. "But the coolest thing I've ever done is gone on a date with the . . ." *What did she call it?* "Junior co-captain of the cheerleading squad." Her widening smile told me I'd gotten her title right.

And then, because I was feeling both confident and bold, I reached down for her hand, curling my fingers around hers. I held my breath, wondering if she would pull away.

She didn't. In fact, she leaned closer. My heart was racing when she tilted her head toward mine and kissed me.

This was no dark parking-lot kiss. This was a public, in-school, in-front-of-her-classmates kiss. A gossip-starting, relationship-cementing kiss.

I'm telling you, a good relationship is all about finding common ground.

And then making out on it.

I nearly jumped out of my skin when the knuckles rapped on the lockers right next to my ear. "Break it up, Miss Hewitt,"

Mr. Hennigan said, not slowing as he strode by.

Sera's cheeks flushed a little, but I wasn't even fazed.

I scored another quick kiss as I dropped Sera off at her history class. As far as I was concerned, this was the green light for our relationship to get going full speed ahead. The possibilities were endless. I dropped into my seat and started planning my weekends.

Long movies in a dark theater, long drives in a dark car, long . . . talks . . . in dark parks.

I was sensing an emerging theme.

"Okay, I got 'em," Kimberlee said, startling me from my daydream.

I just stared stupidly up at her, not yet out of my lust-induced haze.

"Would you get out your pencil?" she yelled. "I can't remember all these numbers forever!"

Locker combos—right. Hello, reality.

Fifteen

"WE CAN'T DO THIS MUCH LONGER," I hissed to Kimberlee as we left the classroom and speed-walked down the hall. "My teachers are all going to think I have some kind of bladder infection or something."

"I don't see you coming up with any bright ideas," she said, her voice both strained and desperate. I was reminded how few options *she* had.

"I'll work on it," I said as I reached the first locker. "Is this Khail's?" I'd been carrying around Khail's bag since Tuesday. But for three days in a row Kimberlee refused to get the combo for reasons I couldn't even begin to guess at. Only after I threatened to stop returning stuff did she finally bring me his numbers. I felt like I owed it to Sera as her shiny new boyfriend to get her brother's stuff back to him.

"Yes, I promise. Just do it and let's move on."

"Keep watch."

She walked several feet away and peered down the hallway.

Unfortunately, people can come from both directions. I didn't even hear Khail's footsteps until he'd grabbed the front of my shirt and slammed me against the lockers. "What the hell do you think you're doing?"

I was too terrified to make a sound.

With his iron fists still holding me prisoner, Khail took two steps toward the bathroom door and used me to push it open.

Next I got slammed up against the tiled bathroom walls. Much more painful than lockers, but thankfully also more private.

Kimberlee wandered in sheepishly and stood in the corner, watching.

"Why were you breaking into my locker?" Khail asked.

His voice was incredibly calm—*scary* calm. I still couldn't speak, but I managed to gather enough wits to hold up my hand, still clutching the bag containing his belongings.

Khail's eyes darted to the bag, and widened. He loosened his grip. A little.

With one hand still on my collar, he reached out and snatched the bag from me. After looking at it for a minute he released me entirely. "You stay right there," he said, jabbing one sausage-sized finger against my chest.

Yes, sir!

He opened the bag and pulled out a worn black Yankees hat. "No way," he said, almost too quietly to hear. As he was staring at the hat, a pair of red silk boxers fell out and onto the floor. He eyed them for just a second before recognition dawned on his face and his hand darted out to grab them and shove them in his pocket.

Then he saw the sticker on the bag.

His eyes narrowed and in about half a second his hand was back at my throat. "Tell me what you think you know."

Know? "I don't know anything!"

"Then why did you take these?"

"I didn't steal them. I'm just giving stuff back."

He paused for a second. "Did you give Sera her skirt and shoes?"

"Yes." Honesty seemed like the best policy at the moment, even though Kimberlee was yelling, "Deny! Deny!" at the top of her lungs.

"Where did you get them?"

"I just found them," I said in a much higher voice than I usually use as his grip tightened around my neck. I'd always felt that my six-foot-two height gave me an advantage over bullies. Apparently it made no difference to this five-foot-eight mass of muscles.

"I've been watching you hit on my sister all week."

Oh shit.

"And I haven't stopped you. You seemed like a nice guy. But now? Give me one reason why I shouldn't give you two black eyes and promise to break your arms if you even speak to her again."

Then he raised his fist of death and I experienced a level of desperation at which I would do or say anything in order to stop the inescapable pain rushing toward me.

"Kimberlee Schaffer's a ghost!" I shouted, then covered my face with my hands. As if that would help. I'd probably just wind up with two black eyes *and* two broken hands.

But Khail's arm stilled. "What the hell are you talking about?"

"No, no!" Kimberlee shrieked. "He is the *last* person in the world you want to tell that to!"

But I babbled on anyway. "Kimberlee's a ghost but I can see her and she won't leave me alone unless I help her return all the stuff that she stole I have no choice in the matter and I'm not trying to hurt anyone I thought I was being the good guy." The words rushed out in a single breath.

Khail glared at me for a long time. "How stupid do you think I am?"

"It's true. There's this big cave on her parents' beach and it's full of stuff I have to give back and every day Kimberlee gets locker combos for me."

"Kimberlee. The *dead* Kimberlee?"

Kimberlee tossed her hair in offense but I nodded. "Kimberlee Schaffer. I shouldn't even know about her; I just moved here. I'm not lying."

"You're out of your mind."

"No, no, I'll show you. Look." I remembered the tactic Kimberlee had tried to use on me that first day. "Hold up a number behind your back."

"What?"

"A number. On your fingers," I said. "Hold it up behind your back. I'll close my eyes and Kimberlee will tell me what it is and I'll tell you."

Khail rolled his eyes. "You think I'm an idiot?"

"Please? Just once."

Khail glared. "Don't you dare try to run."

"I won't."

He sighed and I covered my eyes with both hands.

"Ready," Khail said, sounding bored.

"Kimberlee?"

She crossed her arms over her chest. "This is the lamest thing ever. I'm not helping you; I am not helping him!"

I pointed my finger at her—or at least I tried to; it was kind of hard to be sure with my eyes closed—and hissed, "You tell me right this minute or I am done. I swear I am done!"

She let out an annoyed sigh. "I hate you!"

"Hate me all you want. What's the number?"

"You are a head case," Khail muttered.

"Kimberlee, he hits me, I ditch you, and you walk the earth for*ever*," I growled through my teeth.

Kimberlee was silent for several excruciatingly long seconds, but finally she told me what I needed to know.

"You're not holding up a number," I said. "You just have a fist."

Khail didn't say anything for a few seconds. Then he spun me around, not only holding me tight in a headlock, but with his forearm pressed tight against my eyes. "Do it again," he said, his voice soft, controlled, and with a deadly edge that scared the shit out of me.

"Two," I whispered, grateful beyond reason when Kimberlee spat the number right out.

A moment passed and nothing happened.

Nothing.

Then the enormous forearm retreated and sunlight pierced my eyes. After blinking a few times I looked over at Khail. He looked like he'd swallowed something too big for his throat.

"You honestly believe what you're telling me, don't you?"

I was too scared to talk. I felt like the whole rest of my life might balance on this moment. I just nodded.

Khail licked his lips. "Ask her what I gave her for her tenth birthday," he said after a long pause.

"Um, dude, she's not deaf."

Killer eyes swung at me.

I raised my hands. "Sorry."

Kimberlee rolled her eyes. "Trick question. He hasn't come to one of my birthday parties since I was, like, eight."

I conveyed the message.

Khail's jaw clenched, his jaw muscles—even *they* were huge!—working furiously along the side of his face. "Ask her . . . ask her . . ." Then he was silent.

The bathroom was silent for a long time and I couldn't tell if Khail was leaning more toward believing me, or swinging back to wanting to kill me.

"Jeff," Kimberlee piped up softly. "Tell him he doesn't have to ask."

"What?" I said, turning my head away from Khail, but feeling him jump at the sudden noise anyway.

"Tell him he doesn't have to ask."

"Uh . . . she says you don't have to ask."

"What the hell does that mean?" Khail asked, but his voice was quiet now.

"Tell him I haven't told anyone. Not even you." It was the most sincere thing I'd ever heard Kimberlee say, and she was staring at Khail like it hurt her eyes to look at him.

I faced Khail again. "She said she hasn't told anyone." I

shrugged. "Even me." I hoped I sounded as clueless as I felt.

His eyes widened and suddenly it looked a little like he was having an asthma attack. His breathing went ragged and he looked around the bathroom like a man hunted.

Or haunted.

"Where is she?" he asked.

I pointed off to my left where Kimberlee stood.

Khail's gaze flicked to where I'd pointed and his eyes narrowed like he could will himself to see her. Finally he released the front of my shirt. "Tell her I hate her."

"She can—"

"I want *you* to tell her."

"He hates you," I parroted obediently.

Instead of looking defiant, or bored, like I expected, Kimberlee stared at the ground, cowed.

"Tell her she has no idea how badly she messed things up and how glad I am that she's dead."

I repeated his words again.

When I was done Kimberlee's head was so far down I couldn't see her face anymore. After a few moments a sob wracked through her chest and she gasped against it. I swallowed hard; I'd only heard that sound a couple of times in my life—once from my mom, at her sister's funeral.

"I didn't do it," Kimberlee choked out.

"She said she didn't do it," I whispered, wishing Khail

could hear her himself. "I think she means it." I wanted to mention the tears, that awful sound, but I had a feeling Kimberlee would kill me if I did.

But Khail didn't look fazed at all. "She's a liar," he said, his voice like iced steel.

Kimberlee fled the bathroom without another word.

"This isn't over," Khail said. "I don't want *her*"—he said it like it was a nasty word—"in Sera's life, even as your invisible friend." He hesitated. "Don't tell Sera about this," he warned. "Not a word." Then he was gone, the door closing noisily behind him before I could even catch my breath.

"Not a problem," I whispered to the empty space.

Sixteen

I WENT TO THE CAVE BY MYSELF that afternoon; Kimberlee hadn't shown her face since our bathroom run-in with Khail. It was the first time I'd been there alone. Annoying or not, Kimberlee's yapping had made the beach feel more . . . *alive*. Now it was too quiet and more than a little creepy. I nearly jumped out of my skin when a seagull swooped low and let out a piercing caw. Today it was easy to imagine someone dying here. It felt lonely and empty. I wondered how much time Kimberlee had spent down here by herself when she was alive, and if she had felt lonely and empty too.

I climbed into the cave and blinked in the darkness. The never-ending boxes stared back. As I gathered a bunch of bags from a box simply marked *Whitestone*, I was nearly overwhelmed by the hopelessness of my task.

I couldn't keep doing things this way. We'd scarcely begun and I'd already been caught once. No one was going to believe

I had to piss that much, and eventually someone was going to realize I was doing something sneaky.

But what else was I supposed to do? I'd agreed to help and even if I didn't have the threat of a crazy ghost hanging over me, I had to admit, it was kind of nice giving stuff back to people. It made them happy.

Well, except Sera.

And Khail.

But even he seemed pleased to actually have his stuff back. A hat and silk boxers. Now *that* was a story I wished I knew.

Still, at this rate, I was going to graduate from *college* before I got everything done.

When I got home I poked my head through the garage door and checked for any signs of life before speed-walking through the kitchen, my arms loaded with stolen stuff, and hurrying up the stairs to my room. I managed to only drop two bags while I tried to get my bedroom door open. I swore under my breath and kicked them into my room, hoping they didn't contain anything too fragile.

Kimberlee was sitting on one of the ginormous bean-bags I got for Christmas. I tell you, it's the weirdest thing to see someone sitting in a beanbag without making a dent. At all. And why didn't she just sink right through it? Or right through my floor, for that matter? The physics of

Kimberlee's ghostliness continued to elude me. But then, what about Kimberlee *did* make sense? Ever?

My knee-jerk reaction was to demand an explanation, or maybe give her a sarcastic greeting after being ditched all day, but I remembered the way she'd sobbed in the bathroom and settled for a quiet "Hi" instead. I stashed the stuff in a corner of my closet and closed the door before turning to face her. "You okay?"

"Yeah, of course," Kimberlee said, sounding completely emotionless.

I was silent, waiting for her to say . . . I don't know. Something. "So," I finally blurted, "crazy day, huh?"

She just raised one eyebrow and shrugged.

I sat down on the bed and began unlacing my Docs. "Come on. You don't get to have a scene like that with Khail, disappear for the whole afternoon, and then just shrug. What's up with you and Khail?"

"Nothing," Kimberlee said flatly. "There is absolutely nothing between us."

"Well, not anymore. But—"

"There wasn't anything between us in life, either."

"Oh please. He hates you; you hate him—unless you want to claim you hated everyone in life then there is def—"

"I don't hate him," Kimberlee said. Her voice still had that eerie, flat tone. "I just can't stand to be around him."

Oh. Now I got it. "You *liked* him?"

She swallowed. Answer enough.

"Okay," I said, trying to keep my tone light. "So you liked him and then you died. Is that it?"

"Basically."

Basically my ass. "So why does he hate *you*?"

"Because I'm a bitch," she said simply, as though it were the most obvious answer in the world.

"Come on," I said, trying to look her in the eyes. "You have no one to talk to except me and I can't tell anyone in the world about you."

"Except Khail."

I bit back a sharp retort. "Except Khail, who I hope to never speak to again lest I die young. So spill."

"I liked him, I tried to get with him, he rejected me, and I . . ." She rolled her eyes and I couldn't tell if it was because she didn't believe what she was saying, or because she couldn't believe she was saying it. "I reacted badly."

"What do you mean, badly?"

"I was mean to him. I kinda held some stuff over his head; I picked on his sister," she snapped. "I am a spiteful, terrible person, okay? There, I said it. Happy?"

"What did you hold over his head?"

She shook her head. "No way. I've learned my lesson—it's his business, not mine. Just . . . I was a bitch; end of story."

"Okay." Then the rest of her admission sank in. "You picked on his sister?" I said, too loudly.

Kimberlee slid back against my pillows with an irritated sigh. "It's ancient history; would you just leave it alone?"

"I can't leave it alone when it keeps coming back and slapping me in the face. Today, almost literally. Is there anything else you'd like to tell me while you're in confessional mode? Like why *do* all the kids at my lunch table hate you? What did you do to them? Did you pick on them, too?"

"No!" Kimberlee said, getting pissed. Somehow pissed was better than sad. Less scary. "I was the queen of the school. In case you are unfamiliar with the pecking order, that means I was that person that everyone either adored or hated because they were jealous out of their minds. That is *not* my fault."

"Jealousy? That explains *everything*," I said sarcastically. "Who *did* like you?"

"Langdon!"

"Oh good, Langdon the asshole. I'm so proud of you."

"And Neil," she continued almost desperately. "Kyndra liked me too. We kinda ran the school, okay?"

"With an iron fist, maybe? I'm starting to think you were just a bully with sticky fingers."

"I was not a bully!" Kimberlee protested.

"Oh yeah? I find that a little hard to believe from someone

149

who admits she was mean to someone she *liked*. How did you treat people you *didn't* like?"

"Screw you!" Kimberlee said, standing on my bed. "You have no idea what it's like to be me!"

"That's because half the time you won't tell me anything, and the other half you're lying!" I yelled back, not considering until the words were out of my mouth that my dad, at least, was almost certainly home. If I made it through this ghost ordeal without getting thrown in a padded room, I was going to be seriously proud of myself.

Kimberlee glared at me for a second and then sank *through* my bed and out of my room via the floor. Despite everything that had happened in the last couple weeks, my hands started to shake at the creepiness of that moment. I managed about two and a half calming breaths before my phone rang, making my heart go erratic all over again.

And seeing Sera's name on the caller ID may have sped it up even more than that.

"Hey," I said, hoping my voice wasn't shaky.

"Hi. My parents are driving me nuts. You want to do something tonight? Preferably outside of my house?"

"I'm fine; thanks for asking. And how are you?"

She started to laugh and the stress of the last few hours seemed to melt away. "Sorry," she said. "Long day. Long week, really. I wish I got to see you more."

"Me too," I said, the sad truth of those words sinking right into my bones.

"So can we please, please, please do something tonight?"

I loved how she asked like I would even dream about saying no. "Well, since you said please. Did you have anything in mind?"

"Something completely brainless," she replied. "How about we actually go to a movie this time?"

"Sounds good to me. What's playing?"

"Does it matter?" Sera asked in a tone of voice that suddenly made me feel very anxious to leave.

"No, no, it doesn't," I replied. "When can we go?"

"In an hour?" she suggested.

"Half," I replied with a grin.

"You're on."

I laughed as my mom knocked softly and popped her head through my doorway. "You have a guest," she said, in a weird-ass cheerful tone that made me suspect she had heard me yelling at Kimberlee. My poor mom.

"I'll be down in a sec, Mom," I said, but she opened the door farther, revealing Khail's steely gaze. His shoulders were as wide as my doorway.

Just to add to the weirdness, Kimberlee was standing behind him with her arms folded over her chest. I suspected they had "run into" each other in the front yard. My mouth went dry and I think my throat may have started closing up. "Hey, listen," I said to Sera, the words pouring out of my mouth. "On second thought, let's go in an hour. I'll pick you up, okay?"

As soon as she made some kind of positive response, I hung up with a quick "Bye."

"Hey, Khail," I said, trying—unsuccessfully, I might add—not to let my voice crack.

My mom departed and Khail let the door swing shut behind him, pushing it until the latch clicked. Probably just wanted to beat me up in private. Understandable.

Neither he nor Kimberlee spoke, resulting in a moment of silence, like at a funeral. In this case, *my* funeral.

"I want to see the cave," Khail finally said in a surprisingly quiet voice.

"The cave?"

Khail pointed a meaty finger at me. "You said there was a cave," he said, his tone full of accusation.

"Oh, Kimberlee's cave. Yeah, sure, of course." Like I was going to say no? "Uh . . . let's go now." I walked past him and opened the door—it felt more like opening the gate to a cage—and led my little entourage down the stairs, Khail clomping along resolutely and Kimberlee noiselessly pouting.

I threw off something about the mall to my mom and headed out to the garage. As the door was rising I asked, "You want to, um, ride with me or . . . ?" I let the sentence hang in the air.

"I'll follow," Khail said, heading toward a jacked-up, chrome-wheeled, neon-tricked truck parked on the curb. Seemed fitting.

I backed Halle out and headed toward Kimberlee's house.

"This is not a good idea," Kimberlee said, her voice panicky. "Besides, who the hell said you could bring him on my property?"

"You gonna call the cops?"

Kimberlee crossed her arms over her chest and stopped talking.

Khail's truck was close behind me as we made our way through the gate and down to the small parking lot. Both Kimberlee and Khail were silent while I led the way to the cave and scaled the wall—quite impressively, in my opinion. The practice was paying off.

Khail, on the other hand, climbed up at least as effectively as I had, and it was his first try. *Jocks. Meh.*

I gestured as if introducing Khail to the rows and rows of boxes. Strange how the cave still looked exactly the same despite having cleaned out almost eight boxes.

"Are you serious?" Khail asked.

"Uh . . ." I had no idea what he was asking.

"All these boxes are full of stuff that Kimberlee stole?"

"Yeah."

"Sera was right," he said quietly. "She told me Kimberlee stole her cheer skirt and shoes and bet that she was behind this big theft thing at the school a while back. I didn't believe her. I mean, I believed that Kimberlee stole Sera's stuff—Sera wouldn't just flat-out lie to me like that—but I didn't think Kimberlee would be involved in something this big." He turned to me now. "Someone must have helped her."

"As far as I can tell, no."

Khail whistled. "Damn, she really *was* messed up."

I kind of coughed and looked away.

"What?"

I shrugged and pointed my thumb in Kimberlee's direction.

"She's here?"

"She has nothing else to do and just follows me around most of the time."

"Don't worry about making me sound like a loser or anything," Kimberlee said caustically. "I was just leaving." And before I could stop her, she walked to the edge of the cave and jumped gracefully down and out of sight.

"Okay, *now* she's gone," I said.

Khail had his fists on his hips, staring—as far as I could tell—at the rocks against the wall instead of the mounds of stolen stuff.

I wouldn't want to look at them either.

"I still don't know what to think," he said quietly. "You have all the right answers. Things you shouldn't know—hell, this whole cave should be proof enough. But . . ."

"I know," I said when he didn't continue. "It's completely unbelievable." I shrugged. "I still sometimes think I'm going to wake up soon. Possibly in an insane asylum somewhere."

"It's so much stuff!"

I nodded miserably.

"Man, you need help."

I sputtered for a few second. "Oh, come on. I'm *not* the one who stole it; I told you that. I—"

"I didn't mean it that way," Khail said, interrupting me. "I mean you're never going to get all this stuff returned on your own."

I remembered the truck that was sitting out in the parking lot. That was one big-ass truck.

Don't get ahead of yourself. I hazarded the question. "Is that an offer?"

His eyes darted toward me, then back to the boxes. "Maybe." He picked his way carefully to the back of the cave and I could see him counting silently as he estimated how many boxes there were. I already knew the answer. A hundred and thirty-seven. I'd counted them about ten times. "She'll go away as soon as all this stuff is returned, right?"

I nodded. "That's the idea."

He walked back over to me and stood close. "How much do you like my sister?"

I swallowed. "A lot."

"Enough to do whatever it takes to get Kimberlee's ghost out of her life?"

As if that wasn't what I wanted too. "Absolutely."

"Okay. Meet me at Perennial Park at noon tomorrow. I'll bring the truck, and I'll see if I can get together a bunch of guys. We'll take half—" He paused, looked back at the boxes, and qualified his statement. "We'll take a chunk of this stuff back on Monday." Then he turned and began lowering himself down the edge of the cliff.

"Monday? But wait!" I scrambled over down the rock wall after him, banging my knee. "Who are these guys? How am I supposed to plan something this big by Monday? I mean, we can't just waltz in there and say, 'Hi, this is from that dead girl.' I might not get to see life outside of bars again."

Khail didn't even slow his step. "That's the deal," he said brusquely. "I provide the manpower and the truck. You come up with a plan, smart-ass. Work with me, get this done, or Sera is off-limits until you patch things up on your own." He turned to fix me with a glare. "You understand what I'm saying?"

I hesitated, but what choice did I have? Besides, it *would* go way faster this way. "Tomorrow at noon," I agreed.

And with a squeal of tires, he was gone.

I slid into the car beside Kimberlee and started the engine. We were almost out of her cul-de-sac before she spoke.

"Well?"

"Well, what?"

"What happened? You were in there a long time."

"He came, he saw, he offered to help."

"He offered to *help?*"

"Did I stutter?"

She sat back in her seat again, her face full of confusion. "It's a trick. He'll get you caught," she finally concluded.

"I don't think it is."

"Trust me. He hates me."

"That's why he wants to help, actually. Get you out of here so he doesn't have to live in the same world as you anymore."

"That was real sensitive," she muttered.

"Look, it will take me months to get through all that stuff in there on my own, and I'll probably get caught before it's all gone. Do you want to move on, or whatever, or don't you?"

"Of course I do," she said in a tone that didn't quite have me convinced.

"Then this is the best way to go. Khail is going to meet me tomorrow with a bunch of guys and—"

"A bunch of guys? You are *begging* to get caught. People

157

around here *cannot* keep secrets, Jeff. This is all going to blow up in your face."

"Maybe it is, but what choice do I have? I can't do this alone and I'm not going to try anymore." I hesitated before adding, under my breath, "And it's not like you can stop me anyway."

"Me getting stuck with you is *so* unfair," she responded.

"So true."

Seventeen

I GOT TO PERENNIAL PARK a full fifteen minutes before noon the next day. I'd convinced Kimberlee to stay home this time. For real. I didn't want her chattering in my ear while I was trying to concentrate. I couldn't help but feel like something big was about to happen. That, or I was about to get caught and expelled, and go down on record as having the shortest enrollment in Whitestone ever. Either way, I didn't want any distractions.

It didn't take long before cars started pulling up. A bunch of guys, most of them built like Khail, got out and leaned against their vehicles. Finally Khail's big black truck rolled in and the guys headed toward it like homing missiles. Khail stepped out and his eyes locked immediately with mine. He gestured to the group and they all walked over to me; there must have been about fifteen of them. For the first time, I felt confident.

This might actually work.

"Jeff," Khail said, walking up with a box under his arm, "meet the varsity wrestling team. Team? Jeff." He rattled off a bunch of names, but I hoped he didn't expect me to remember any of them.

We wandered over to a pavilion with a bunch of picnic tables under it and Khail set the box down as everyone else took a seat. When the team was settled, Khail reached in. "Stevens," he barked, and one of the guys looked up right before a bag hit him in the chest. "Moore." Another guy, another bag. Soon every wrestler but one had a bag. "Sorry, Sig," Khail said, and I had a moment to briefly wonder if Sig was short for Sigfried or maybe Sigmund—what was wrong with parents out here? "I didn't find one for you."

I'd told Khail the code for the beach gate, but I hadn't expected him to actually go back to the cave. I wondered how many hours he'd spent last night finding the bags for his teammates. I had clearly underestimated his commitment to this project.

Or maybe his hatred for Kimberlee.

The wrestlers started rooting in their bags, some pulling out one item, others two or three, with murmurs of surprise and even some laughter before one guy—the one Khail had called Moore—looked up at Khail and said, "What the hell is this?"

"This is all stuff that got stolen from you guys over the last few years," Khail said.

"I can see that," the guy replied, clearly not satisfied. "Why do *you* have it?"

Khail looked over at me. "Jeff was doing some cave exploration a couple weeks back—science geek," he added, and the whole team nodded like that was explanation enough. "And he found a cave full of this stuff."

"A cave?" another guy piped up.

"A cave," Khail said firmly. "I've been there; I've seen it. You got a problem?"

The guy raised his hands in dismissal, but his face was still cloaked in disbelief.

"It's full of tons of stuff," Khail said, "like what I just gave you." He stood a little taller. "I want to give it all back. Everyone deserves to have their belongings returned."

"So give 'em back. What do you need us for?"

"Come here," Khail said, gesturing for us to follow him. We walked over to his truck and I noticed for the first time that there was a big green tarp in the back. Khail leaned over the edge of the truck bed and lifted a corner of the plastic, revealing a sea of bags. "This is only . . . maybe ten or fifteen percent of the stuff in that cave," Khail said. "That's why I need you. There's something for practically everyone at Whitestone, including teachers." He tossed the tarp back over the loot and looked out at the wrestlers. "So, you guys in or not?"

"This is the stuff from the big theft ring, isn't it?" one of the smaller guys asked.

Khail nodded.

The guy shook his head. "I can't have anything to do with this. Hennigan already had me on his list for that because I have shoplifting on my record from when I was in middle school. He'll blame me. Hell, he'll probably *expel* me."

"That's the risk," Khail said, nodding. "And not just for you. You all know how obsessed Hennigan was. He still can't talk about it without blowing a vessel. He won't care who *really* stole this stuff. *Any* of us get caught and we're dead meat."

"So why bother?"

"It's the right thing to do," Khail said calmly, not missing a beat. "I was happy to get my stuff back—weren't you?"

He looked around the circle as each wrestler eyed his bag of stuff.

"How do we know you didn't steal it all in the first place?" asked one guy who I didn't think looked nearly large enough to accuse Khail so directly.

"I have my faults, but I would never steal from my teammates, and I think you all know that," Khail said, not looking offended at all.

"What about him?" the little guy piped up again. "I don't even know him."

I opened my mouth to defend myself, but Khail spoke over me. "Jeff just moved here. I think being four hundred miles away is a damn tight alibi."

"Why don't you take it to the cops?" asked another guy.

"You think the cops are going to give anything back to anyone?" Khail said coolly. "They'll confiscate everything, label it as evidence, and no one will see it again." He paused. "I want all this stuff to go back where it *belongs*. No one likes being stolen from." He paused for a second, then cleared his throat. "So I'm in, whether you guys are or not. But anyone is free to walk away right now." He pointed a finger at the group. "You're all bound to secrecy about what I've told you so far; don't get me wrong. I will make sure anyone who rats pays—even you, Vincent," he said, looking at the only guy there bigger than himself. "But I won't force anyone to join us. Me and Jeff'll do it ourselves if we have to." He stopped and looked across the semicircle of guys. "Who's in?"

The guys looked back and forth at one another and then down at their bags of stuff. Finally the big guy—Vincent?—raised his chin. "I am."

One of the shorter guys nodded. "Me too."

A couple more guys echoed him and after about thirty seconds, everyone had agreed to join—even the guy with the shoplifting record. I felt a tangible weight float off my shoulders as I looked around at the team who had all just agreed to help me. Well, help Khail. Hell, I didn't care; they were helping.

"Okay," Khail said. "Anyone who spills gets jumped by the rest of the team and don't think that doesn't include you, Jeff."

"What? *I'm* not telling!"

"Just setting the rules," Khail said.

"So what are we going to do?" one skinny guy finally asked.

Khail turned to look at me and everyone else followed his lead.

I think I broke out in an instant sweat.

"Um." I scratched at the back of my neck and hoped it wasn't turning red. "I didn't really have a ton of time to plan last night." I suddenly hoped Khail didn't know I'd been out on a date with his sister. And for the first time I wondered just how much she'd told him about me. Specifically, about what we'd been doing throughout the entire movie. My ears were starting to heat up at the thought. "But I thought if we loaded a ton of the stuff into the truck and labeled it well, we could probably just leave it in a huge pile in the gym." I looked at Khail. "You know, start simple."

"Like Christmas?" a guy piped up from the back.

"Sure, moron," another shot back. "Maybe we should get a Christmas tree to top the whole thing off."

The two guys started arguing, but Khail's eyes lit up and a half grin formed on his face. "Guys, knock it off. That would be awesome, don't you think?"

"What, a Christmas tree?" I asked. "But it's January."

"No, seriously, picture it. We have an assembly tomorrow for our Northridge match. That would give us all excuses to be out of class. So right before lunch, everybody walks into the gym and there's a ten-foot-tall Christmas tree with piles of those bags underneath. The school would go crazy!"

The guys were starting to smile and talk and I leaned in a little closer to Khail. "The point isn't to make *anyone* go crazy. I wanted to get this done with as little attention as possible."

"Jeff," Khail said seriously, "you've got over a hundred boxes of stolen shit to return. There is no way to do that without having anyone notice. I'm already starting to hear people talk about stuff that's suddenly coming back and you've hardly returned anything. You don't understand how big a deal this thief was. Kids being pulled from the school, police patrolling the parking lots. It was massive. Trust me, people will talk. If we do this—and it's going to get noticed anyway . . ." He trailed off, then finished with a grin and a flourish. "We may as well do it with style."

"Where we gonna get a Christmas tree this time of year?" one of the wrestlers asked.

"My parents always line our front walk with ten-footers.

They're in storage. They'll never know one's missing," Khail offered.

A Christmas tree. The idea was growing on me. After all, there was nothing wrong with *style*, as Khail put it. We huddled closer and began to hammer out details, mostly how we were going to get everything into the gym without getting caught. But between a bunch of jocks with huge duffel bags who hung out in the gym a lot anyway, and Kimberlee to keep invisible watch, I figured we'd be able to pull it off.

"Okay," Khail said as we started to break it up, "there are enough bags here for everyone to take fifteen. Fill up your gym bags, backpacks, whatever. Bring 'em Monday."

"Oh!" I said, remembering. "You'll need these." I pulled out my big roll of "Sorry" stickers and ripped off a strip for each guy.

"Why do we have to put these on here?" one of the shorter guys asked.

"Don't you think whoever did this is sorry?" I asked. Totally lame.

The guy looked dubiously up at the huge pile of bags. "Maybe?" he said, more a question than an answer.

"It's a logo," I said, still holding the stickers out to Shortie. "The stuff I've already returned had the stickers on them and if we don't put them on these, too, no one'll know it's the same person."

"So?"

"Dude, it's cool," Khail interjected. "We're going to be totally famous around school."

"Yeah, but no one will know it's us."

"That's half of the point. We'll be like a secret society. A league." He was really getting into this.

Shortie looked dubiously down at the strip of stickers in his hand. "I guess," he mumbled.

Khail and I both helped hand out the bags. Slowly, Khail's teammates returned to their cars and drove away. Finally it was just Khail and me and fifteen bags.

"You counted them out exactly," I said, watching as Khail stuffed the remaining bags into his own duffel.

"Couldn't sleep last night," Khail said evasively.

"How did you know everyone would agree?"

"Because I know my team. They're good guys."

"I see that," I said quietly, wondering if I would put myself on the line for someone I didn't know. I barely agreed to do it under threat of psycho haunting. "I never did say thanks," I added.

"Well, I don't exactly have totally selfless motives," he said, brushing it off.

"Yeah, actually, you do," I countered. "You're not getting anything out of it. Even if it's for Sera, that still doesn't directly benefit you."

"Whatever. I have my own reasons," he said, turning his back on me.

Note to self: Do not get personal with Khail.

Third hour had never felt so long. I sat there listening to Mrs. Wilkinson drone on about economics and didn't hear a single word. Khail had insisted that, this once, I couldn't help.

"You gotta be the one with an alibi," he said seriously. "The rest of us can all claim that we thought we were just helping with the assembly. But if the trail leads back to you, you have to have proof you weren't involved."

"But I'm the only one who can talk to Kimberlee," I argued. Kimberlee had agreed—volunteered, even—to be on watch for teachers, custodians, and especially Principal Hennigan while the wrestlers were pulling off their antiheist.

She seemed more focused since Khail had become involved. I think that she—like me—had almost given up on the idea of ever getting everything returned. There was just too much for one person. But now, with a whole team of wrestlers helping, we could be done in a couple of weeks! I thought she would be happy, but she seemed more serious. Maybe that was good, actually.

"Dude, she can go through walls; she can run right to you if there are any problems—which there won't be," he tacked on confidently, "and you can grab the piss-pass and come warn us."

I still wasn't convinced. But Khail was sure they could pull it off alone, and he did have a point about the alibi thing.

The bell rang for the assembly and I forced myself to pack my backpack at a normal pace before joining the rest of my classmates, merging into the crowd of students ambling toward the gym. My heart started to race as we approached the double doors, where people were already filing through. Was there more noise than usual? Less? It was my first assembly at Whitestone. I had no idea.

I clenched my fists as I walked through the doors.

My jaw dropped.

Khail had truly outdone himself. A ten-foot Christmas tree stood in the center of the gym, hastily decorated in the school colors. There were streamers and balloons and some-one had thrown handfuls of confetti over the whole thing.

And beneath the tree, stacks and stacks of Ziploc bags—also covered in confetti. There were already people sifting through the contents, calling out names, and tossing the bags to one another. Kids were smiling and laughing as the few teachers who were there tried fruitlessly to clear them away from the tree.

"Nice, huh," Kimberlee said, suddenly right by my ear. I was extremely proud that I didn't fall down on the floor and go into convulsions.

"They did a pretty good job," she continued coolly. I stepped away from the doorway so the crush of students wouldn't trample me, and leaned against the wall with Kimberlee.

"This is amazing," I whispered out of the side of my mouth.

"Khail's such a show-off." But she sounded pleased.

Sera was standing off to the side of the crowd, observing everything with her arms crossed over her chest. I walked over to her and slid my arm around her waist.

She didn't react—just stared straight ahead. I wondered if I should pull my arms back. But finally I leaned down a little closer to her ear and whispered, "Everything okay?"

She looked up as though just noticing I was there. "Yeah," she said, turning her head back to the crowd. "I just . . . I mean, really. What is this?"

I managed to shrug casually.

"I'd bet money this is more stuff that Kimberlee stole. And here everyone is all excited. Why aren't they mad? They should be totally pissed. This is . . . this is just sick." She pulled away with an apologetic frown, headed for the exit. "I'm gonna get some air. I'll see you in a bit."

I turned back to the tree. It didn't look quite so festive anymore.

It took almost the entire half hour allotted for the assembly to get the student body away from the tree and up on the bleachers where they belonged. Mr. Hennigan was breathless and flushed after ten minutes of trying to sweep the kids away from the tree. But it was useless. He'd yell at five or six kids on one side and get them to leave, only to have them replaced by five more kids on the other side.

Once order was restored, we were treated to a long lecture on appropriate behavior and following rules and the proper use of school facilities. "I know who's doing this," Hennigan said in a soft, barely controlled voice. I shivered, wondering if that could possibly be true. "It's clearly the same person or persons who were involved in the theft ring last year."

A small murmur went through the crowd. But all I could feel was relief. Hennigan had no clue.

"When I catch whoever the guilty persons are," he said—and I was a little shocked at how angry he looked, "there will be suspensions. Expulsions. And prosecutions! This," he said, flinging his arm in the direction of the tree, "involved truancy from class and breaking and entering school property. To say nothing of pilfering these items to begin with."

Fear churned in my stomach. Khail had warned me that Hennigan had been obsessed with the thief, but I had apparently underestimated him.

"Do not think this will be treated lightly just because of these ridiculous apology notes," he continued, holding up a torn sticker. "Whoever this student or students are, you will be caught, and you will be punished." He stepped away from the microphone and the room was silent save for the crinkling of a hundred bags.

Still, I couldn't help but feel a little bit of pride as the cheerleaders finally ran in—officially beginning the very late assembly—and there wasn't a single bag left under the tree.

Eighteen

I WENT TO MY FIRST wrestling meet that night. I wanted to support Khail and the guys after what they'd done. I mean, what they had accomplished on one day would have taken me *months* to do on my own.

And Sera was there cheering.

Kind of. They all sat on the edge of the mat in their uniforms and yelled and waved pom-poms. I guess I'd appreciate it if I were a wrestler.

I certainly appreciated it as a spectator.

The actual wrestling, perhaps not as much. Watching Khail wrestle made me remember that I was mortal. Seriously. He wasn't being offered wrestling scholarships right and left for nothing. I always knew he was huge and ripped, but you don't quite understand the meaning of *ripped* until you see someone in those little wrestling outfits. Layers of muscles, masses of muscles, muscles *with* muscles, and only one tiny leotard thingy to cover it all up. I think Khail's opponent must have contemplated his own mortality as well, in the twenty-four seconds it took Khail to twist him into something a contortionist might squeal at before his shoulders hit the mat.

I had visions of myself down on the floor if anything in our little scheme went sour. Talk about terrifying.

After the match Sera ran up to hug me, said something about her ridiculous outfit, then hurried off to change before I could comment that there was no need. Oh well, maybe another time.

I was just leaning against the wall when I heard someone whisper my name, and before I could turn, Khail yanked my arm and pulled me around the corner into the darkened hallway.

"If you wanted some time alone, all you had to do was ask," I joked, rubbing my shoulder.

He just looked at me.

"Uh, good . . . wrestle," I said awkwardly.

"Hardly," Khail said with a snort. "The guy's a freshman. Only got to be on varsity because the guy I was *supposed* to match with didn't make weight. I hate it when that happens."

"Um, yeah. That sucks." I had no idea what he was talking about. "Anyway, man, that Christmas tree was awesome."

Khail broke into a grin. "It was, wasn't it? It was Stevens's idea to do the streamers and shit and, I gotta tell you, I wasn't convinced it would look right. But it totally did!"

"It did; it was awesome."

"So what's next?"

"What do you mean next?"

"The next *return*," Khail said with a grin. "We're all ready!"

My throat went dry. "What's the hurry?"

"I want this done!" Khail said. He took a deep breath. "Also, we've only got two weeks till State. Then wrestling season is over. You'd be surprised how much freedom we have to wander around the school in-season. A teacher stops me and I just hold up my bag and say, 'Coach wanted me to . . . whatever.' They totally buy it. But after wrestling, we go back to being like everyone else. We have enough time to do a drop this week and a drop next week. Early the week after if we have to, but that's pushing it."

"Listen," I said, shoving my hands in my pockets. "Everything today was really cool and you guys helped me so much, but—" I hesitated. The fact of the matter was I *wanted* them to keep helping me. But it wasn't fair to ask. "I don't think you guys should do this anymore."

Khail's face snapped serious. "Why not?"

"Hennigan's talking expulsion, Khail. And I don't think he's kidding. I can't ask you guys to risk that for me. It's not fair."

Khail sighed and leaned against the wall. "I know you're

concerned for us, Jeff, but we don't want out."

I looked up. "Really?"

"I talked to the guys before the match tonight. I was worried about Hennigan too, so I told them that they had a one-time free pass out. And all of them want to stay."

I didn't understand. "Why?"

"You're new and you don't know all these kids, so they aren't talking to you about the stuff they got back. Some of this is important stuff. Actually, *most* of it. This guy in my calc class got back an action figure worth almost a thousand bucks that he brought to school for a display for one day. A girl in my history class got a hat knitted by her best friend who moved. There was one guy who got back a pair of gloves that his mom gave him for Christmas a few months before she died in a car accident. Dude was in tears, Jeff."

"Wow." I didn't know what else to say. I'd been so focused on Kimberlee, I hadn't thought what returning the stolen items might mean to other people.

"The guys all feel like they're helping with something that really has meaning, you know?" He slapped my shoulder and I tried not to show how much it hurt. "We're with you, bro." He started to walk back toward the locker room, then turned just before reaching the corner. "Unless *you* want to wimp out."

I shook my head quickly. "No, that's not it. I just don't want to drag you all down with me if anything goes wrong."

Khail took a step back. "We'll be careful," he said earnestly. "Real careful. We'll lay low for the rest of the week. Won't return anything. Then it's back to business."

"How am I supposed to come up with something that fast?"

Khail just grinned. "Desperate times call for desperate measures." He turned and started to walk away. "Oh," he said, reaching into his pocket. "I got you something." He handed me a cheap, nondescript cell phone.

"What's this for?" I asked.

"I don't want you to think I'm taking Hennigan's threat lightly. All the guys have this number and it can't be traced; I paid cash for it. When we're done, toss it in a Dumpster in Chino or something, okay?"

I felt strangely touched that Khail was kind of looking out for me. "Thanks," I said quietly.

"We're going to see this through to the end. You come up with a plan and we'll be there." He continued walking this time, around the corner and out of sight.

I let out a breath I didn't realize I had been holding. "Good," I said shakily. "Good." I waited for a few more seconds to give Khail a chance to make it to the locker room so no one would realize we'd been talking.

My conscience was seriously conflicted. I mean, it was great to have all these guys on my side and really feeling like they were doing something noble, but it didn't make me feel any better about the possibility of getting them expelled. And I hated hiding the whole thing from Sera. But not only had I promised Khail I wouldn't tell her, judging from her reaction to the Christmas tree that morning I wasn't sure she would like me being involved at all. Never mind being the person in charge.

I peeked around the corner to make sure Khail was gone, and pulled my head back when Sera came out of the girls' locker room. Feeling like an idiot for hiding from my girlfriend, I was about to walk out when someone called Sera's name. "We're all going to O'Brien's, you coming?"

"Not tonight," Sera said. "I'm going somewhere with Jeff."

"Okay," the girl said hesitantly. She started to walk away and I got ready to pop out again, but then the girl stopped and turned back. "Can I talk to you for a sec?"

Great. My timing was fabulous. I didn't want to eavesdrop, but now did *not* seem like a good time to suddenly appear.

"Uh, sure," Sera said hesitantly.

"You know I love you, and I've been there for you since you first got on the squad even through, well, everything. But . . . Jeff? Really?"

"What about him?" Sera asked defensively.

"Don't be that way," the girl said, sounding like she cared, although I didn't think it was any of her business. "I'm just concerned. He's not like the guys you used to date."

"It's his best feature," I heard Sera reply dryly.

"I don't want you throwing yourself at some new nerdy guy just 'cause it's been a while."

Wow. Harsh. I wasn't completely sure if her bluntness was a sign of a true friend, or someone to seriously avoid.

"It's not like that," Sera said softly. "He—he's really nice. He listens to me and seems to actually care what I think. He doesn't push me to do stuff I don't like and . . . I need someone like that right now. And I admit: It's nice to have a fresh start. Almost everyone at Whitestone has known me since I was in diapers. It's . . . I think I need someone who only knows who I am now."

"I just wanted to check," the other girl said. "Let you know I'm still watching out for you." There was a pause that I could only assume held some kind of hug or girly gesture, but even in the silence I could sense a sincerity there that I weirdly appreciated. For Sera.

"Thanks. Really," Sera replied.

"Okay. Well, see ya," she said.

I waited a few seconds, then walked out from the darkened hallway, glad to see Sera's back was still turned. I had a feeling she wouldn't be supercomfortable knowing I'd just overheard that conversation. I wasn't sure how comfortable *I* was with it. *New start?* I hated that it made me wonder if any of what

Kimberlee was constantly spouting about Sera was true. Trying to push those thoughts away, I stepped up behind her and laid a soft hand on her waist.

And barely managed to catch her hand before it smacked me in the face.

"Oh, I'm so sorry!" she said, her hands covering her mouth. "You scared me!"

I grinned down at her. It was kind of fun to see her ruffled. "It's okay. You didn't get me. I should make a noise before I sneak up on you."

"I'm just nervous," she said with a sigh, starting to walk toward the front doors. "This whole stolen stuff coming back thing is creeping me out. It's like every time I turn around I expect to see . . . I don't know. A ghost or something."

I laughed in a way that I hope didn't sound too fake. *Hoo, boy, if she only knew.*

"Stupid, I know." She shrugged. "I'm totally on edge."

I slung an arm over her shoulder. "Well, let's get you off that edge." I have the lamest pickup lines in the world.

Luckily, Sera didn't laugh, probably due to having just almost smacked me in the head. "So what are we doing?"

"I know you've only got an hour, but are you hungry? Like, not just halfway hungry, but real hungry?"

She cocked her head to one side. "Actually, yeah. You?"

"Starving."

"Then let's go."

I took her hand and led her to my car, remembering at the last second to open her door, and we drove out of the parking lot. When we got to the In-N-Out, I pulled into the drive-thru. I ordered for us both and handed the warm bags to Sera as she looked at me with a curious smile. She seemed to sense that I had something planned, so she didn't comment as I pulled away from the restaurant.

Then I drove to the park.

Yes, *that* park. The one where I had the disastrous night that turned out about a zillion times better than any night should have, considering its dubious beginning.

I had hoped to do this on our first date, but I couldn't find the park. Being semi-sober as she drove me home didn't change the fact that I had no idea where I was. I'd spent hours driving around looking for it over the past week or so. And I was at least eighty percent sure this was the right one.

That eighty turned into a hundred when Sera smiled and said, "Here?"

I exited the car without answering and came over to her side, taking the bags. "Everybody gets an occasional do-over, right?" I said with a smile. "This one's mine."

We ate at the picnic table as if it were the middle of the day instead of nearing ten o'clock at night. "You sure cheer a lot," I said, reaching for a fry. "Basketball games, wrestling matches. Plus you have practice, too, right?"

"Every day after school. Plus competitions, which are coming up at the end of the month."

"It seems like a lot of time for someone who says she doesn't like cheering."

Her hand hesitated; then she broke a fry in two and studied the ends. "It's not that I *don't* like it. I just like parts of it better than others."

"Like watching Khail wrestle?"

"Yeah. That's nice. But it also just gives me an excuse to get out of the house. And my parents like it when I'm busy. They stay off my case. Now *that* is worth it," she said, pointing at me with her broken French fry.

"No joke," I said, thinking of the brief interludes I'd had with her parents.

"They like you, I think."

"How can you tell?" I asked with a laugh.

"Oh, it's subtle," she retorted. "It helps that you always get me home on time."

"No that I want to," I said, leaning forward for a quick kiss. "Ever. Come on," I said, tilting my head toward the swings. "We can both swing tonight."

Despite her giggling protests, I pulled her down on my lap and we swung together for a while. I liked the feel of her weight on my legs, the wind blowing the curled ends of her hair against my face. After a while she got on her own swing, and we raced, seeing who could go the highest and fastest.

"I bet I can jump farther than you," I called over to her, her hair streaming behind her as she pumped back and forth.

"Not a chance!" she yelled back.

I focused on the sand in front of me as Sera counted. On three we both let go of our chains, and for just a second, I remembered the feeling of flying that I hadn't had since I was a kid, and the thrill of the earth rushing toward me. I hit the ground and rolled while Sera landed gracefully on her feet, but I got six inches farther.

"I win!" I said, pointing to the mark my knees had made when I fell.

"No way," Sera said, giggling. "You have to measure from here, where your feet landed."

"You're only saying that because you didn't think of falling forward to get farther," I said, wrapping my arms around her and picking her up to spin her around. Once we were both too dizzy to spin anymore I took her hand and pulled her to the hill we'd walked up after the party. I sat down on the cool grass and patted the spot beside me. She smiled and joined me and I put my arm around her shoulder, drawing her close and laying my head against her hair.

"So was it a good do-over?" I asked, more serious now. "Can we just forget that the other night happened?"

She hesitated and I got a little nervous.

"Is it going to happen again?" she asked seriously.

"What? Going to a Harrison Hill party? Uh, no. Believe me."

"Not just Harrison Hill," she said. "Are you going to keep partying?"

I laughed. "You make it sound like I have a habit. Even back in Phoenix, I didn't go to many parties."

"I don't mean it like that," she said. "I just . . . I've tried a lot of stuff." She chuckled softly. "A *lot* of stuff. And . . . it's all bad news, Jeff. It'll mess you up. It messed me up," she added softly. "And in the end, I got off easy." She swallowed hard and for a second the secret-filled silence chilled me. "I think you're great, but . . . I can't get involved in that world again. Not even through you. So if getting toasted every weekend is your idea of fun, then . . ." She let the sentence hang.

Although my brain was screaming at me to ask her what *a lot of stuff* was—combined with what the other cheerleader had just said about *watching out for her*—I knew this wasn't the time. "The hangover sucked big time," I confessed. "I think I'm off that kind of partying for a while. A *long* while."

"Okay," she said, turning and leaning her head against my shoulder.

"*Now* can we forget it happened?" I asked.

"Forgotten," she whispered. I lay back on the grass, wishing

I'd thought to bring a blanket, and Sera curled her body against me and rested her forehead against my cheek. One of her hands rested on my chest for a moment, then after a bit of hesitation, she pushed her hand under my shirt, laying it against my bare stomach and awakening pretty much every nerve in my entire body.

"My hand is cold," she offered as an excuse.

That was just fine with me.

I brushed her hair away from her face. "Thanks for rescuing me."

"From the party?" she asked.

"That, too," I said, leaning close. I wanted this kiss to mean something—to show her how much she meant. I didn't quite know how to put all that into a kiss, but I tried.

Somehow, she seemed to understand. Beneath the vanilla of her lip gloss I swear I could *feel* how much she wanted me at that moment, and the thrill of it made me light-headed. I wasn't just kissing her—*she* was kissing *me*. And she really, really meant it.

And that made everything else worth it.

Nineteen

"ARE YOU CRAZY?"

Khail's words echoed in my ear even though I pulled the phone away.

"Khail, just lis—"

"We can*not* break into the school!"

"Quiet!" I hissed. Who knew who might hear him in his house?

Sera, at the very least.

"I told you he wouldn't go for it," Kimberlee said from the passenger seat.

"You're the one who wanted to do this with *style*," I said into the phone, waving at Kimberlee to hush. Not that anyone could hear her.

"That's, like, a professional job, though. And illegal," he added, as though I hadn't thought of that.

"And easy when you're working with an invisible person," I said.

That stopped him. "Kimberlee? Seriously?"

"Yes! She can get us all the security codes, watch for anyone coming, make sure the school is empty—you know, all that stuff."

"Just one problem, brain-boy. Master key. Alarm codes are all well and good, but all those doors still need a key, and from what I understand, your little friend can't touch anything."

"Bailey," I said, naming our assistant principal. "She's got keys to everything, but she's never in charge of actually locking up. I bet we could steal her master key and she wouldn't notice it missing for weeks."

Khail was silent for a long time.

Since he wasn't arguing with me, I took advantage of it. "Think about it: We go in at night, like, Monday, maybe, open the front doors, you go put in the alarm code, I start unlocking classrooms, we leave a stack of stuff on every teacher's desk," I said, grinning even as I laid out the coup de grâce.

"Why the hell would we leave stuff on the teachers' desks," Khail said flatly.

"That's the beauty of it. The thing about getting stuff back is that, like you said, sometimes it's really important stuff. If even a fraction of the stuff we give back to the teachers is important, they're going to stop caring so much about catching us and we can take a bunch of student stuff back in the process."

Silence again, and I forced myself to breathe slowly as Khail considered it. "Okay," he said slowly. "I get it. This . . . this'll work! See, this is why you're the brains of the operation. That is genius, Jeff. Genius!"

I decided against telling him it was Kimberlee's idea. Her great dream to pull off a true heist.

Only, in this case, it would be an antiheist.

"There are a bunch of details we'll have to get exactly right, though," Khail said, sobering now. "Cameras."

"There's only the four everyone knows about," I said, acting as though I *had* known about them all before Kimberlee told me. "Front doors, cafeteria, office, computer lab."

"We can avoid all of them except the front doors."

"And the office."

"Why do we have to go into the office?"

"That's where the alarm panel is."

Long pause. "And you know this how?"

I shot Kimberlee an apologetic glance and then said, "I'm working with the klepto; she knows where everything is." *Everything.* When she first came to me with the idea, I had about a billion arguments, and she had an answer to every single one. A clearly well-thought-out answer. The irony of fulfilling her biggest stealing dream to undo hundreds of small thefts wasn't lost on me.

"So . . . what about those?"

"That's the risky bit. Someone's got to get close enough to cover them, and I think it should be me."

I could practically hear Khail bristling. "Why you?"

"Because your build is too distinctive. All you guys. Face it: You look like wrestlers."

"I guess so," he said grudgingly.

"And everyone will have to wear gloves."

"Obviously," Khail said, and I wondered if he was pacing. I stayed quiet, letting him mull it over. "So," he said after a while, "you and Kimberlee lift the key and get the codes and then what, we all just gather at the school?"

"In your truck. Everyone in the back, where they can't be seen. I run up and unlock the doors, go enter the codes, and cover both cameras. After that I'll start unlocking classrooms with the master key and the guys can come in and be assigned one, or maybe two classrooms each."

"That'll take too long. You need to let me help, Jeff."

I pursed my lips, not wanting Khail to risk himself for me anymore.

"How about this: You handle the key; I'll handle the codes and the cameras. Twice as fast—we'll be out of there in ten minutes, tops."

I hesitated, wondering briefly how in the world I'd

managed to get myself in this predicament at all. "Fine," I said softly. "But you have to promise me you'll stay off camera as much as possible."

"You think I *want* to get caught?"

Talking to Khail was near impossible when his ego made an appearance.

"When?" Khail said when I didn't reply.

"How about Monday? I'll try to lift the key this week, when the opportunity comes along."

"I'll tell the guys. Can you sneak out at two a.m.?"

"I think so," I said. I *hope* so.

"Okay," Khail said. "We're on." Then he hung up without saying good-bye.

I held the phone against my ear for a long time before relaxing my arm and letting it fall. I looked over at Kimberlee, sitting anxiously at the edge of my bed. "He said yes," I said weakly, realizing that I was hoping Khail would refuse.

Kimberlee just grinned.

"We should do something different today," Kimberlee said from her spot on my bedroom floor, where she was lounging on her stomach, watching me brush my teeth.

"Yeah, because we haven't done anything exciting lately," I said dryly. Kimberlee had finally managed to figure out Mrs. Bailey's schedule, and when she would be away from her desk.

With Kimberlee acting as lookout, I'd managed to sneak into her office and find her key ring lying oh-so-innocently on top of her desk.

Now minus one key.

Twenty-four hours later my nerves still hadn't recovered.

"Well, it's Saturday, so how about we hit the mall?"

The mall? Last time I'd mentioned the mall to Kimberlee, she'd been less than enthusiastic. "I don't need anything."

"Not to shop; to take stuff back."

I groaned as I turned my razor off. "You're kidding, right?"

She shot me a glare.

"Seriously, Kimberlee, when are you going to figure out that *I* am the one doing *you* a favor and not the other way around?" I studied the mirror again and added quietly, but loud enough for her to hear, "Probably not until you see those bright lights everyone is always talking about."

Despite my best arguments, several hours later I stood in front of a corner store in the mall and studied the list in my hand. "Claire's?"

"Oh yeah," Kimberlee said from behind me. "This place is so easy to steal from. They have these total airhead cashiers who are more interested in their nails than what you're doing. They don't even have cameras."

"Thus the reason you have *four* bags of stuff from them?"

I asked out of the corner of my mouth.

"What can I say?" she asked, already striding toward the store. "It was just too tempting."

I let out a very long sigh and followed her. We'd been at the mall for about two hours already and my feet hurt. I'd loaded the backseat of my car up with three boxes of merchandise and I would fill my backpack, take stuff into the store, drop it off, usually with an obliging but confused clerk, and move on. I started my returns small, mostly because I was nervous—to little kiosks that Kimberlee had only stolen maybe a set of earrings or some kind of makeup from. Little trips; a thing or two. Nothing to draw attention.

But it was time to start taking merch back to the stores that were bigger. And had multiple *bags* of stuff.

Claire's was first.

Sure enough, the girl behind the counter was much shorter than me and looked like she was younger than me too. A lot younger.

"Yes?" she asked in a squeaky voice after I stood at the counter for about five minutes trying to get her attention.

"Hi," I said with what I hoped was an extremely non-threatening smile. "I've got something for you."

She watched wide-eyed as I placed the first gallon-sized storage bag on the counter.

"Do I know you?"

I looked down at her, confused. "Oh no, these aren't for you personally—they're for the store."

"The store?"

"Yeah. I'm returning some things."

"Um, do you have receipts?" she asked doubtfully.

"Nope, these are free." I placed the last bag on the counter and smiled. "Have a nice day."

"Wait!" she called. "Come back."

Sucker that I am, I turned. Stupid me. "Yeah?"

She hesitated, opening the bag and sifting through the contents, lifting a few items. "I don't even recognize most of this stuff. How old is it?"

"Uh . . ." I glanced sideways at Kimberlee.

She shrugged.

"Two, three years some of it . . . I guess."

She held a pair of silver hoops up to her scanner. Nothing. "I don't think I can take this back," she said. "It doesn't even register on my computer. How am I supposed to sell it?"

I shrugged. "I just thought the store should have it, that's all."

"Do you know how long it's going to take me to inventory all this?"

"Sorry, not my problem," I said.

"Wait, I really can't take this stuff," she said, coming around the counter and trying to dump it back into my arms.

Oh, no you don't.

I hurried my step a little more and reached the double doors at the same time she did. "Really, you should—" She sucked in a breath as my bag hit something big and solid.

I turned around and found myself facing a white shirt with a blue badge-shaped logo on it. *Perfect. Just perfect.*

Twenty

TURNS OUT MALL SECURITY HAS its own little
interrogation room. Okay, so it's not really an interrogation
room; but it sure felt like one as I sat on a chair with two
security guards looking down at me.

"Now, son—"

"I'm not your son," I insisted in a surge of bravery.

The two guards exchanged a meaningful glance. I'm sure
the meaning was something along the lines of *stupid smart-ass
kid.* "All right, *Jeff,* I need you to tell us again why you have a
backpack full of women's jewelry. And a car full of brand-new
clothes."

"How do you know about my car?" I asked. Way to stay
cool under pressure. *Fail, fail, fail.*

"We've been watching you. Clutching at your backpack, looking nervous, browsing aimlessly. You may as well
wear a sign that says *thief.* You kept walking outside to your
car, and coming back. So we checked it out. There's a lot

of merchandise in there. Would you like to explain that to me?"

This is so embarrassing. "I have a . . . friend . . . and she's a girl," I added stupidly. "And a couple of years ago she went through this theft stage. She's had a change of heart and I agreed to help her give the stuff back."

"Uh-huh. And *your friend* apparently doesn't have a name."

"Of course she has a name," I snorted. "I'm just not going to give to you." *Because then I'll look like a loon, and it won't be juvie where you toss me before you throw away the key.*

The guards shared another long look. "Stay strong," Kimberlee coached from the corner. "They're not cops; they can't do anything except escort you from the premises."

I took a long, slow breath.

"Or call the real cops, I guess."

I could hardly look at Kimberlee, I was so mad. She was the master thief; couldn't she have given me some kind of, I don't know, pointers on not getting caught? Or at least not doing stuff that makes the mall security *follow you around?*

Big Guard pulled out a notebook. "Okay, kid. I need her name and you're going to give it to me."

"I would love to, sir, but I'm afraid I gave my word to keep her identity anonymous."

"Kid, you *have* to tell me."

"No, I don't." I crossed my arms over my chest. "I have the right to remain silent."

The two guards stared at me for a long time as Kimberlee laughed raucously from her corner. I shot her a glare.

The security guards told me to stay put and left the room. I heard them muttering on the other side of the door but I didn't get up and try to spy. Honestly, I don't think I *could* have gotten up at the moment if I tried. Kimberlee may have been in this room a dozen times, but I'd never been in trouble like this. Never.

The bigger guard came in and crossed his beefy arms over his chest. "Here's what we're gonna do. Joe's calling the police and they're going to send someone over to take you home. To make sure you get there and tell your parents what you've been doing."

Crap.

"I don't want to see you back at the mall for a few weeks. And I don't *ever* want to see you causing trouble again, or the cops'll do more than just take you home. You understand?"

"Yessir," I whispered.

"That's better," he grunted. "Now we'll just sit tight till the higher authorities get here."

He leaned over and switched on a television. "Y'like baseball, Jeffrey?"

Great.

. . .

Officer Herrera suppressed a grin as he looked through the contents of my backpack. "I'll take care of this, gentlemen," he said to the hovering security officers, dismissing them.

Both guards gave me a nasty look before retreating behind their door. To the baseball game, I was sure. "Let's go out this way," the deputy said quietly, gesturing toward a back exit. Kimberlee walked ahead of us, sliding right through the wall before the cop got there.

"Where's your car?" he asked, hands on his hips. It was probably a casual stance, but all I could focus on was the gun that was now mere inches from his fist.

"That way," I said, pointing toward the parking row where Halle was. We walked over and Officer Herrera had me unlock all the doors, then stand with my hands on the trunk while he sorted through the contents. At least he didn't cuff me.

"Okay," he said. "I've seen enough. Let's go to my car."

My face must have gone white because Kimberlee said, "You worry too much," as she playfully tried to grab at the cop's gun. "This guy obviously thinks the security morons are idiots. He's just going to give you a ride. I get shotgun!" she called.

But when we reached the car, Officer Herrera opened the passenger door for me.

"I don't have to ride in back?" I asked, inclining my head

toward the seat behind a sturdy mesh of metal.

"Well, I guess that's up to you," he said. "But if you sit there, I have to turn my lights on."

As Herrera walked around to the other side I looked at Kimberlee and jerked my thumb covertly toward the backseat.

"You suck," she said, settling in behind the bars. I couldn't help but smile. Technically, that was where she belonged.

Officer Herrera was quiet for several minutes after entering my address into his GPS. "Well, the security guys seem to think you're a menace to society and a liar on top of that," he said, starting to run down familiar streets. "Personally, I believe your story. Especially since your backseat is full of girly stuff. So, am I going to have any more luck getting you to rat out your friend than they did?"

I sighed. "She's dead, okay? I just thought the stuff she stole should go back to where it came from." Oh, man, it felt good to just tell someone that! Even if it wasn't the *whole* truth.

Herrera chuckled. "You sound like you just walked out of confession in church after a wild Saturday night. Makes sense, though. The merchandise is old. And I guess if she's dead the actual theft problem is taken care of. Except that you now have a carload of stolen stuff."

"Tell me about it," I muttered.

"Your parents know you're doing this?"

"No." I sat up straighter. "Listen, I know you have to tell

them, but could you skip the part about my friend being dead? I haven't told anyone else and I don't want her to get a reputation for being a thief." Admittedly, that wasn't my main concern, but I thought it sounded rational.

The cop shrugged. "I don't like to speak ill of the dead. Bad luck. I can keep that to myself." He turned a little. "I come down here a couple times a week and take kids home on calls like this and I've gotten a pretty good sense of who's guilty and who's not. And I gotta say, not-guilty waves are pouring off you."

Thank you, universe!

"Let me tell you something, Jeff. I see a lot of victims in my line of work. Victims of muggings, robberies . . . when people get stolen from, they don't just lose their stuff. They lose a piece of their security, their ability to believe things are right in the world. I've seen very few of those victims have their belongings returned. But when it does happen?" He paused and smiled. "It's amazing. They get their confidence back. And sometimes more than they had before. Suddenly humanity isn't so bad; the world isn't so dark."

His impassioned speech made me suddenly—irrationally—want to tell him about the other stuff I'd given back. But I wasn't going to push my luck.

"You seem like a good kid," Officer Herrera said, "so I'm going to give you a suggestion. None of these stores is going to benefit from what you're doing; the merchandise is too out-of-date. At best the employees will take it home, but it'll probably just get trashed. If you're really as sincere as you say you are, find a charity secondhand store and donate it. Goodwill, Deseret Industries, Saint Vincent DePaul, that sort of thing. I think that's a better salute to your friend's memory than taking a bunch of hair clips back to a corporation that wrote this stuff off last year. This way, maybe it'll do someone some good."

"That's a really good idea, actually," I said, thinking of the six other boxes full of merchandise that were still in the cave.

When we reached my cul-de-sac, Officer Herrera shifted into park and looked over at me. "I have to take you in and explain things to your parents, but I'll try to help them see that this was mostly just a misunderstanding."

Despite his assurances, I don't think anything can make that moment when your mom opens the door to find you on the porch with a cop easier. Her face went pale and she looked up at Officer Herrera with a dazed expression. "Don't worry, ma'am, your son's not in trouble." He chuckled. "Not with us, anyway."

Har, har.

"What happened?" Mom asked.

"Jeff was caught by mall security trying to return some merchandise a friend of his stole. The security guards didn't believe him and called me. Personally, I think he's telling the truth. But escorting him home is standard protocol, so here we are." He paused for just a second and then dug into his wallet and handed me a business card with his name and number listed. "If you get into any more trouble over this—the security guys hassle you or anything—let me know. Okay?" He handed me my backpack and nodded at my mom before heading back to his car.

Her eyes followed the tall cop down the driveway and then watched as his car disappeared from the cul-de-sac. Only when she had nowhere else to look did she turn her eyes to me. "Wow," she said. "That may be the hottest cop I've ever seen."

"Mom!"

"I'm married, not dead." Did I mention that my parents freak me out sometimes? She glanced one last time down the cul-de-sac before putting on her Mom face. "So?"

"So . . . what?"

She raised an eyebrow. "Don't even try to play dumb."

My eyes darted out to the well-lit sidewalk where old people seemed to always be walking their dogs and—at the moment—eyeing me. "Can we at least close the door?"

Mom rolled her eyes at me and swung the door closed. "Wish granted. *Now* spill."

Man, I hate lying to my mom. But what else could I do? "It's like Officer Herrera said. I found a bunch of stolen stuff and I'm trying to get it back where it belongs."

"You just *found* a bunch of stolen stuff. Someone delivered it to your doorstep or something?"

"Mom." I paused, trying to decide what to say. "Have I ever been a problem child?"

Her eyes softened. "No," she admitted.

"And I tell you everything, right? I mean, I even told you about getting drunk."

"That's true. You did earn some points there."

"Okay. So I want you to understand how weird it feels to I say that I can't tell you. But," I added as she started to interrupt, "I *will* tell you that I'm trying really hard to do the right thing. And I want to cash in all my good-kid chips from the last sixteen years and ask you to just trust me." It was all I could do.

"Are you in trouble, Jeff?"

"No. I'm not. I promise." *Trouble* really wasn't the right word for it.

Mom looked up at me, her lips pursed. But I could tell she was considering it. "Okay," she finally conceded. "But please don't get brought home by the cops again. It kinda strains the trust thing."

"I will do my very best," I said.

Mom looked at me hard for a moment longer before stepping forward to hug me. Then she patted my cheek—something she'd done for as long as I could remember. It usually made me feel like a little kid, but tonight it didn't bother me so much. "I love you, Jeff."

"I love you, too, Mom." I smiled at her and a movement just above her head caught my eye. I glanced up and saw Kimberlee at the top of the stairs. The instant my eyes met hers she dropped her gaze, pivoted on one heel, and disappeared into my room.

Twenty-One

FIVE O'CLOCK COMES WAY EARLY on Sunday morning. "I don't know why we have to do this at the butt-crack of dawn," Kimberlee whined as I pulled a T-shirt over my head and attempted to lace my shoes with fumbly fingers.

"So nobody sees me. You may not be facing expulsion, but I certainly am."

"Why do *I* have to come? It's not like I can help."

"Consider it penance. And you can keep watch," I said, very quietly. My parents were sleeping like every other reasonable person in Santa Monica. I'd decided Officer Herrera was right; returning Kimberlee's shoplifted items to corporate America over a year later wasn't going to help anyone. Surely whatever cosmic power was keeping Kimberlee hostage here on earth would understand a little creativity in this instance. But thrift stores still turned around and sold stuff, cheap or not. I had a better idea. We were headed to a homeless shelter. I'd looked up the closest one.

It wasn't very close.

Granted, I wasn't completely sure what a bunch of homeless people were going to do with designer clothes and fashion accessories, but I've heard silk is warm.

Kimberlee griped the whole way down to her parents' house. "Holy hell, Kimberlee!" I said, my patience finally snapping. "I don't know what you're bitching about. You'd think you actually could sleep or something. *I'm* the one who's exhausted out of my mind!"

She glared at me. "Just because I can't sleep doesn't mean I automatically like mornings." But I could tell that even she knew it was a weak retort.

"Face it," I said as I trudged through the sand, the chilly morning air cutting right through my hoodie. "This is your project as much as it is mine. What the hell am I talking about? This is your project way *more* than it is mine. What am I getting out of this? Nothing. Nada." I turned and looked at her. "I honestly do not know why the hell I am still doing this!" I shouted. I am *not* a morning person.

"Be quiet," Kimberlee said, glancing up to where you could just see the rooftop of her house. "My parents are actually home right now."

I rolled my eyes. "Good! Maybe someone can catch me, find what's in the cave, and take it away. Then I could get out of this whole crazy situation."

"Look, I'm sorry, okay?" Kimberlee said, clearly more

interested in placating me than actually apologizing.

"Whatever," I grumbled.

It took me five trips to load my car up with the rest of the merchandise from stores. And even though I had totally altruistic motives, I had to admit it was a nice bonus that I would be able to take so much stuff back in one trip.

I pulled the rapidly dwindling roll of stickers out of my pocket and slapped one onto each box.

"Why are you doing that?" Kimberlee asked. "With Hennigan on the rampage, you're more likely to get caught if you're using those stickers on everything, even if this isn't in school."

"It's my trademark," I said. "I *like* it," I added icily. Maybe I just liked that they still annoyed her. Small victories.

"Well, when Hennigan kicks your ass out of school, don't say I didn't warn you."

We drove for almost half an hour before we reached the homeless-shelter-slash-soup-kitchen I'd found online. There was no one at the back door, despite the huge line out front. I'd apparently caught the staff between garbage runs and cigarette breaks. That could last minutes . . . or seconds.

With my heart pounding I ran back and forth from my car to the porch, stacking boxes as fast as I could. I practically threw the last box on the top of the pile, and as I turned I heard it crash to the ground. I glanced back and saw something glittery and gold roll out onto the cement, but didn't dare go back. I was already a little worried I'd been caught on some kind of camera and was about to experience my first manhunt. And I doubted every cop would be as nice or understanding as Officer Herrera.

I think I was a full ten minutes back on the road before I began breathing normally again. And, miracle of miracles, Kimberlee stayed quiet that whole time.

I glanced down at the dashboard clock. 6:21. "Sweet. I have enough time to go home and sleep for a few more hours," I said, trying to stifle a yawn.

"What am I supposed to do?"

I shrugged. "Whatever you want. I'm not your social advisor."

"Yeah, but I'm bored. You're never around. If I let you sleep, can we watch a movie tonight?"

I just wanted her to stop talking. "Can't. Have a date with Sera." Assuming I could get home before I fell asleep and crashed my car.

"Edged out by the junkie cheerleader again," she muttered.

"Would you shut up!" I half surprised myself when the words came shouting out of my mouth.

Kimberlee looked over at me with wide eyes. "What?"

"Nothing—not a word about Sera ever again, do you understand?"

"I have a right to not like her."

"Then keep it to yourself!" I gripped the steering wheel harder. "The fact that *you* don't like her is probably a compliment."

"Screw you!" Kimberlee snapped.

"All you have done since I met Sera is rag on her and try to keep me away from her. But guess what? I like her. I like her a *lot*. You know who I like her a lot more than? You!"

"Yeah, 'cause she's sooo much better than me."

"That's for sure."

"Because she's so innocent? Stuff happened before you got here that you can't even *begin* to understand, and she was right in the middle of it. She's lucky she's not in *jail*. My dad would have put her away in a second."

I briefly remembered Sera's words the other night—*It'll mess you up. It messed me up*—but pushed them to the back of my mind. "And I'm just supposed to believe that?"

"Why would I lie?"

"Why would you steal? I don't know! Because you are a freaking *psychopath*!" I was out-and-out yelling now and it felt good. Weeks of holding my temper, despite everything, exploded out my mouth. "You're mean and petty and spiteful! You hate everyone—as far as I can tell you've *always* hated everyone—and I don't know why you can't understand when everyone hates you back!"

"At least I'm not the one stumbling blindly down a path led by nothing but a pretty face and a nice ass, refusing to listen to anyone around me!"

I slammed on my brakes and skidded to the side of the road. "That's it. Get out."

Kimberlee looked out the window. "Here?" she said, wrinkling her nose. Her voice was calm—as if the entire conversation had never taken place.

"Here. Get out and don't come back until you're ready to accept my relationship with Sera. Because if you say one more thing about her—and I mean it—*one* more thing, I will take everything else in that cave and throw it in the ocean and you will *never* move on."

It was an empty threat, but something in my voice must have convinced her I was serious, because her jaw dropped and for a second I thought she might cry. Then her eyes narrowed and her glare was all daggers. "Fine," she hissed. "But when she breaks your heart into a million pieces because she's not the perfect angel you think she is don't come whining to me, because all I'll say is I. Told. You. So." She spun away from me, hair flying, and slid through the passenger-seat door. I peeled onto the freeway and forced myself not to look in my rearview, afraid that seeing her standing on the side of the highway might make me change my mind.

. . .

I was still a little grumpy when I rang the doorbell at Sera's house that afternoon.

"Oh, Jeff," her mom said, obviously not all that pleased to see me. "Come on in. Are you early?"

"Maybe a little," I admitted. Fine. Half an hour. But I got sick of hanging around my house jumping at every noise, afraid it might be Kimberlee.

"Let me go see if Sera's still in the gym."

Oh man, I was so not going to miss this. I hurried to follow Sera's mom through the hallways. Last week Sera told me about the gym. Not like with basketball hoops and tennis courts, but a spring floor and a bunch of gymnastics and weight equipment and big foamy mats that roll out so Khail can do wrestling stuff. It sounded amazing, but so far I hadn't managed to get far enough into the house to actually see it. I was practically rubbing my hands in anticipation when Sera's mom opened a totally normal-looking door.

And there she was.

Her back was to us and I don't think she heard us come in. She was wearing a dark blue leotard with tiny black shorts over it. And she was doing pull-ups on a set of uneven bars. I counted as she struggled through her sixth one before dropping onto the ground, rubbing at her arms.

I couldn't decide if it was sexy or intimidating to have a girlfriend who could do more pull-ups than me.

Sexy, I finally decided. So long as we never had to go up against each other in some kind of public contest. That would be beyond humiliating.

Then her mom spoiled everything by clearing her throat. Sera turned and as soon as she saw me, she ducked her head and her whole face and neck flushed bright red.

"Jeff's a little early," her mom said as though that weren't the most obvious thing in the world.

"Hey," I said, giving a totally lame-ass wave.

But Sera just looked at her mom. "I'll be done in about five minutes; then I'll send him back to the kitchen before I shower."

"Please do," Sera's mother said as she left the gym, but not before pulling a little hand weight over and propping the door open.

I stepped closer to Sera and gestured at the open door. "Seriously?" I whispered, in case her mom was still in earshot.

Sera rolled her eyes. "She keeps me on a pretty short leash. At least when she's in town. I love it when she goes on business trips with Dad. The longer, the better."

"Why such a short leash?"

Sera was quiet for a few seconds. "I got into trouble a couple years ago," she said quietly.

I had to shove my hands in my pockets to keep from

fidgeting. "What kind of trouble?" I asked, not wanting to believe anything Kimberlee said, but not stupid enough to have missed all the little hints I'd been hearing the last couple weeks.

Sera waved the question away as she picked up a sweatshirt and pulled it over her head.

"You don't have to dress up for me," I said with a grin, reaching an arm out to loop around her waist.

She settled the sweatshirt down over her chest slowly before whispering, "If it were for you, I wouldn't be putting clothes *on.*"

Oh. Hell. Yes.

"But I'm cold." To prove her point she laid chilly fingers along both sides of my face. I pulled her close and kissed her nose, and when she giggled I went for her mouth.

"The door," she whispered, twisting away.

"So," I said, checking out the expansive spring floor. "Are you going to do something cool for me?"

She shook her head. "Sorry, I just finished the weight part of my workout and you should never tumble after weights. Way more likely to injure something." She pushed up onto her toes and pressed a soft kiss to my cheek. "You go and make nice with my mom and I'll get ready. I'll be down in fifteen minutes."

I snorted in disbelief.

"What? My mom's not that bad. She'll mostly just ignore you."

"Not that. Fifteen minutes? I've never seen a girl get showered and ready in fifteen minutes."

She flipped a confident look over her shoulder. "Time me."

It took Sera exactly fourteen minutes and thirty seconds to get ready and I know because I looked at my watch every fifteen seconds the entire time she was gone. It wasn't like Mrs. Hewitt grilled me. . . . She just didn't do *anything*. Within the first thirty seconds after I walked into the kitchen she plunked down a glass of ice water in front of me—on a coaster, natch—and then said nothing. She straightened the countertops, flipped through a magazine, made notes about something in a notebook—I could only hope the notes weren't about me—and nothing else. Not a word, not a sound.

So when I say that Sera was a sight for sore eyes, I mean she was really a sight, and that my eyes were seriously sore.

"You ready?" I asked as I stood. I didn't take her hand or even touch her. I figured that could come later, out of sight of the mother.

"Back by ten," her mom said, looking up from her magazine. "School tomorrow."

Sera sighed as soon as she was safely ensconced in my car. "My mother," she said. "I know she means well, but she's such a perfectionist."

214

"Well, she's not here now," I said, covering her hand with mine. "Just you and me."

When we arrived at the movie theater, we walked up to the ticket booth and began looking through the titles.

"I think I've seen all of these," Sera said.

"Like three times," I replied. "I'm kind of surprised there's nothing new. All of this has got to be on its way out."

"Do you mind watching one again?"

I hesitated. "Maybe I'm not in the mood for a movie after all."

"Well, I figure if we've seen it before, it won't be as . . . distracting," she said, her fingers skimming over my stomach as she wrapped her arm around my waist.

My voice was a little shaky as I turned to the ticket guy. I don't remember which movie I picked.

But it was way better the fourth time.

Twenty-Two

I WAS CROUCHED BY MY front bushes a few minutes before two a.m. when Khail's truck swung by and the passenger door popped open. Turned out it was harder to sneak out of *my own house* than I expected it to be to break into the school. And even when I got around the alarm and the gate, I managed to get a faceful of motion-triggered security light at the last second.

As the truck pulled up, I sprinted to jump in and felt like a kid trying to avoid the monster under the bed.

"You ready?" Khail asked, sounding utterly calm. I have no idea how he did it.

"Yeah," I said, feeling my pits break out in a sweat even as I gripped the key so hard it made my hand hurt. *I'm such a liar.* "Where are the guys?"

"In the back, all loaded up." I peered through the back window and saw them, hoodies shadowing their faces, jammed into the bed of the truck like sardines, arms around duffels.

I'd sorted items with Khail that afternoon and filled almost his entire truck bed with the other wrestlers' duffels, each labeled with a teacher's name and stuffed to the brim with bags. We cleared out enough stuff that it would only take one more return to get everything in the cave gone for good.

I couldn't think about that now, though. One return at a time.

"Is . . . is she here?"

Guilt burned in my chest. I hadn't seen Kimberlee since Sunday, when I'd abandoned her on the side of the road. She was still mad . . . somewhere. "She'll meet us there," I mumbled.

And I wondered if I was telling the truth. She'd been so excited about it; surely she'd come back. Hell, it was *her* idea.

She'd never stayed away this long, but everything was set and if Kimberlee still didn't show, I didn't think I had the guts to back out.

Besides, her big part was the codes and that was done. We'd be okay either way.

Probably.

Khail killed his lights as we pulled into the school parking lot and steered into the shadow of a big elm tree. "You ready?" he whispered.

Hell no. "Yeah." I grabbed an old ski mask I'd found in the garage that barely fit over my head, and yanked it into place.

217

With a quick nod Khail slipped from the car and jogged to the front doors. By the time I got there, he'd scrambled up onto the stairway railing, shoved a paper bag over the lens of the camera, and secured it with a piece of tape.

My turn.

I dug the key out and, after a shaky breath, slid it into the lock. I turned it clockwise and for a moment, I thought it wouldn't go. But a tiny bit more pressure and the unmistakable hollow click of a bolt sliding filled the dark space between Khail and me.

"Ghost girl says it's all clear?" Khail whispered.

I nodded without thinking. But the guilt hit me half a second later. Still, it *probably* was all clear at this time of night.

Morning.

Whatever.

"Then move it," Khail said, brushing past and pushing the doors open. A steady beeping greeted us, just like Kimberlee said.

"Get the doors. I got the code. We're *gone* in ten minutes."

Right.

I gripped the key harder and sprinted through the darkness with the key in one hand, a tiny penlight in the other.

Nothing bigger than a penlight, Kimberlee had warned. *Or someone might see the lights through the windows.*

I shook thoughts of Kimberlee out of my head and slid

the key into the first classroom door. Ten doors on each side of the hallway, two floors. Forty doors, ten minutes.

I was on the second door when the beeping of the alarm stopped. Perfect. I continued unlocking doors and flinging them open, straining my ears for the other wrestlers' footsteps.

And almost ran right into one before I heard him.

"Keep moving," he whispered as he brushed past me, barely making a sound. I realized they were all wearing their soft-soled wrestling shoes.

Brilliant, I thought with a grin as I took the stairs two at a time. More than halfway done now.

I zigzagged across the second-floor hallway and the smallest wrestler caught up with me just as I got to the last door—the advanced-chemistry lab.

"This is it," he whispered. "Head back to the truck."

I was almost to the stairs when I heard the glass shatter.

I spun and pointed my penlight toward the last classroom along with a couple of other wrestlers emerging from their own classrooms with limp, empty duffels. The little guy popped out. And a bunch of tiny beams of light shone on him.

"It's okay!" he said, blocking the lights with his hands. "Just a beaker or . . . something. Campbell had a bunch of crap on her desk; I knocked it over. Just go!" he said, sprinting past us.

219

Don't have to tell me twice.

A group of about six of us were almost to the door when a piercing wail slammed into my eardrums.

"Dammit, Khail," I called over the noise when I reached the door where he was waving guys out the door. "I thought you took care of the alarm."

"I did; what the hell did *you* do?" He pointed down the hall, where a bright white light was flashing. "It's the *fire* alarm, genius."

I clenched my eyes shut. "The chemistry lab. Shortie broke something."

Khail punched the door and let out a string of swears that would have earned him about six detentions. "It must have had chemicals in it."

"I have to go check it out." I turned and Khail nearly pulled my arm out of my socket yanking me back.

"There's nothing you can do and the firemen will be here in three minutes. Maybe less. We gotta get out of here."

"But—"

Khail grabbed me by both shoulders and put his face close to mine. "Are you a fireman, Jeff?"

I shook my head convulsively.

"Then leave it to the professionals. Send ghost girl to check it out if you have to, but we are leaving *now*."

We ran to the truck and Khail took about three seconds

to do a quick head count before starting the engine and peeling out of the parking lot.

Hands down the fastest and most nerve-racking ten minutes of my life. Maybe twelve.

And Kimberlee wasn't here to see it.

She'd have loved it.

But she never showed up.

We were driving at a very reasonable three miles above the speed limit when I heard the sirens. Khail turned off the main road before I saw them, but in my mind's eye they pulled up in front of a Whitestone completely engulfed in flames.

Khail dropped me off about three minutes later, barely slowing down enough for me to get out of the car safely. I managed to make my way back through the security obstacle course that is my house, but my nerves were still crackling so I plugged my noise-canceling headphones into my iPod and cranked it. I lay on my bed, my eardrums throbbing with the volume of my music and slowly—very, very slowly—started to relax.

It was almost an hour before I finally felt the disposable phone vibrate in my pocket. I sat up and yanked off my headphones. "Yeah?" I said in a low voice.

"We're good," Khail said softly. "All the guys are home—everything got delivered, and when I drove by the school it looked like the fire trucks were packing up."

"You saw the school? Did it look like anyone else was there? Hennigan? Bailey?"

"No clue. I didn't even slow down. Besides, *she'll* tell you everything later."

"Yeah, yeah, of course," I said evasively. "I just wondered." I hesitated. "So we're good? The school didn't burn down and no one got caught, right?"

"We are golden, bro. Totally golden."

Twenty-Three

THE NEXT MORNING WAS LIKE a nightmare come true.

When I arrived at school, hired security guards were standing at the doors, directing us to go to the gym for a last-minute assembly. I knew it had to be about us. I wished I could talk to Khail . . . or even Shortie. But we had all decided that, at least until all of this was over, we had to act like we didn't know one another in school.

I did manage to find Sera, though. "What do you think's going on?" she asked after greeting me with a kiss that had me desperately wishing we could ditch the assembly.

"Not a clue," I lied.

She slipped her hand into mine and we walked into the gym together, me trying to subtly sniff the air for smoke. But everything looked and smelled okay. So far.

All around me were confused whispers and people asking what was happening. I heard a few people mention the fire trucks, but half of the students seemed to think that was an exaggerated rumor.

Once most of the students had taken their seats, Mr. Hennigan walked to the middle of the gym, where a podium was set up.

Then he just stood there.

The students quieted at first, and then got fidgety as the silence continued to stretch. I swear he stood up there in front of us for ten minutes. When he finally did speak, it was in a low, simmering tone that sent shivers up my spine.

"A terrible—not to mention expensive—act of vandalism was committed yesterday," he said.

Expensive? That made my stomach do rather uncomfortable things.

"The details are unimportant. I won't glamorize this incident by spreading rumors that will only encourage the perpetrator. Perpetrators, I should say." He straightened and cleared his throat, becoming almost businesslike. "You will have one chance, and one chance only, to turn yourself in. If you choose to do so, I will be lenient with the consequences."

Something in his tone told me that was a barefaced lie.

"But after today, I will use every resource I can to catch you, and I will make you pay." He paused and his eyes swept the bleachers, seeming to take in every student. "I want everyone to understand that just because this person is returning things that were once stolen from you does not make him a hero. He is not the good guy here. And," Mr. Hennigan added, "if anyone here wants to *help* this person do the right thing, well"—a dry chuckle escaped his throat—"you know where my office is. Also, Mrs. Campbell's classes will be meeting in Mr. Lewis's lab today. That is all."

Without another word, Mr. Hennigan left the podium and strode purposefully toward the double doors.

Leaving Kimberlee in his place.

"Indeed!" she shouted, waving her fist. "You are all my slaves and will help me catch this terrible, terrible person who—by the way—eats babies for lunch. Babies!" she shouted again.

I knew no one else could see or hear her, but I was already overly paranoid and couldn't help glancing covertly around to make sure.

But everyone was busily whispering about what might have happened, and even Sera was calmly reapplying her lip gloss.

I wanted to stay—to ask Kimberlee where she'd been, to tell her about what we'd done, to apologize for what I'd said.

But I couldn't now. Today was not the day to act weird.

I managed to make eye contact with Kimberlee for a just a second before being swept out of the gymnasium with the rest of the students. She paused in her ranting. Then she smiled tightly—almost apologetically—and started to bid the completely unaware crowd a lavish good-bye.

Sera's hand pulled on mine, bringing my attention back to her. "What the hell do you think that was about?"

I tried to look clueless. "I don't know."

"Sounds like it's another hit by whoever is returning all that stuff." She rolled her eyes. "It's so lame."

"Why is it lame? It sounds like they're doing a good thing." *And, you know, racking up expensive damages.*

She shrugged. "I guess so. But after over a *year*, I think you should just throw everything in the trash and find peace with yourself. This just stirs needless drama up all over again."

Someone behind us cleared his throat. "Miss Hewitt?" Mr. Hennigan said, his voice carrying through the hallway as only principals' voices do.

We turned and looked at him together.

"Would you please step into my office?" he said, gesturing.

Sera flipped her hair and—sounding completely chill—said, "Sure. Whatever." But she turned and whispered in my ear, "Wait for me?" and I could hear the panic she wasn't showing.

"Of course," I said automatically. Screw Bleekman. I only had one tardy in his class anyway.

The door closed with a click and I pushed my back against the wall to wait.

Kimberlee walked up and assumed the same position just

a few inches away from my shoulder. "Hey," she said softly.

I glanced up to acknowledge her, but said nothing.

She paused and looked down at the ground for a few seconds before reluctantly meeting my gaze. "I'm sorry I wasn't there. I—shouldn't have stayed away. You probably could have used my help."

I swallowed hard and nodded again.

She looked down again. "You were right," she finally said. "You're doing me this huge favor and the least I can do is be grateful—or at least interested—and stay out of your social life. I—I'll try to do that from now on."

I thought I'd heard everything from Kimberlee. Yelling, screaming, crying, bad jokes, criticism, whining, shrieking, laughing, but never, ever apologizing.

It was kind of strange. And I didn't know if I could trust it.

But I wanted to.

I sighed and looked up at her with a small grin, and shrugged. Apology accepted, I guess. What else could I do?

We stood, shoulders almost touching, for a few companionable seconds. "I can't believe you set off the fire alarm."

"It was an accident," I whispered out of the side of my mouth. "Shortie broke something. There must have been chemicals in it."

"Well, whatever it was melted a hole right through the linoleum. The lab's a huge, soggy mess."

Great. Just great.

After another stretch of silence Kimberlee turned to me. "Do you want me to . . . you know?" she asked, pointing her thumb toward the principal's office. I was trying to decide just how much of a breach of privacy it was to send a ghost to spy on your girlfriend, when the door opened and Sera walked out.

"You think long and hard about that," Mr. Hennigan said firmly.

Sera didn't answer but her eyes were wide and dark against her pale skin.

I waited a few seconds until Hennigan closed his door again. "Are you okay?" I asked, slipping my hand into hers. It was cold.

She looked up at me and blinked, and in a matter of a second, her face changed. It was still pale and I could see a trace of worry in her eyes, but her smile was steady and the stressed creases on her forehead flattened out. "Yeah, I'm fine. Um, Hennigan was just worried about me getting enough credits to graduate next year. Thought I needed an extra math class, but it was a mistake." She turned away and started walking down the hall, with me in tow. "Hurry, we're going to be late."

My spider senses were tingling. I didn't want to believe that my girlfriend was lying to me, but I was pretty sure the threat of an extra math class wouldn't turn her face terrified like that.

I dropped her off at her class, and when she tried to leave I threaded my fingers through hers and pulled her back. I kissed her softly and then looked into her eyes, hoping she'd change her mind and tell me what really happened in there. But she just smiled and finger-waved at me before letting the classroom door close, blocking her from my view.

"Wow," Kimberlee said in a voice that sounded—for once—more concerned than mocking. "That was not good."

"No shit."

Returning stuff to the teachers had worked even better than I'd hoped. Almost all the teachers were in a good mood and had no problem helping to get the piles of bags on their desks to the right students. Several of them displayed their own returned objects on their desks like trophies. In English, Mr. Bleekman actually spent half a class period relating the history of the small sculpture that had been returned to its place on his desk after a two-year absence.

It made me want to take it back.

The really interesting part was that, thanks to the roses on the stickers, the whole school was talking about the Red Rose Returner—seriously, in capital letters. The conversations would totally dissipate if Hennigan came anywhere near—and man, he was patrolling the hallways constantly—but everyone was whispering about us . . . me . . . like we were heroes. Hardly anyone grumbled about the assumption that the Returner was probably also the thief. Like it didn't matter now that stuff was coming back.

There were a lot of interesting theories, ranging from the thief-slash-Returner being the ancient school janitor, Mr. Benson, to the wildest one, that it was Mr. Hennigan himself and that his rages against it were just to keep himself out of the spotlight. Unfortunately, the rumors about a senior trying to atone for high-school sins before graduation—the ones that made me worry for Khail and some of his teammates— were still the most popular. And the most logical.

"Would you turn them in if you found out who it was?" I asked our lunch table two days later, in what I hoped was an innocent tone.

"Are you kidding?" Wilson said. "And get lynched by the rest of the school? No way. Whoever this Red Returner guy is, he's doing everybody a favor."

"I would so make out with him," Jasmine said a little dreamily, stroking a keychain rabbit's foot she'd gotten back in the Christmas-tree stunt. She seemed unnaturally attached to it. But hey, I don't judge.

"What if it's a girl?" I asked.

Sera kicked me under the table. "You just want to see Jasmine make out with a chick," she said dryly.

"Sorry, I was totally kidding," I said, defending myself.

"Well, no one knows who it is and even if they do, they're

not telling." She stood without waiting for a response, and dumped most of her lunch in the garbage before striding out of the lunchroom.

The table was quiet and everyone's eyes slowly turned toward me. This was a clearly a boyfriend-duty moment. "See ya," I mumbled before throwing away a significant portion of my own lunch to follow Sera down the hallway.

I had to jog to catch up with her as she pushed through the doors at the back of the school and dropped down onto a cement parking barrier. I sat beside her, feeling more than a little awkward.

"Man, I wish I still smoked," she said after a long sigh as she unwrapped a piece of gum and popped it into her mouth.

"You used to smoke?" I said, genuinely shocked.

She laughed tersely. "Like I said, I wasn't always a good kid."

The wind blew a few stray hairs across her face. I reached out and gently brushed them back. "Why are you so upset over this?"

She sighed again and rubbed at her temples for a few seconds. "I don't expect you to understand," she said. "I really don't. But Kimberlee Schaffer has to be involved with this. I know she's dead, but somehow, she's *linked* and I have . . ." She hesitated. "I have some bad history with her and now everything has returned to smack me in the face and I just can't handle it all right now."

"Well," I said, hoping I didn't sound like I knew too much, "it has to be over soon, right? She can't possibly have stolen *that* much stuff. And then you can just forget about it, right?"

"No," Sera said with startling firmness. "I have to find out who's doing this. I *have* to." She rested her forehead on her knees, already hugged tight against her chest. When she spoke again her voice was muffled. "Maybe she has, like, a cousin or something. There's got to be a connection."

I rubbed Sera's arms gently, feeling like the worst boyfriend in the whole world. I was practically ready to confess. Even leaned my head down toward her ear when she sniffed and said, "I would rat the bastard out in a second if I knew. In a second!"

Laying my cheek on her back, I did the only thing I could. I said nothing.

Twenty-Four

"DUDE, I'M TELLING YOU, it'll work," I said to Khail on the phone—as I drove toward *his* house, strangely enough—after school. "You've heard everyone talking. They love us!"

"I don't know, man. Not many people can keep a secret. And you're talking about trusting, like, five hundred of them all at once."

"Yeah, but if we time it right, there's no way we can get caught."

I had come up with the idea while not paying nearly enough attention in calculus after lunch. We needed a way to return everything else in the cave all in one go so I could stop being a lying, dirtbag boyfriend. But other than Sera, the fact was that everyone was on our side.

And we could use that.

"If we start buzzing on Friday that there's going to be a big return on Monday, everyone will do our work for us over the weekend."

"Yeah, but then Hennigan'll lock down the school. He'll probably patrol it himself just to catch us."

"But the drop-off point doesn't have to be at the school. That's the beauty of it. We start the buzz and Hennigan will find out. He'll put loads of pressure on the school, but it won't *be* at the school." I waited for a second for effect. I think I inherited my mother's affinity for drama and was only now seeing it. "It'll be at Hennigan's house."

"What? Are you *trying* to get caught?"

"No, seriously. That's the one place that Hennigan would never expect. I heard from some guys in English that he lives just a block or so away from school, and Kimberlee's following him home today to make sure. But if it's true, kids could totally storm the place during lunch and Hennigan wouldn't be able to do a thing about it."

A long silence followed. "You may have something there," Khail finally said.

"Yes! So you're in?"

"Let me give it some thought," he said. "I gotta go shower. I reek."

"Okay. I'll be at your house soon, just so you know. I don't want you to turn around and freak out or anything."

"Whatever. I'll just keep pretending I don't know you, nerd boy."

"Thanks," I said dryly.

I turned onto Sera's street and pulled into my usual spot just south of the long driveway. Mrs. Hewitt was outside clipping roses. "Jeff," she said a little tersely. I had assumed that the more I hung around the house the more comfortable she would get with me. Apparently I was wrong.

"Hi, Mrs. Hewitt," I said, forcing myself to smile.

She looked down at her soiled gardening gloves and then back up at me like she was facing an earth-shattering problem. "Sera's up in her room. I don't want to track dirt in the house."

Oh. Got it.

"I suppose under the circumstances you can go in and get her, but come right back down. Also," she added, her voice vaguely threatening, "Khail's up there too."

I tried to look a little intimidated as I nodded and headed inside.

The house felt particularly quiet as I tromped up the steps. I'd been a little too cowed to tell Sera's mom that I didn't actually know which room was Sera's, so I was hoping there would be one of those signs on her door that said *Sera's Room*. No such luck.

I peered carefully into the first open door I came to. It was obviously a guest room. Perfectly made bed, paintings on the wall, two matching armchairs—but nothing personal. The next two doors were closed but the last one was ajar. I poked my head around the doorway and heard the faint sound of water running. The black, masculine furnishings—complete with a messy, unmade bed that could easily have been mine— told me there was no way this was Sera's room, so it took me a moment to realize that the auburn hair I was staring at was indeed the back of Sera's head.

Then I noticed what she was doing. She was holding a pair of jeans that were obviously Khail's in one hand, and she had his cell phone in the other and was rapidly pushing buttons.

"Sera?"

She shrieked as I spoke and jammed the phone into the jeans pocket.

"What are you doing?"

Her face turned bright red and she kept rifling through the jeans in her hands. "You scared me! I was, uh, looking for some gum," she said. "I was out and Khail usually has some, but nope, okay, let's go." She dropped the pants on the floor and pushed me out of the room, closing the door hard behind her.

"What are you doing up here?" she asked, not looking at me as she made her way to one of the closed doors. "My mom never lets guys come up here alone. Actually, she almost never lets guys come up here even if they're supervised."

She swung the door open and I fumbled for words as I

walked into her room. It was like every stereotypical rebellious-teenager bedroom you see in the movies. The walls were covered in rock-band posters, the bed was unmade, black stars dotted the ceiling, and the only light was from a lamp on a messy desk. "Um, she was doing roses, or something. D-dirt, you know," I stuttered. "Whoa," I said when I saw the enormous poster of Cryptopsy over her bed. "Is that . . .?" I just pointed wordlessly.

Sera looked at me funny. "What? Because I'm a cheerleader I can't like death metal?"

"No, it's fine, but . . . I don't know . . . this is, like, all emo and shit."

"Yeah, well, truth is I'm not really into most of this stuff anymore, but it bugs the hell out of my mom, so I keep it up."

I just kept looking around. I'm not sure what I expected, exactly, but it wasn't posters of girls in miniskirts screaming into microphones next to guy-linered, spiky-haired percussionists. It was too weird. Of course, when you go to a school with uniforms, it is a little hard to tell who's preppy and who's goth. But I saw Sera almost every day—in *and* out of school—and she'd always been the semi-preppy, casual type. Not . . . this.

"Speaking of my mom, we better head downstairs before she goes ballistic. Is *your* mom home?"

"She was when I left."

"Good enough. I can't do my homework here; not today." Sera's mom had this rule about Sera not going to a guy's house unless his parents were home. I was starting to believe that Sera's mom had rules for every situation imaginable. As she'd predicted, the first question Sera's mom asked was if my mom was home. I hoped I wasn't lying when I said yes. My parents tended to come and go as they pleased.

As I drove and Sera chatted, I tried to put the picture of her snooping in her brother's phone out of my mind. I mean, if I had a sister, I'd probably snoop in her phone too. But at the moment Khail was much more than just Sera's brother. He was . . . I guess you'd call him my first mate.

Turned out my mom *was* home, but she's way more lenient than Sera's mom, so we went up to my room and Sera and I did homework for an hour.

And by homework, I mean we made out.

Close enough.

"Is it safe to come in yet?" Kimberlee asked, poking her head through my bedroom door with her hands over her eyes.

Kimberlee and I had apparently arrived at some kind of truce. She kept her distance when Sera was around and if she wasn't exactly *nice* to me, at least she wasn't actively trying to insult me. She seemed genuinely impressed by our little break-in—that and I suspect she went to the cave and saw how little stuff was left. I guess not even the epically unappeasable Kimberlee Schaffer could argue with results.

"I took Sera home an hour ago. Chillax."

"Chillax? Please, nobody *actually* says *chillax*, loser." But even her insults had taken on a teasing tone in the last couple days.

Seeing that the coast was clear, she walked the rest of the way in and sank down on one of the beanbags. *Her spot*, she'd dubbed it.

"Were they right?" I asked. "About Hennigan's house?"

"Yes!" Kimberlee said, eyes sparkling. "I have no idea how I didn't know this while I was alive, but his house is just barely out of sight of the parking lot. It's perfect."

"Awesome," I said, and reached into my pocket for my phone to jet a text off to Khail. I hesitated before I hit send, remembering Sera going through Khail's phone, but this number was unlisted anyway; that was the whole point. I was probably just being paranoid.

"So," Kimberlee said hesitantly as I put my phone away, "speaking of Hennigan, did you ask Sera what happened today?"

"No," I said, not looking up from my history homework.

"Why not?"

"It's her business, not mine. If she wants to tell me, she can."

"Real proactive."

"What do you mean?"

But Kimberlee just shrugged. "The timing just seems like a little too convenient, if you ask me."

"Which I *didn't*," I said.

"Whatever. I just thought it sent up some warning signs."

"Because it's actually weird, or because it's Sera?"

"Because it's *weird*," Kimberlee said. "I'm serious, Jeff, if you were dating anyone else, I would be just as worried. Think about it; *your* girlfriend—who also happens to be the *sister* of the guy you're working with—gets called into the psycho principal's office on the day after a big return and then starts acting all weird. If you took the names out and forgot our history, wouldn't it totally make you suspicious?"

"No. I think you're reading way too much into it," I said. "Besides, we're doing the last drop on Monday and then it will be over."

"I don't understand you, Jeff."

"I'm speaking English, *Kimberlee*."

She gave me one of her melodramatic sighs. "I understand the words you are saying; I don't understand *you*. You think everyone's good and noble and whatever. You're sure Sera is innocent and you totally believe that Khail has no motivation except being a *swell* older brother." When she said *swell*, she pumped one fist like the protagonist of a 1950s sitcom.

"What's wrong with that?"

"You're living in a fantasy world. And the longer you pretend, the harder it's gonna be when you find out we're all miserable screwups. Especially *her.*"

I looked up from my homework. "And you vilify people. Is that any more realistic?"

"I don't vilify people," Kimberlee argued. "I see them as they are."

"Sure you do."

"I do!"

"So Langdon's a nice guy and Sera's a bitch? I don't think that has any ground in reality whatsoever."

"He was nice to me," she muttered.

"What about Khail?"

"What about him?" Kimberlee asked, looking suddenly quite interested in the *TV Guide* I had left open on the floor.

"He didn't do anything to you."

"Hell hath no fury like a woman scorned," Kimberlee said, waving me off.

"I don't believe that," I replied flatly. "You can't tell me that getting rejected made you so mad you took it out on Khail's little sister. That doesn't even make sense."

"When does love ever make sense?" Kimberlee grumbled.

"Why does he hate you?"

She hesitated. "I can't tell you."

I should have known better than to try to have a serious

discussion with Kimberlee. "Okay, well, I have a buttload of homework tonight—what channel do you want?" I asked, picking up the remote.

"I'm not lying!"

"You're *always* lying," I said, as I channel surfed.

"Not this time."

"Yeah, okay," I muttered, tossing down the remote and turning back to my calc book.

Kimberlee watched about two minutes of a tooth-whitener infomercial before breaking the silence. "Khail's . . . significant other got sent to brat camp. He thinks I was responsible."

"Brat camp?" I'd heard of parents who sent their "problem children" to special wilderness "retreats" for superharsh discipline, but I'd also heard that most of them got shut down—too many abuse scandals and a couple of deaths or something. I'd certainly never known anyone who'd gone. "Why would Khail think you had anything to do with his girlfriend being sent to brat camp?"

Kimberlee had a strange look on her face, like she was trying to both breathe and hold her breath at the same time. "It wasn't a girlfriend," she finally said before burying her face in the beanbag.

"What do you mean it wasn't a—oh. Oh!" Comprehension dawned on me. "*Khail?* Are you shitting me?"

Her head remained buried in the beanbag, her words

muffled and barely comprehensible. "Preston's parents are superfanatic something-or-others. . . . Somehow they found out what was going on and totally went off the deep end about it. Khail thinks that *somehow* was me."

"Why would he think that?" But what I wanted to ask was, *What did you do this time?*

Kimberlee glared up at me. "I already told you. I really liked him and he brushed me off. *Nobody* brushes me off! I wanted to find out what the deal was and I kind of started . . . following him."

"You stalked him?"

"It was *not* stalking!"

I waved my hands in an attempt to placate her. "Continue."

"It wasn't stalking. Years of stealing have just made me very good at not being seen."

"I bet." Everything had just taken a nosedive into surreal.

"And I . . . found out that his best friend . . . was more than a friend."

"And he *knew* you found out?"

"Duh," she said, looking at me like I was particularly remedial. "What's the point of finding out a deep, dark secret if you don't gloat about it? And a couple weeks later Preston got sent away."

"Convenient," I drawled.

"I didn't do it!" she yelled. "I didn't tell *anyone* what I knew. Well, except Khail."

"Why don't I believe you?"

"I don't know!" she protested. "No one believes me! Khail cornered me after school one day and tried to get me to admit I'd squealed, but I didn't have anything to do with it!"

"And that's why he still hates you a year after you died?"

She paused.

Oh no.

"Well . . . maybe that's not the *only* reason."

Just when I thought it couldn't get any worse. "What?" I said, more to my book than her.

"Preston's parents sent him off before he could say goodbye to anyone, so all Khail had to remember him by were the two things he'd left at Khail's house."

"Lemme guess," I said, not even bothering to put any inflection in my voice. "A Yankees hat and red boxers."

Kimberlee had the decency to look chagrined.

My first run-in with Khail made a whole lot more sense now. "How does Sera fit into all this?" I asked, not sure I wanted to know.

She shrugged.

"Oh, come on. Let's not play this game again."

"What do you want me to say? Preston was gone and Khail acted like he didn't even care, and so I started picking on Sera instead because I knew it would bug the hell out of him. And maybe I got carried away. It was more fun to pick

244

on Sera; she got all mad and flustery," Kimberlee said, as if we were talking about the weather instead of how she'd bullied my girlfriend. "Bullying Khail is like beating on a brick wall, but turn on Sera and they *both* go off the deep end. It's surprisingly satisfying."

"You really are crazy." I meant it. I was seriously horrified.

Kimberlee rolled her eyes and turned back to the television. "Whatever. I wasn't Miss Nice to Everyone. That's hardly news. But I *never* told anyone except you about Khail or Preston."

"Oh yes, you're *completely* innocent." My head spun. *Tell her I hate her.* Khail had meant every word.

And now I knew why.

"Why'd you tell me anyway? Are you hoping I'll go plead your case to Khail?" I asked, already dreading *that* conversation.

"No!" Kimberlee said, turning around to face me again, her eyes deadly serious. "You cannot tell him! You have to promise. I don't know if even Sera knows about him. So he'll figure out exactly who told you and then he'll *never* believe I didn't out him and Preston."

"Why do you care what he thinks? I mean this in the nicest way possible; you are *dead*."

Her expression immediately snapped to a practiced neutral. "I just do, okay?" she said, turning back to the infomercial.

Someone's crush didn't die with her. In her own warped way, Kimberlee really did care for Khail. Still. Talk about doomed love. *He's gay, she's dead, stay tuned.*

I turned back to my calculus homework, but was having trouble focusing. I felt like I was keeping secrets from everyone. Sera, my parents—now Khail, the one person who knew everything about Kimberlee. Weirder, it was his own secret I was keeping from him.

One more drop, I told myself. Then I could go back to my life, and Khail could go back to his, and he'd never have to find out that I knew the one thing he apparently didn't want *anyone* to know.

Three days. And this would all be over.

Twenty-Five

FRIDAY MORNING THE PLAN WENT into action. Step one was ridiculously simple. Khail leaned over to a girl in his first-hour class and said, "I heard the Red Rose Returner is going to pull something big on Monday."

It took off from there. By lunchtime the whole student body was buzzing about it.

I expected Sera to be pissy as usual about anything having to do with the Red Returner, but she didn't seem mad. She seemed *scared*. I tried to bring up the possibility of a date, but she brushed me off for the first time since we'd gotten together.

"I have tons of homework," she said vaguely. "I can't do anything this weekend."

"But you just finished your big project for history and you haven't mentioned anything else."

"Yeah, well, my homework is hardly the most exciting thing to talk about," she insisted.

"You have to eat sometime," I pressed. "Can't I take you out for a quick lunch on Saturday or Sunday?"

"I just don't have time," she said, pushing past me toward her next class.

I grabbed her hand and pulled her to a stop. "Did I do something wrong?" I asked quietly.

Her eyes softened. "No, not at all." She pulled my face down to hers and kissed me. "You're wonderful. I just . . . I have a special project I'm working on this weekend and I have to do it alone. Okay? Next weekend we'll get back to normal, I promise."

"Okay," I said, defeated for the moment. "I'll see you on Monday, then." I watched her hips sway as she walked, blinking only when the door closed behind her.

"I don't like it," Kimberlee said over my left shoulder.

I jumped and knocked into some freshmen, who looked at me funny but didn't say anything. I *had* to be getting a rep for being totally spastic. "I wish you wouldn't do that," I hissed as quietly as possible. I headed toward calculus and Kimberlee caught up with me.

Kimberlee glanced back at the door Sera had disappeared through. "She's acting weird. You can't tell me you haven't noticed."

"It's midterms. Everyone's stressed."

"How long has she been acting this way?"

"I don't know," I shot back. "Since midterms started?"

"How about since she got called into Hennigan's office?"

I turned to look at Kimberlee, glad the halls were mostly empty—even if it was because I was late for class. "I admit, the timing is weird, and whatever Hennigan said obviously upset her a lot. But she seems to know that you were the person who stole all this stuff that's making a sudden reappearance. Can you think of *any reason* why she might be so upset at the thought of you?"

For a few seconds Kimberlee looked everywhere but at me. Finally she met my eyes. "She could be spying for Hennigan."

I snorted in disbelief, a second before the direness of the possibility hit me. "No way. She wouldn't do that."

"You'd be surprised what people will do under the right kind of pressure."

"You're biased, and—"

"I know," Kimberlee said with a sigh. "I'm just saying— I'm not even accusing. I want you to be careful. You're almost done—everything will be over by Monday." Her cocky demeanor clicked back on as quickly as it had vanished. "Just try not to get your ass caught in the meantime, okay?"

Saturday morning I met Khail down at the cave to load everything up. As we worked, we went over our plan for Monday.

True to his promise to be extra careful, he'd borrowed a truck from a friend in Santa Barbara to load all the bags into. He'd stow it in his parents' guesthouse garage before they got home and retrieve it after they left for work Monday morning.

"So at eight ten I'll be all ready to go," he said, dragging out the last box. As in, the last box in the whole godforsaken cave.

I'd been trying to build up the courage to say it for an hour, and this was my last chance. "Watch out for Sera," I blurted.

Khail paused and I could see the muscles in his arms flex. "Why?" he said with a forced nonchalance.

"I think there might be . . . a possibility—a small possibility," I revised, "that she's trying to find out who we are."

Khail's head lifted and he glared at me. "What are you talking about? Like *spying*?"

"Forget it," I said. "It was a stupid thing to say."

Khail jumped down from the truck and walked around to face me. "No, explain," he said, crossing his massive forearms over his chest. "I want to know what makes you think she'd spy on us."

"Don't worry about it," I repeated.

"No, you wouldn't bring it up if you didn't have a good reason; I want to hear what it is."

I sighed. "She got called into Hennigan's office right after the break-in and she's been acting really weird ever since."

"So?"

"She was looking in your pockets while you were in the shower when I came over—going through your cell phone."

Khail laughed openly now. "This is how I can tell you're an only child, Jeff. That's totally normal. I snoop on her all the time, too." He grinned. "Oh man, the things I could tell you."

I hesitated for a few seconds before playing my final card. It was the only way I was going to find out for sure. "I bet you could. I've heard some things about Sera . . . um, freshman year . . . ?" I left the question open.

Khail's smile immediately melted away. "You can't hold that against her, Jeff. She didn't know what was happening. You of all people know she would never deliberately let someone die."

Holy shit! "What?"

Khail's jaw clamped shut. "Damn it," he whispered, running his fingers through his hair. "I shouldn't have said anything. I just assumed Kimberlee would have told you. She's not exact a good secret-keeper," he almost growled.

Oh boy, this is awkward. I figured my best course of action was to just keep my mouth shut.

Khail pursed his lips, then something changed in his eyes. "I'm only telling you this so you hear the truth, understand?" He glanced around like someone might be listening. "It was a rough time. My dad got fired; he said we might lose the house and everything. . . . He and my mom were talking divorce—yelling divorce, really. They fought constantly. Like the bad fighting you see on TV, except that it was real and it was our life. Sera was only fourteen, and she took it really hard. I . . . I got involved with someone, so I wasn't around. I've always wondered if things would have turned out differently if I'd been there for her." He shrugged. "But I wasn't and I can't change that now.

"Sera stopped doing anything anyone wanted her to do. My parents have always pushed her hard in gymnastics, so she quit—refused to even do a cartwheel for her coach. Failed classes she didn't used to have to even try in. Dropped her old friends and found new ones. Bad ones. Way older than her. She had money and they were happy to use her for it. They got her on weed, then coke, and one night they all got high and tried heroin." He shrugged. "She was tripping hardcore when the only other girl her age OD'd." Khail sighed and leaned back against the truck. "If anyone had been lucid enough to call 911, they probably could have saved her."

"Holy shit." I couldn't think of anything else to say.

"My parents finally realized their stupid problems were having an effect on their kids. Sera went to court-mandated rehab for two months, Mom and Dad started seeing a counselor, worked some stuff out, didn't get divorced after all, but it was a little late by then—we were already screwed up," he said in a quiet voice that simmered with anger.

I didn't say anything. *Couldn't* say anything. Sera had told me she'd been a mess, but I figured she meant something . . . I don't know . . . tamer. She seemed too good and pure to be involved in anything even remotely like this.

"She's worked really hard to get over this. And, trust me, it hasn't been easy. Some things she's *never* going to get back. Her clean conscience, for one. I know that night still haunts her. On top of that she lost her shot at competing nationally in gymnastics. She'll brush it off if you ever mention it, but it's a major sore spot for her. She has a lot of regrets, but she's dealt with them and moved on." He hopped up onto the tailgate and fixed me with a hard glare. "That's why I started watching you so closely when Sera told me she liked you. Why do you think someone as pretty as her hasn't had a boyfriend in almost two years? She doesn't trust herself to choose someone good. Someone who'll understand that she's made mistakes and let her keep moving forward. And if *you* can't, then you should—"

I held up my hand defensively. "No, you don't get it. I don't hold it against her at all." I hoped I was telling the truth, but I had a little ache in the pit of my stomach. Coke? Heroin? I had never even *seen* that kind of stuff, much less tried it. "But . . . what if Hennigan tried to use that against her? To put pressure on her?" I hedged.

But Khail was already shaking his head. "She owns her past—owns her mistakes. And she would never let someone else suffer for what she did. Besides," he added as he jumped back onto the tailgate and lifted another box, "most people at Whitestone either know or have heard rumors. Who would Hennigan threaten to tell? You?"

He had a point. It really didn't make a lot of sense. But . . .

"She would hate that we were helping Kimberlee," Khail said. "But I guarantee she'd never rat me out." He let the box fall hard into the bed of the truck. "And I don't think she'd rat you out either."

I nodded and tried to squelch the feeling that something still wasn't right, but doubt haunted me . . . rather like a drowned girl's ghost.

Twenty-Six

"DO YOU WANT TO DO something else?" Kimberlee asked peevishly after I failed yet another attempt to conceal a yawn.

"No, I'm good," I said, trying to sit up and look interested.

"Right," Kimberlee muttered.

Since Sera was busy, I'd been watching TV with my only other nonsecret friend—loser much?—and she was on this nostalgia-for-childhood kick so we were on about our tenth episode of *My Little Pony*. I argued that she wasn't even alive when *My Little Pony* originally aired, but she retorted that she wasn't alive now, either, and there's just no good comeback to that.

After a few more minutes of pink sparkle ponies, she turned to me. "It's all going to be gone on Monday, right?"

I had to jerk to attention a bit. I *may* have been snoozing. And possibly drooling. "Wha—? The stuff? Like in the cave? Yeah. We'll finish it all up on Monday."

"Then what?"

"Huh?"

Kimberlee turned her whole body to me now. "Then. What?" she repeated, as though the problem was with my ears.

"I heard you," I said, rolling my eyes, "but I don't understand what you're asking. We return the stuff, you go poof, I get my life back, the end." I rolled over and closed my eyes again.

She was silent for a few seconds, then asked, "Yeah, but what happens to me?"

I figured that if she actually asked me a question three times maybe she was ready to hear a serious answer. But it wasn't really an answer I knew myself. "Honestly?" I said hesitantly. "I think you'll just fade out. Become at peace and then cease to be."

She sat straight up. "What the hell do you mean, 'cease to be'?"

Perhaps that was a bit *too* serious. "Okay," I said, rolling over to face her, resting my chin on my crossed arms. "I always figured when someone died, they were probably just done. But now there's you. I mean, are you an angel or a spirit or what?" None of those words sounded anything remotely like Kimberlee. "My theory is you're kind of like an echo of a person. And you're still here because you can't find peace. So once you do, maybe you'll slowly slip away, like drifting off to sleep."

"So you're doing this all because you want me to just *disappear!*" She looked genuinely horrified.

"No, it's not like that. *I* like the idea of drifting away after I die. If you don't, then believe something else."

"But *you* think I'm going to disappear?"

Yeah, so maybe as an agnostic I'm not the most comforting spiritual advisor around. What did she want me to say? "I don't think anything. I was just . . . presenting one possibility. You could also turn into the abominable snowman and terrorize skiers for all eternity."

She narrowed her eyes. "Now you're just being stupid."

I let out a frustrated breath. "Look. I don't *know* what's going to happen to you—I don't actually care about the details. I don't know; that's what *agnostic* means."

"So you just live your life not knowing anything?"

"I know a lot of things," I countered, then shrugged. "Whether or not there's a god just doesn't happen to be one of them. It doesn't seem that important to me."

Her jaw muscles flexed and she looked back at the television, although I doubt she realized the credits had started to roll. "Well, it seems awfully important to *me* right now."

"I can understand that."

"And even being confronted with a *ghost* doesn't make you want to find out now?"

"Not really. Nothing in this world is going to prove or

disprove that there's a god. At least, *I* don't think so. Religion is really good for some people, but being agnostic works for me. Like Einstein."

"Einstein was agnostic?"

"Very."

"Hmmm." She was silent for a while. "What makes you want to be good?"

"I don't know. I just want to."

"That's dumb. Why bother?"

I had to stop and think on that one. *Because I always have* seemed a little trite. "I believe that there's enough bad in the world and that you should do what you can to put some good in there, because it's the right thing to do."

"You're just a good person, I guess."

I shrugged. "Maybe."

Another endless silence. "So . . ." I said, scrolling down to the next episode. "You ready for another?"

She stared intently at the now-blank television screen as if it might hold the answers to all of her questions. Then she shook her head. "I'm not in the mood. I'm gonna go." Without waiting for a response, she started toward the window.

"Wait a sec," I said, scrambling to my feet. "When are you coming back?"

She gazed out at the streetlights illuminating the sidewalk in front of my house. "I don't know. Tomorrow, maybe?"

I nodded but said nothing.

With a scarcely audible "Bye," she slid through the window and dropped to the ground. I watched her go. Her head was bent and her shoulders curled forward. She looked so real, and—at that moment—so *heavy*. Weighted. You'd have never thought to see her that she was less than a wisp of air.

Twenty-Seven

MONDAY MORNING I WOKE UP early and couldn't get back to sleep. This was it: the day I got rid of my spectral friend.

Kimberlee didn't say a word about our conversation Saturday night or her disappearance all day Sunday, and I had a feeling she wouldn't appreciate me bringing it up—especially on her *special* day. "This is the most awesome plan!" she gushed in what was possibly her very first sincere compliment to me ever. "Hennigan is going to be so pissed. He might just keel over and have a heart attack right then and there."

"Oh good," I grumbled, "then I can have that on my conscience for the rest of my life." I wasn't sure why I couldn't get into the spirit of it like she could. Maybe it was because the drop wasn't finished yet or because of everything I'd learned in the last week.

"It would *so* not be a loss," Kimberlee said, studying herself in the mirror. "He's such an asshole. I wish I could wear something else. Some kind of party clothes. Or at least do my hair," she added, swirling it around and piling it on the top of her head. But as soon as she let go it slipped back down around her shoulders. "Oh well." She turned away from the mirror. "Maybe I'll be able to do more wherever it is I'm going."

"Yeah," I said hoping my sarcasm would cover my nerves. "It's a big day for *you*." It was easy to be cavalier when you weren't the one risking your neck.

If Kimberlee noticed my tone, she gave no indication.

The timing was delicate. I drove to school, parked in the school parking lot, and ran over to the south side, where Khail was waiting for me in the borrowed truck.

Then we headed to Hennigan's.

Kimberlee was *actually* keeping watch today. She was going back and forth between making sure Hennigan was still roaming the halls suspiciously and checking that no one was watching his house.

The actual drop-off took less than a minute. That was mostly Khail's brain at work. We stacked everything on the tarp and laid another tarp on top of the whole thing. At eight thirty-five we backed the truck over the curb onto Hennigan's lawn. Then Khail and I ran to the tailgate, unlatched it, gave a good tug, and the tarp—loaded with bags—came sliding right out.

It took about ten more seconds to grab a big sign from

261

the truck bed that had a huge version of the little stickers: the red rose and a scripted *I'm sorry*.

That part was actually Kimberlee's idea. She said it was like a billboard and that some student late for school was bound to see it.

Khail and I jumped back in and hurried away from Hennigan's house. He pulled over behind the school and let me out so he could go ditch the truck, driving off almost before I could close the door. Hennigan would probably get suspicious when Khail missed his first class, but Khail assured me he could handle it.

I wished I shared his confidence. If I got him busted, Sera would never forgive me.

Either way, I had to get my ass to class before I got caught too. I was only about seven minutes late, but if I slid into my seat more than ten minutes late, it would count as an absence.

And then they would call my mother, which was almost scarier than expulsion after the promise I'd made that I would stay out of trouble. After which, of course, I broke into the school.

"Jeff, wait!" Kimberlee called, but I didn't have time to stop and knew she could catch up.

I almost ran into Mr. Hennigan before I saw him. The one time I really *should* have listened to Kimberlee.

"In a hurry, are we?" Mr. Hennigan said pointedly.

I put on my best I-am-an-idiot voice and pointed at my watch. "Late," I said.

Mr. Hennigan circled me like a vulture. "This wouldn't have anything to do with the alleged returning of stolen items today, would it?"

"Huh?" I said, trying to look confused. "Oh, the lost stuff. Yeah, no. If I was missing anything, it would still be in Phoenix. I just moved here." Smooth, suave, and totally stupid-sounding. Perfect.

Hennigan looked over the edge of his glasses and studied me. "Oh, yes. Mr. . . . Mr. Clayson, is it?"

"Yeah, that's me."

Frustration passed over Mr. Hennigan's face, but he only allowed himself a small sigh before he snapped back to attention. "On your way, then," he said dismissively. "You've got one minute to get to class before you're marked absent."

I took off the second his eyes left me, walking as quickly as possible, and managed to slip into the door of Mr. Bleekman's class just as the clock turned to eight forty.

Mr. Bleekman looked up at me and his eyes darted to the clock. With obvious disappointment, he marked a tardy down in his grade book.

Twenty minutes after the bell, a girl named Katie—which, since she lives in Santa Monica, is short for Katerina, not

Katherine—burst into class, her face pink.

Mr. Bleekman smiled very slightly and walked over to his grade book. "More than ten minutes late, Miss Chardon; you'll be counted absent for this class period."

"Sorry," Katie said, sounding distracted.

As soon as she sat down I watched her pull a Ziploc bag out of her backpack and—after a quick glance at Bleekman's back—hand it to the girl across the aisle.

The girl giggled quietly and asked—in a voice so loud half the class could hear—"Where?"

"Hennigan's!" Katie squealed, drawing a stern look from Mr. Bleekman. But no one was paying attention to him anymore.

"Hennigan's?" another guy asked. "Like, his house?"

"Yeah. Right in his yard! There's a big sign and everything. I saw it on the way to school. That's why I was so late," she added in a whisper. As if we couldn't all figure *that* out.

In the front row a girl's hand shot into the air.

Bleekman ignored her.

"Mr. Bleekman," she said, refusing to be put off so easily.

Bleekman sighed. "Yes, Miss Sanderson?"

"I gotta go. Like, to the bathroom," she added.

He glared at her for a long time, but no teacher in his right mind tells a girl she can't go to the bathroom. Finally he sighed and motioned to his desk. "Take the pass."

She positively bounced to the desk for the pass and almost ran out the door.

"I'm next when she gets back," a low, threatening voice said.

I knew who the voice was before I turned, but it surprised me so much I had to look anyway.

Langdon.

Unfortunately for him, he wouldn't find anything there. Langdon was one of the only students I knew of who Kimberlee had never stolen from. I guess friendship meant *something* to her.

By the time lunch rolled around, the school was buzzing and full of stickered bags, half the kids were tardy to my third-hour class, and Mr. Hennigan was storming around the halls in a rage.

But we were done.

Kimberlee popped up beside me. "There are six bags left," she said nervously. "What if no one takes them? What if they're absent today?"

"Don't worry," I whispered, while pretending to arrange books in my locker. "Even if they're gone, one of their friends will take them. I guarantee."

She nodded reluctantly. "I guess you're right. I'm going back, though, just to be sure."

I watched her speed off and chuckled as I shook my head.

I grabbed my backpack and headed toward the lunchroom to meet Sera. I hadn't seen her since Friday. Which meant that I hadn't actually spoken to her since Khail admitted she was involved in a friend's death.

I had to admit, I was nervous. I didn't *want* to think badly of Sera—it really wasn't her fault—but was I actually a big enough person to just let it go? I figured seeing her face-to-face was the only way to know for sure.

I was about to turn the corner when I heard Mr. Hennigan call her name. "Miss Hewitt," he said, his voice stern, but also a little raw. I suspected he'd been yelling at kids all day. Not that there was anything he could do about the legions of bags entering the school. Nothing in them was a banned item, and he couldn't suspend anyone unless he could prove they were involved.

After a pause Mr. Hennigan said icily, "We need to talk."

I peeked around and saw Sera standing in front of Mr. Hennigan's office. But she didn't have the confident, straight posture I was used to seeing. Her shoulders were slumped and her head hung forward, her hair almost blocking out her face.

She looked . . . guilty. And it killed me inside.

I didn't want her to know I'd seen her get called into Mr. Hennigan's office again, so after the door closed I continued on past the front office and into the lunchroom to the table where we normally sat.

She didn't come back the whole lunch period. I had to

catch her on her way into her history class. "Hey," I said, laying a hand on her shoulder.

She turned and smiled, but I realized it looked a lot like Kimberlee's smiles. The fake ones.

"Hey!" she said, her voice sharply chipper.

"You didn't come to lunch," I said, refusing to actually ask her where she'd been. I wanted to see what she would say.

"Oh," she said, waving a hand dismissively, "I had to stay after in English. I totally screwed up an assignment and had to work with Bleekman to make it up. Sorry I didn't tell you. I didn't know till right then."

She wouldn't meet my eyes.

"Oh, okay," I said, looking down at my shoes.

"But we can do something tomorrow after school," she suggested.

I nodded and accepted a kiss before she disappeared into her history class. It tasted strangely sour.

She lied.

But then, who was I to judge? Technically, I'd been lying to her from day one. I tried to remember that as I walked into my own class.

Twenty-Eight

WHEN I ARRIVED HOME, KIMBERLEE was restlessly pacing in my room. "What if it doesn't work?" she said, without a greeting. "What if something got lost, or someone stole somebody else's bag and I'm stuck here forever!"

"Fate wouldn't hold you responsible for someone else's actions," I grumbled, already in a bad mood; what the hell did I know about fate? "You can only be held accountable for things you actually did." I was pretty sure I'd seen that in a movie once. Or something.

She paused and looked down at me where I had dropped into a beanbag with a pint of Ben & Jerry's I'd grabbed from the kitchen on the way in. Sugar therapy.

"Are you sure the cave was completely empty?"

"Kimberlee," I said firmly, "you checked twice. It was *totally* empty. Everything you stole has been returned or donated to a good cause."

But my mind wasn't on our latest stunt. I couldn't help

but be angry that Sera hadn't admitted to being called into Hennigan's office. And if she'd lied this time, she'd probably lied last time, too. If she *had* been pressured to help him, it didn't matter anymore. But the thought of Sera in league with Hennigan made me look at her differently. It pissed me off.

More than the drug thing. I could think of a million excuses for that. She made some bad friends, bad choices, and then got dumped in a situation where she had no choices at all.

But this felt weirdly personal.

And if she was lying about him, what else was she lying about? After all, she had never told me about the girl who died. I had to drag it out of Khail. And she hadn't said anything about her problems with Kimberlee at all. She was the victim in that situation—why *wouldn't* she tell me? Didn't I have the right to know? I was her boyfriend.

But then ... did that mean she owed me a full life's confession? I didn't want to think that way either. My sense of right and wrong—of justified and unforgiveable—felt completely screwed up.

Kimberlee sat down in the other beanbag. "Why hasn't it happened?" she said in a very small voice. "Shouldn't it have happened by now?"

I shrugged, my mind whirling so fast I could hardly concentrate on what Kimberlee was saying. "Maybe it's one of those things that happens at midnight, or at night when you—I'm sleeping. It'll happen," I said, stretching my arms over my head.

Khail and I had managed a very brief conversation in the bathroom—it was a bit nostalgic, actually, considering our first conversation—and talk around the school confirmed that before fifth hour, everything on Hennigan's lawn was gone. Including the tarp. The deed was most definitely done.

All we had to do was wait for Kimberlee to pop.

"Sit," I told Kimberlee. "I have a surprise."

She sat—albeit a little warily—and I reached into a bag beside me. I stopped by the video store on the way home—a little farewell . . . present, I guess . . . seemed appropriate. With a little *ta-da!* I pulled out a cheesy romance movie, one she'd managed to talk me into way back at the beginning of all this. Kimberlee's face fell.

"What?" I said. I looked at the movie case. I had gotten the right one, hadn't I? All the sappy romances look pretty much the same to me.

"No, no," she said, waving her hands. "It's great really. It's just, you've been so nice to me. After everything. Me almost getting you beat up that first day, and bothering you about Sera, and having to take so much stuff back. And you still brought me a movie you hate. I guess I . . . well . . . for a nerd, you're pretty cool."

She was getting weepy now, and not the fake-weepy she used to get what she wanted out of me. This was new, and not entirely comfortable. I didn't want to embarrass her by making a big deal out of it—okay, I *wanted* to, but I knew it wasn't the nice thing to do—so I just smiled and nodded before turning and putting the movie into the player.

I think chick flicks have superpowers. Really. They're so boring that I theorize supersleep waves actually come rolling out of the television screen when you watch them. Because I know the movie didn't get over any later than eight o'clock and by the time the credits rolled, I was out. Like out, out. I didn't wake up until the next morning at six a.m.

With Kimberlee in my face, shouting. Not her usual mad shouting, but wild, crazy, panicked shouting.

"It didn't work. Jeff, wake up! It didn't work. I've been watching the minutes click by and nothing. Nothing!"

She continued ranting as I attempted to sit up. It felt like every bone in my back was out of alignment and my neck couldn't turn more than about forty-five degrees to the left. My mouth tasted dry and sour after eating so much ice cream before falling asleep, but I managed to make it work and mumbled, "Wait a sec; I don't get it."

"I'm still here!" she shrieked, sounding much more like her normal, angry self.

"I can see that," I said, shaking my head. It was starting to

271

unfog and behind the fog lurked a sense of unease. This was *not* what I had planned.

I finally managed to stagger to my feet—still wearing my full uniform, including tie, mind you—and rubbed one eye, then the other as I looked at the clock and then at the window, where weak sunlight was starting to light the edge of the sky.

Kimberlee was silent—for once—and stared at me with an empty, hollow look in her eyes. "I'm not gone," she finally said, voice trembling.

I let out a big breath. "No, you're definitely not." I walked over and sat on the edge of my bed. "Maybe . . . maybe it takes longer."

But Kimberlee only shook her head. "I should have been gone yesterday, or at least by midnight." She dropped onto the bed beside me and tears, real tears—I could tell by now—streaked down her face. "I'm stuck," she whispered shakily. "It's been over a year and I've done everything I can think of, and now I'm stuck."

"You're not stuck," I said with very little conviction. "Ghosts don't just get stuck." But really, what did I know? I hadn't even believed in ghosts until I met Kimberlee. The doubt I couldn't keep out of my voice shattered whatever hope she'd been holding on to. Her chin dropped to her chest and her shoulders curled in as sobs shook her whole body.

"Kim," I said softly. "Don't—"

"I hate this," she said, her voice a little muffled. "I hate everything about my life. My unlife, what-the-hell-ever! It's torture every day and I'm so *tired*."

"It's not that bad," I said, wishing I could pat her shoulder or something.

She looked up and pushed her hair away. "No, you don't understand. I'm a nutcase. I'm a serious, lock-me-in-a-padded-room klepto and being a ghost is killing me."

For a second I thought I'd misunderstood. "Wait, you're pissed because you *can't steal?*" The look on her face was answer enough. "Kimberlee!"

She wouldn't meet my eyes. "I thought dying would make everything easier."

What? "You thought *dying* would make everything easier? You told me you got caught in a riptide!"

"I did. I didn't commit suicide, okay? Chill." She was silent for a long moment, but tears continued trailing their way down her face. "But I thought about it," she confessed in a whisper. "I was down at our beach, my parents were gone—as always—and I was superdepressed. I stole, like, six things that day trying to feel better and nothing was working. And I . . . I considered it. Who hasn't?"

I shrugged rather than answering. But thinking and doing are two very different things.

273

"It was sunny, but the water was freezing and I went out anyway. I was out way too deep in the water by myself—me, the water, and my chattering teeth. And I may have been a little drunk, so I wasn't thinking very clearly. And I laid back floating with this little noodle thing, and I looked at the sky and wished I could just float out into the ocean and die."

I checked my spider senses, but they didn't seem to be tingling. I cautiously concluded that she was telling the truth. For now.

"So I . . . I had a good cry and started swimming in. And I noticed I was out farther than I thought and I tried to fight the stupid current—which you're not supposed to do—and after a while I was so cold and tired I couldn't hold on to the noodle anymore and I sank." She looked up at me, her eyes wet. "And it turns out that all of your problems are actually worse when you're dead. Stealing included."

"But you *couldn't* steal stuff anymore. Wasn't that better?"

"I wish," she said. "Cold-turkey withdrawals are a bitch. I couldn't touch anything. The first few months were hell. No, really," she said, turning to me for a second. "I thought I was in hell. Everything in me screamed out to grab things, to take things, and I. Just. Couldn't. And it *hurt*. I spent so much time yelling and screaming and cursing God, and Buddha, and Allah, and anyone else who might have made me a ghost. But it was no use." She gestured to herself. "Obviously."

"Did the urges finally wear off?"

She shrugged noncommittally. "Yes and no. I mean, I found ways to deal with it—I had no choice—but it's like being an alcoholic or a chain-smoker or something. You can quit, but you never lose that urge, especially when you're around the good stuff. And I'm around *stuff* all the time. The best I can do is distract myself with other things. I can go wherever I want and listen to private conversations. Spy on private moments. Sometimes stealing people's privacy feels almost as good as taking their stuff. But it's not . . . it's not the same. And it's—" She paused for a second to take a few breaths and get a hold of her emotions. "It's just so damn *hard.*"

"I didn't know," I said quietly. "I mean, I *knew* about the kleptomania, but I didn't know it affected you like this. I . . . I'm sorry."

"I didn't want you to know. I just wanted to get the stuff returned and move on, whatever that means." She shrugged helplessly. "And now that's not going to happen." She flopped back onto my bed and started to cry again.

"Don't cry, Kim, please," I implored. "We'll find a way. We'll make things happen."

She opened her wet, black-lined eyes and looked at me. "Do you think so?"

I knew the life or death of her hope lay in my answer. An answer I already knew was going to have to be a lie. "I know it," I said, with as much conviction as I could muster. Faith was never my strong suit; I'd never had any use for it. But even when all I really felt was doubt, Kimberlee needed more than *ifs* and *maybes*. "We'll find a way. I—" *This was the hardest part to say.* "I'll help you."

A little part of me died inside at that. I knew I *would* help her—in the past month we'd become . . . I wasn't sure *friends* was the right word, but we were *something*. So I'd help. But what would it cost me? At the very least I'd have to lie to both Khail and Sera. And until when? I was out of ideas.

But she had no one else.

"Really?" She pushed up on her elbows, her eyes brightening a little.

"Yeah," I said, trying to sound casual. "Of course." I smiled. "I'm the one who can see you; that must mean that I can help you. We just have to figure out how."

She crossed her arms over her chest. "If taking all that stuff back didn't work, I don't know what will."

"We'll think about it for a few days," I said, trying to stave off the panic while keeping my expression totally impassive. "Something will come up. We'll find the answer."

Kimberlee looked down at the floor for a long time before looking me in the eyes. "Thank you," she said, her voice low. Then her eyes darted away.

"You're welcome." I cocked my head toward the bathroom.

276

"I gotta get in the shower," I said. "Turns out, it is another day."

Kimberlee rubbed her arm across her face, swiping away her tears. She had put her game face back on. Her face that held the world at bay and didn't let anyone get too close—or know how much she was hurting. The face I was used to.

Kimberlee was back.

Twenty-Nine

KIMBERLEE FOLLOWED ME around school all day again, but she kept her distance and didn't speak. Even with her brave front, she wasn't exactly jovial, and a cloud of gloom seemed to encompass her. After all these weeks with a ghost in my life, I was finally feeling *haunted*.

And she wasn't the only one acting weird.

"You want to come over after school today?" Sera asked, a little too cheerily. "My parents are both out of town and Khail has a big party after wrestling to celebrate the guys going to State."

State. I am such a bad friend. I hadn't even asked which of my guys had made it to State. I'd been so concerned about the last return that I didn't ask how the qualifying match went.

"We could have some actual alone time," she said, snuggling against me.

Any other time I would have been all over that idea, but everything felt strange today. My whole life felt was upside down, and my brain kept reminding me that Sera had lied and I hated that. Still . . . I wasn't going to turn down an invitation like this.

I tried to give Kimberlee an apologetic look as I walked out the door with Sera after school, but I wasn't sure she caught it. Still, she'd forgive me. She didn't really have a choice. She was stuck with me. Forever, maybe.

Or was I stuck with her?

I tried to push thoughts of *forever* to the back of my head, but they were there, lurking just out of sight. Sera let us into her house and we went into the kitchen to grab something to eat. She chattered as she did, but I had a hard time following her conversation for more than about ten seconds. The third time I said something like, "Huh? Yeah. What?" she sighed and looked at me with one hand on her hip.

"You're so distracted today. Come here." She grabbed my hand and pulled me along behind her.

The Hewitts had an awesome media room, dominated by a sectional with an enormous middle piece that was like five feet wide and turned the whole sofa into what looked like the most massive bed ever. You could just sink into it and it molded around your body with the perfect combination of softness and support. Seriously, best make-out couch ever.

And, as yet, untried by me.

Sera put on a movie, but I figured it was just for back-ground noise when she lay down beside me and wrapped her arms around my ribs and let one leg slide up to rest on my thigh.

I leaned toward her and pressed my face against her neck. She started to kiss me and for a while I kissed her back, start-ing to feel like I could let everything else in my life go and just focus on her, but my thoughts kept returning to Kimberlee, going through everything she had told me. I tried to figure out what could be left for her to do.

And why me? Why was I, of all people, supposed to help her? Was there something special about me that related to what she had to do? It made sense, but I couldn't figure out just what it was. Maybe if we had a long talk tonight I could find out something she hadn't wanted to tell me yet. Something she—

"Hello?" Sera said, waving a hand in front of her face.

My eyes snapped back down to her and I groaned. I'd wanted a day like this forever and I just couldn't enjoy it. "I'm sorry," I said. "This is great and you're awesome and I've wanted to be alone like this for ages, and I'm just so—"

"Distracted?" Sera offered.

I nodded glumly.

Sera settled herself beside me. "Me too," she said quietly. "I've been planning this since I found out last week that both my parents were leaving," she said, looking up at me from underneath her eyelashes. "I wanted . . . I wanted this to be really special. But things are kind of weird in my life, and you're obviously stressed about something and . . . well, I should probably stop trying to force it."

"It's okay," I said, slinging an arm around her. She curled herself against me. I knew I should probably keep quiet, but I wanted to tell *someone*. "I've been working on a big problem that I thought I finally fixed, but it turns out I was wrong. I'm back at square one." But rather than making me feel better, saying the words out loud made the hopelessness of the situation seem suddenly overwhelming. If anything, I was *worse* off than when I first met Kimberlee. At least at that point we *thought* we knew what to do. Now we had nothing.

"Care to share?" Sera asked quietly.

I wanted to. I wanted to so badly, but I knew I couldn't. "It's really complicated," I said, stalling. "How about this?" I suggested, leaning to kiss her forehead. "When I figure it out, I'll tell you." *And hopefully by that time, you'll have forgotten all about it.*

"Fair enough."

I was silent for a moment, then it was my turn to press. "What about you?" I asked. "You've been pretty distracted yourself."

I felt her whole body stiffen against me.

"Hey," I said, in my most gentle voice, hoping that being nonconfrontational might encourage her to confide in me. I hesitated, then decided to confess what I knew. "Listen, I saw you get called into Hennigan's office again on Friday. And you don't have to tell me what happened, but you don't have to lie, either." *Please just don't lie.*

She sat up, her jaw clenched. "It's no big deal," she said, scooting herself off the couch.

"It *is* a big deal," I said, following her. "It's a big deal because it upsets you so much. I don't like things upsetting you like this. Especially not Mr. Loser-Hennigan."

"He's not a loser; he's a snake," Sera retorted so sharply I backed away a little. "He's a sneaky, blackmailing snake and I hate him!" The flare of anger settled into a bitter cold as she paced. "Not that it's really *his* fault. I'm not going to fall in the trap like everybody else in the school. Just being all happy about all this stuff coming back," she said in a singsong voice, "and not realizing that they shouldn't be happy. They should be pissed at the person who started everything. Everything is her fault. Hennigan, the stupid returns, everything. I swear, I am never going to be free of Kimberlee Schaffer."

At the mention of Kimberlee's name I sat up and swore under my breath.

"What?" Sera said, looking at me in a way that made me glad I didn't have a mirror.

"Why . . . how . . . I don't . . ." I paused and tried to collect my thoughts. "Why do you hate her so much? Why can't you just move on and let this go? You don't know what kind of life she had. Maybe she had problems, Sera."

"Everyone does; that doesn't mean they treat the world like shit."

"Maybe her problems were that big." Big enough to contemplate suicide and then to keep her here as a ghost.

"And maybe it doesn't matter. Some things aren't justifiable, Jeff."

"I'm not trying to justify anything. But sometimes there's more to people than you think." Who was I lecturing now? I felt like this was what I needed to hear, not Sera.

"And you know this why? She was dead by the time you moved here."

"But I—" I paused and chose my words carefully. "I've been hearing a lot of stories. It sounds like she was really messed up—like she had problems and no one bothered to understand."

"Well, she didn't make it very easy."

"It sounds that way. But she's gone now. Wouldn't it be healthier for you to let her go? She's dead. Isn't it bad to speak ill of the dead?"

"What do you care? You don't even believe in an afterlife."

"I care because I care about *you!*" When had I started yelling?

"And she was awful to me. Doesn't that mean anything to you?"

"Maybe it would mean more if you would just tell me what's going on!"

Sera was yelling back now. "No offense but you've known me for, what, a month? Boyfriend or not, maybe I'm not ready to spill my life story, okay?"

Why was I demanding Sera level with me even though I hadn't been honest with her? But I couldn't seem to stop. After the way Kimberlee had fallen apart when she didn't move on, I felt like I had to stand up for her. "She stole your stupid shoes and skirt. I can't believe you're still holding a grudge over that!"

Two red spots stood out on Sera's face. "You have no idea what she did to me, Jeff. I'm warning you; don't go there."

But the picture of Kimberlee sobbing on my bed was too fresh. "Did you ever consider that maybe you can hurt people even after they're dead? That people's feelings live forever? You don't ever think about how she feels. You're just like everyone else. You want to be forgiven for what you did but you won't forgive her." I clamped my mouth shut. I hadn't intended to confess that I knew.

Her cheeks flushed bright red. "Who told you?"

"I wish *you* had," I said quietly.

She swallowed hard. "I couldn't. I knew you wouldn't . . . you wouldn't—"

"Forgive you? Well, you were wrong."

She looked down at her feet.

"I don't care about your past, Sera. But I care about now. And if you won't let go of this thing with Kimberlee, then I don't know if we can—" I clamped my mouth shut. I'd been about to say *I don't know if we can be together*. But I'd stopped too late; she knew where that sentence was going.

She was quiet for a long time, her eyes drilling into mine. When she spoke, her voice was soft, controlled, and full of fury. "You don't know anything. No one does." She hesitated. "Even my parents and Khail don't know everything. You want me to forgive her? Believe me, I'm working on it." Her voice rose now. "I'm trying because I can't live with these awful feelings inside me. She was terrible, Jeff. Completely inhuman. She would shove me in the halls, break into my locker and soak my backpack, destroy my assignments and books. She beat me up in the locker room one day—slammed me against the lockers so hard I blacked out for a couple seconds. And I *never* understood why."

I did. Or, at least, I knew the reasons. *Understand* was something I would probably never manage. "Why didn't you tell someone?" I choked out.

285

"I did, eventually. But—" She hesitated. "Let's just say my parents weren't very interested in *me* at that point. And that didn't help either. I felt abandoned on all fronts. When things got really bad I was into some pretty messed-up stuff, and I was superhigh one night when Khail found me and worked the whole story out of me. I hadn't told anyone because Kimberlee was basically untouchable, since her parents paid for like half the school. That was about the time I . . . got shipped off to rehab," she said, not meeting my eyes. "When I came back I was determined to be clean and start over, but I was terrified of Kimberlee. Khail promised me he'd . . . he'd taken care of it, and that Kimberlee wouldn't bother me anymore, but I wasn't sure I could believe him."

"And then she died," I said weakly. I knew the end of this story.

But Sera shook her head. "My first week back she cornered me in the parking lot before the game and *cut off my hair,* Jeff. She grabbed my braid and chopped it off. Who does that? A monster, that's who."

I stared at her in horror, not wanting to believe. But everything in her eyes told me she was telling the truth. This was it—what I'd been trying to get them both to confess from the beginning.

And it made my whole mouth sour.

"I never told Khail. Never told anyone. Just said I decided

to get it cut—into a *really* extreme A-line," she added with a grumble. I don't think Khail suspected anything. I was tired of needing him to fix my problems, so I decided to just take it. And I did. For a couple weeks. Then . . . then she died." Sera walked forward, her eyes glittering with anger. "And you know what I felt, Jeff? Relief. No, it was more than that. I felt safe. For the first time in ages, I felt *safe.*"

"I—"

"Don't. Don't say anything. Just go get into your car and leave. I can't talk to you right now."

"Sera, I—"

"Please go," she whispered.

I was in my car, driving aimlessly, a few minutes later. What had I done? After feeling sure that I had learned to see Kimberlee for what she was—especially this morning—she'd completely suckered me. She wasn't a lost soul waiting to move on; she was a demon cursed to live a hollow eternity on earth.

I stopped the car in front of my house and stared up at my bedroom window. She'd be there. Where else would she be? As I pulled into the garage I went over Sera's story in my head, stoking my anger. I punched the button to close the garage door and slammed the kitchen door open. No one was home and I was glad. I couldn't have kept this quiet if I had wanted to—and I didn't. I stomped up the stairs and threw open my bedroom door. Kimberlee was sprawled in front of the TV that I had started just leaving on when I left for school. I grabbed the remote and turned it off, flooding the room with silence. Kimberlee looked up at me, her eyes wide and questioning. And maybe a little scared.

"What did you do?"

"Do? I can't *do* anything."

"To Sera, when you were alive? What did you do!" I'd never been a shouter, but something about Kimberlee brought that side of me out.

Kimberlee rolled her eyes. "Is the little princess making up stories?"

"They're not stories, Kimberlee, and you know it."

Her face closed into an unreadable expression.

I took a step back and put my hands on my hips. "I want to hear it from you."

She forced a smile, but fakeness radiated from her so brightly I couldn't believe I'd ever been fooled. "I stole her skirt and shoes. I already admitted I shouldn't have done that."

"Don't give me that!"

"What?"

"This I'm-just-a-poor-demented-klepto crap. Stealing was the least of your problems, Kimberlee. And I should have realized it a long time ago."

Something must have changed in my voice, because

Kimberlee stared silently up at me for a long time. "I wasn't very nice to her. We talked about this already."

"No, it was more than that. You did everything you could to sabotage her. You can't stand to hear me talk about her. You *hate* her. Why?"

"I just do. Some people rub you the wrong way and—"

"Why!" I shouted.

Her lips pressed into a straight line and her hands found her hips as if pulled by a magnet. "Because some people just need to be brought down a peg," Kimberlee said, sneering. "She thinks she's so good, so above everyone else. I heard her bragging one day how she was stoned the day she tried out for cheer. And she *still* made it. That's how superior she thinks she is. And she believes it so much, everyone else started believing it, too! Even you. But I know what she did. I know who she *really* is. She let someone *die*, Jeff!" Kimberlee laughed, a short, scoffing breath. "And she can blame it on drugs all she wants, but it's an act. Everything, everyone in this town is acting. And you're fooled by all of them. You think everyone's so genuine. But it's all just *fake*. Everyone is cold and bitter and *fake*! Just like me," she finished in a whisper.

But I was already shaking my head. "No, that's why you hate *yourself*. Maybe she was like that once, but she's changed. She learned how to be better and you can't accept that. You *want* her to be like you."

"She *is* like me," Kimberlee shouted. "You just can't see it. Nobody just changes like that. Not really. She's still a messed-up druggie on the inside. I hate her, she's a bitch, end of story."

"So what's the beginning of the story?"

"What the *hell* are you talking about?"

"Why *her*? Of all the cheerful little freshmen you could decide to warp—why her?"

Her eyes darted away and I knew I'd hit it. "She bugged me—do I need a reason?"

"Why!"

"Shut up!"

"Why!" I yelled so loudly, I was sure our neighbors were going to call the cops soon.

"He adored her the way he would never adore me, okay?" Kimberlee shouted. She sat back on the bed. "After Preston left, what did Khail do? Started hanging out with his *sister* twenty-four seven," she said, scoffing. "And I saw how nice he could be—how careful he was with her. Defended her, protected her, and I hated that I would never have that."

"She's his sister, Kimberlee. It's what brothers do."

"Not all brothers. *Her* brother. She gets everything she wants in life. Waltzed right onto the cheer squad, got off easy when her friend died—rehab? Please. On top of that, after years of stealing, she's still the only person who ever caught me. What is she, Superwoman? It's not fair. She needed to be dropped down a few notches and I took care of it."

"Took care of it? You beat her up. You made her life hell. You chopped off her hair—*after* Khail asked you to leave her alone. Put his secret on the line to get you to stop. That's not bringing her down—that's stomping her into the ground for your own amusement. What is wrong with you?"

"What is wrong with *you*? What, did she finally let you screw her? That's the only thing that makes guys act like this."

I looked straight into her eyes, refusing to yield. "No, Kimberlee, it's not. I don't need that from her to see who she is. A girl who's decent and kind and works hard for what she wants in life. Who doesn't manipulate anyone she thinks can help her, or sabotage whoever gets in her way. A girl I may have lost because I fell for your act."

"Oh, come on. You think she didn't sleep around? Let's just put it this way; I would need to take my shoes off to count how many guys she slept with her freshman year. That's what really gets you. You've made Sera out to be this paradigm of perfection, but in the end, she's *just like me*."

"She's nothing like you," I said through gritted teeth as the twisted truth of her words rocked through me. "Not anymore. She let that life go. She *moved on*, Kimberlee. Something you obviously can't do. Not alive or dead. And maybe, even if you can't see it, *that's* why you hate her." I turned away before I could start yelling again, and headed toward the door. My hand was on the knob when I realized something and looked over my shoulder at Kimberlee. "You're not stuck here because of the stuff you stole. You're here because nothing and no one in the universe wants you."

Thirty

I GAVE THE WOODEN STAKE one more good pound and stood to survey my work. My arms and back hurt from swinging the hammer, but I'd finished early enough to beat the sun going down. I looked up at the dark gray clouds and hoped they would wait just a few more minutes before dumping on me. After two deep, calming breaths I grabbed the last poster, holding it against my chest as I dialed Sera's number on my cell phone.

"I don't want to talk to you, Jeff." *Beep.*

Yeah, I was afraid of that.

I texted her instead, hoping she'd be curious enough to read it. *Please, just come look out your window.*

Two minutes passed, then three. After five minutes I was sure this wasn't going to work. Then I saw her face peek over the windowsill. She stared down at the signs I'd pounded into the lawn; her eyes took in each one slowly. *I'm sorry. I'm an idiot. I shouldn't have yelled. I take it all back. I'm a total jerk. I'm not worthy.* (I swear I saw a tiny smile when her eyes focused on that one.) *Please forgive me. I feel terrible.* Finally her eyes reached me. My heart was pounding as I turned the last poster board around and held it up to her.

I Love You.

She stared at it for a long time.

Then the window opened. "I'm sorry," I yelled before she could speak. "I didn't know, but it shouldn't have mattered. I should have supported you, no matter what. You always trusted me, and I didn't trust you enough." I held my sign up higher. "I mean it," I yelled. "I won't let you down again. I promise."

Sera didn't say anything for a long time, but finally her eyes lifted to meet mine. The gray sky chose that moment to start raining. Great. But I didn't move as small splatters began to pepper my face. Then, without a word, she backed away and closed the window. I let the sign fall and watched as the rain made the colorfully markered words run in small trickles down the poster board. I looked around at my other signs. They looked equally pathetic.

It was a dumb idea anyway.

I had just started pulling up the soggy signs when I heard the door open. Sera stood in the doorway in a light green tank top. As long as I live I don't think I'll ever forget that sight. She'd obviously done some crying after I left and her face had been washed of all traces of makeup. Her hair was down and curled around her almost-bare shoulders.

She walked across the lawn in her bare feet and came to stand in front of me. "I'm so sorry," I whispered. "I—"

"Shhh." She touched a soft finger to my lips. "I love you, too," she said, standing on her toes to press her lips to mine.

I dropped the signs and held her to me. In that moment, nothing else mattered: not the rain, my wet clothes, and especially not Kimberlee. I didn't care what had happened in Sera's past; I loved her for who she was *now*. The person she'd chosen to be. I sighed as her body melded to mine, her curves soft against my chest.

"Come inside," she whispered.

Somehow we managed to get up the stairs without breaking contact. We were both breathing hard when I shut her bedroom door. "You're wet," she said. Her eyes held mine, and she lifted the bottom of my T-shirt and pulled it upward. I raised my arms and let her peel the wet fabric from my skin. She ran her hands over my bare chest and down my arms. Then she took my hands and placed them at the base of her own shirt and raised her arms over her head.

My fingers gripped the soft cotton and hesitated for a moment. "Are you sure?" I whispered. She nodded, and there was no hesitation in her eyes. I slid the tank top over her head and pulled her to me, enjoying the warmth she radiated. She led me to her bed and kissed me as I kicked out of my shoes and heavy, wet jeans. My mind was aware only of the tangle of sheets around us and the feel of her in my arms, against my chest, her hands running through my hair and down my face.

I wanted this more than I could remember ever wanting anything in my life. But although I'd come prepared for everything a good apology could possibly need—I even had chocolates in my car as backup—I hadn't come prepared for it to work quite this well. I looked down at Sera, her eyes wide, a smile crossing her face.

In that moment I think I understood my father more than I ever had before. I wanted to do what he'd done with my mom; throw caution to the wind for the girl I loved. I leaned down to kiss Sera again, clinging desperately to that momentary disregard for any and all consequences.

And for half a minute it almost worked. But I wouldn't make her go through what my mother had. I couldn't even chance it. "Sera?"

"Mmmm?" Her hands drifted lower and for a second I forgot what I'd been about to say.

"I can't," I gasped, and it felt like I was tearing my own arm off. "I didn't bring . . . I don't have—"

"Shhh." Again those soft fingers touched my lips. "It's okay."

She turned from me to dig behind her bed and brought out a small wooden box. She opened it to reveal a colorful display of tiny packages that meant only one thing to me—permission. I understood at that moment that Kimberlee was right; Sera wasn't the innocent I had imagined her to be.

And I realized I didn't care.

I let everything else in the world float away.

I had to work at driving home within the speed limit. For some reason my mind kept wandering and every time it did, my foot sank to the floor. The third time I looked down to find myself twenty over the limit, I slammed on the brakes and pulled over. I had to calm down a little.

I looked up into the rearview mirror and was surprised by how flushed my face still was. And the more I studied it, the redder it got.

It was more than sex. I hadn't lost Sera; I'd found a way to get her back. I was through letting this misguided fate idea run my life. Today I chose Sera, not Kimberlee. It didn't matter that I was the only one who could see her; you can't help someone who doesn't want to change. What I could do was give Sera and me a decent chance at something we both wanted. Isn't that what life is about?

When I hit the garage-door opener I discovered that sometime in the last few hours, my parents had come home. Great. All the calming I'd done on the side of the road immediately went away.

I tried to sneak through the kitchen and up to my room,

but my mom and dad were both still sitting having after-dinner coffee. "Jeff, you missed dinner," my mom said. "I texted you."

Damn.

"Where've you been?"

"Just out," I said, turning from them to hang up my keys.

"You're wet," Mom pressed.

"Yeah, I, uh, got caught in the rain."

They both looked at me for a long time. "It stopped raining two hours ago, Jeff."

"Yeah, well . . ."

"You've been driving around wearing wet clothes for two hours?"

Well, Dad, I wouldn't exactly say I've been wearing *them.* I said nothing.

He looked at me a second longer. "Your hair's dry."

Oh crap. "I gotta go change," I muttered, and turned toward the stairs.

"Well, it's your choice," my mom said cheerfully. "We can have this conversation in wet clothes or in dry. I guess I'd rather be comfortable if I were you, too." She smiled at me, but she was wearing her Mom face. I looked down, uncertain for just a moment that there weren't big letters across my chest that said *I had sex.* But it was just my faded blue T-shirt. "Come back down when you've changed," she said. "I saved some dinner for you."

Now that I thought about it, I was starving.

I took the stairs two at a time, then hesitated outside my door, wondering if *she* was in there. I hadn't actually asked her to leave, but I'd made myself pretty damn clear, hadn't I? I turned the knob very quietly and poked my head in.

No Kimberlee on my bed. No Kimberlee on the beanbags. I closed the door and searched my room. No Kimberlee in my closet. No Kimberlee in my bathroom.

No Kimberlee.

I went straight for my food as soon as I got back downstairs and tried not to look at anyone as I shoved big bites into my mouth.

They waited a few minutes while I cleared most of my plate.

"So," my dad started. "Where've you been?"

I gulped. "At Sera's."

"All afternoon?"

"No, we got into a fight and I left for a little while. But other than that, yeah."

"So you got wet when you left?"

"Pretty much."

"And then you sat around Sera's house in wet clothes for two hours?"

I squirmed. "Kind of."

My parents shared a long look.

"Or maybe you spent two hours sitting around Sera's

house without your wet clothes on?" Mom said.

"It could have happened that way, too." I think my voice cracked.

"Jeff, be serious. Are you and Sera having sex?" That question sounded so dire coming from my dad.

"*Having* might be a bit of an overstatement," I said to my plate.

"Just today?"

This was *so* bad. "Um, yeah."

"Jeff." Disappointment dripped from my mom's voice.

That was too much. "What? You say that like *you* waited."

"Jeff." A clear warning from Dad.

"Well, it's true." I worked hard to keep my voice sincere, not sarcastic. "I'm not trying to be a smart-ass. You guys did it, too; does it really surprise you?"

"I had hoped you would learn from our mistakes," my dad said.

"I did. We . . . we were careful."

"Define *careful*."

"We used protection, Dad. Okay?"

"At least that's something."

I took a few breaths to calm down. I didn't want this to be a fight; I wanted them to understand. And if anyone could understand, it would be my parents. "I love her, Dad. I do." My dad started to speak, but I cut him off. "Maybe I don't love her the way you loved Mom; maybe it's just, uh, a crush or whatever you're going to say. But I love her and you can't tell me I don't."

My dad's mouth closed.

"I thought about you. I did. Just before . . . well, just before. I didn't have anything with me, and I was ready to stop. I told her we had to stop, and I *would have*," I said, looking up and meeting his eyes again.

"Why didn't you?"

"She . . . was prepared."

"Ah, a good Girl Scout." Mom hid her smile behind her coffee cup and coughed when Dad glared at her.

"That's not the point, son—"

"It *is* the point, Dad. You taught me to wait for the right time and the right person, and then to use protection and not leave my life up to chance. That's what I did. I'm still kind of young, I know. But I'm six months older than you were when you met Mom. And you married her! You've been married for over fifteen years. Were *you* wrong?" I asked.

My dad stared at me for a long time before sliding his gaze over to Mom. "No, Jeff, I wasn't wrong." He turned back to me with his mouth set in a hard line. "But condoms are not a hundred percent. If you're not ready to stand by her and do what it takes, don't do it again. Promise?"

I worked to suppress a grin. "I promise."

Thirty-One

I DIDN'T SEE KIMBERLEE AT all the next day. I saw a lot of Sera, but not Kimberlee. Sera still seemed stressed and wouldn't say why, but after yesterday, I stopped worrying. Whatever was going on, she would make the *right choice*. I'd learned that trust isn't always something someone earns; it's a choice you make. Kimberlee taught me that in her caustic, demented way.

It was weird. This whole time I had been assuming that Kimberlee was supposed to learn something from me, but maybe I was supposed to learn something from her.

But where did that leave Kimberlee?

On Thursday morning I walked into school and Kimberlee was lying on the floor in the middle of the hallway again. I was gripped by a twisting sense of déjà vu and had to stop myself from yelling out when a girl in platform heels walked straight toward her. Kimberlee didn't move an inch, but I cringed as that black shoe sank through her face.

"Bitch," Kimberlee said quietly.

The girl looked quizzically down at her foot for a moment, then tossed her hair over her shoulder and kept walking.

I was trying to decide if I should go say something when I felt Sera's warm hand slip into mine.

"Hey." She smiled at me with those green eyes that made me want to find an empty classroom . . . now.

Decision made—I walked past Kimberlee without even looking down. I didn't feel eyes on my back; apparently she was ignoring me, too. Waiting for a new destiny, maybe— though who knows what someone else would help her with. There was nothing left in the cave; no unfinished business left to get her out of limbo.

Still, it was weird not to talk to her, or even acknowledge her. We were two people whose lives had revolved around each other, now drifting apart. I think maybe I even missed her. When she wasn't being crude, mean, sarcastic, or cruel, she was kind of fun to have around.

Friday morning I made up my mind to talk to her. I had everything—I had Sera, my parents, even some friends back home that I still texted sometimes. Kimberlee had no one but me. And like it or not, I still felt obliged to try to help her. If nothing else, to get her finally and completely out of my life.

I parked Halle in her usual spot and tried not to drag my feet as I approached the school. I'd made the decision; I couldn't wimp out now. I even called Sera the night before and told her I'd probably be late and to just meet me at lunch. No turning back now.

I walked into the main foyer and my eyes immediately went to Kimberlee's portrait on the wall. She looked innocent in that picture—happy. I knew better. I wondered if Kimberlee had ever been innocent, and I knew it had been years since she'd been happy.

I steeled myself and walked past the portrait and into the south hall.

But she wasn't there.

I stared at the space on the floor she had occupied yesterday—the place she'd lain when I first saw her. I blinked a few times and wondered if fate had changed its mind. Had I screwed up so badly I wasn't allowed to help anymore? Maybe it was Kimberlee who had screwed up. Okay, fine. *Probably* it was Kimberlee who screwed up.

For a moment I dared to hope she'd been allowed to move on after all, but the idea fled almost as soon as I thought of it. If anything, Kimberlee was *more* conflicted than when we'd first met.

Maybe I just couldn't *see* her anymore. I walked over to her spot and tried to stand there casually. "Kimberlee," I whispered. "Are you there?"

A backpack bumped my shoulder. "Sorry, man," a sopho-more said. "My fault." He hurried on when he saw the look on my face. But my eyes weren't on him; they were fixed on the line his feet had just followed. Straight across where Kimberlee should have been lying. He didn't stop and look down the way everyone did when they made contact with Kimberlee—staring around as the chills went through them. He didn't look at his feet at all.

She wasn't there.

Where was she? She had nowhere else to go.

Did she?

Maybe she'd found someone else who could see her. Maybe there *was* another new kid. The thought made me strangely, irrationally jealous.

I went home alone after school. Sera's parents were having company for afternoon tea—whatever the hell that was— and dinner that night, and Sera's parents had decided that *her presence was required*. So I was left out in the cold. I came home to an empty garage, and a note on the kitchen door told me Mom and Dad had taken off for one of their spontaneous romantic weekends.

They think it improves their marriage—I try to think about it as little as possible.

I was vaguely hungry, but I didn't even stop for a Coke as I headed up to my room. Everything seemed wrong. I should be happy Kimberlee was gone—whether by choice or not. But even though I'd all but given up on her, I hated that she'd given up on me.

I reached for the TV, intending to play something mindless, but after looking through my games for a full five minutes and finding nothing that appealed to me, I turned to my bookshelf instead. When I was little and we lived in Phoenix we didn't have cable or video games or anything like that. Hell, we were so poor we rarely had anything beyond necessities. So I got into comics. I could go to the comic-book store and, as long as I bought one comic when I left, the owner would let me read the rest of them for hours. Spider-Man, Superman, Sandman—guess I was all about the S-Men—and then when I was done, I would choose my favorite and take it home. I didn't have any complete series, just random issues. But it made for good comfort reading.

I pulled out one of my favorite issues of *Spider-Man* and had gotten about ten pages in when my cell phone rang. I pulled it out of my pocket, and was about to hit *Talk* before I realized I was answering the wrong phone.

The ringing was coming from my bedside table drawer. The phone Khail had given me. The one that had only rung maybe three times in the whole time I'd owned it. It rang twice more while I tried to figure out what to do.

I should probably answer it.

Shouldn't I?

Finally, after about eight rings, I brought the phone to my ear. "Yeah," I said in a voice a few tones lower than normal.

A couple of seconds passed in silence. "Is this the guy who's been returning all the stolen stuff?"

I'd have known her voice anywhere. Sera. I didn't say anything. *Couldn't* say anything.

"Don't hang up," she said, and that tiny inflection, the touch of desperation in her voice, made me obey.

"I know this is you and . . . I'm calling to ask for your help on Khail's behalf."

Khail's behalf?

"He got caught."

I felt my throat convulse, making it hard to breathe.

"He doesn't know it, but he did. Hennigan pulled me into his office last Monday and told me that when you guys broke into the school, Khail apparently was trying to turn off the alarm and he lifted his mask and got caught on camera."

"There's not a camera in Hennigan's office," I said, hoping Hennigan had just been bluffing.

"Not an official one. After the theft ring last year Hennigan decided he needed his own security and put in his own camera. Trust me," she said before I could argue, "I've seen the video. It's obviously Khail."

Dammit! "So why didn't he just nab Khail?" I asked, still in the weird, low voice.

"Hennigan knew it wasn't just one person. He wanted to catch the whole ring. Thought he'd put pressure on him later.

But then he figured out Khail couldn't be the ringleader."

"Why not?"

"He went back and checked the schedule. Khail was gone for a three-day wrestling meet the week stuff first started showing up. So Hennigan knew he couldn't have gotten involved until later."

I tried to play it cool. "So what? Khail's not going to squeal. Why do you need my help?"

"You're right. Khail will take his punishment for you and never say a word. I know it. Hennigan knows it. So he leaned on me instead."

"What's he got on you?" I bluffed.

"It's not about me. Hennigan just . . . knows that I won't let anything happen to my brother. The damage from the chemicals and sprinklers in the lab will cost the school almost ten thousand dollars. Hennigan is talking about pressing criminal charges for breaking and entering."

Ten thousand dollars? Criminal charges? I knew there was some damage but I hadn't imagined it was so substantial.

"At first Hennigan said if I could give him the ringleader he'd just give Khail two days' suspension. But he called me into his office again this week." She paused and I could hear her sniffing in the background. "He's so pissed. He's given up on the idea of catching the whole ring. He just wants *someone*. A scapegoat. And if he doesn't have one by Monday morning—"

Her voice caught and her muffled sobs made my chest ache. "He's going to expel Khail. He won't graduate, he'll lose his scholarships . . . I *can't let that happen.*"

And everything came crashing down around me.

I had failed.

Failed so completely and so miserably that there was no way to pick up the pieces.

For a few weeks there, I really thought I was a hero. I was like Robin Hood, or Edmund Dantès, or Percy Blakeney. A daring vigilante.

And now I was just a punk kid who was about to get his friend expelled.

"What can I do?" I asked, my voice barely a whisper.

"Turn yourself in."

Three simple words that struck a fear into my heart so deep I wasn't sure I trusted myself to speak.

"I know it's not fair. None of it is," Sera continued. "But it's even more unfair to let Khail take the fall for this. I don't know why he's involved at all, but I guarantee he's not doing it for himself. He . . ." She stopped and had to get control of her emotions again. "He's the most unselfish person I know. Whatever the hell he was doing with *you*, I promise it was to help someone else. Do *not* let him take the fall." A few seconds passed in silence before she added, "Please?" in a voice so fragile and frail I knew there was no way I could refuse. "He's not just my brother; he's my best friend. I would take his expulsion for him, but I can't. I tried."

"You tried?" In my surprise I almost spoke in my regular voice.

"I owe my brother everything. Of course I tried. But Hennigan knew I was lying. I had no proof, no nothing, and it was a crap story. I'm a terrible liar. You're the only one who can help him now."

It took two tries to get the words to come out of my mouth, but finally I managed to say, "Okay."

"Thank you," she said in that same vulnerable voice. It was almost a question, as if she wasn't completely sure I'd actually said it—or, more likely, that I'd actually meant it.

"But I want you to turn me in," I blurted, before thinking through the consequences of that statement. "I want to make sure you're off the hook."

She sniffled again. "Please don't make me do that," she said.

I almost couldn't believe my ears. "I thought you wanted the Red Rose Returner to get caught."

"I just wanted you to *go away*. You reminded me of a horrible time in my life, and I hated being slapped with it day after day."

Guilt welled up in my chest. I knew now what she was talking about, and honestly, if it had been me, I wouldn't have wanted reminders, either. "I'm sorry," I said.

"Don't be. You made a lot of people happy. Khail included. You . . . you have no idea what the stuff you gave back meant to him."

Actually, I kind of did.

"Still, *you* have to turn me in. That way Hennigan can never hold this against you." She didn't say anything for a few seconds, so I continued. "I'm going in either way. It may as well do someone some good."

More silence. "Okay," she finally said. "What do I do?"

I hadn't really thought that part out. Probably best to just keep it simple. "I'll be at the school at six tonight. I'll meet them in the parking lot and I'll bring stickers if they want proof. You call Hennigan and tell him that."

"And you'll be there?"

The words caught in my throat, but I choked them out, sealing my fate. "I promise."

I stared at the phone for a long time after I hung up. Part of me wished I had thrown the phone away as soon as we'd finished our big return on Monday. Wished that by the time I figured out it was my lying about Kimberlee being on watch that got Khail caught, it was too late to help.

But then I would have to live with the guilt.

I'd told my mom to trust me. Assured her I was a good kid, just trying to do the right thing. And she *had* trusted me. How was I going to tell her I'd repaid that trust by getting myself expelled? And criminal charges—was Hennigan bluffing about that? I flopped back onto my bed and tried to think of a way to get out of this, even though I knew there wasn't one. It was time to pay my dues. No good deed goes unpunished, and all that.

And the biggest irony of all? Kimberlee—the catalyst of everything that had gone wrong—was nowhere to be found.

The worst part was that Sera was going to be devastated when she found out it was me. I wasn't sure which emotion would win out—anger or guilt—but either way, I'd screwed everything up for her, too.

For the first time since I was, like, ten years old, I had the urge to curl up on my bed and cry. Right then, I just wanted to get in Halle and drive back to Phoenix, where stuff like this didn't happen.

But I couldn't.

I looked over at my alarm clock to see how many minutes of my so-called life I had left when my eyes fell on something on my bedside table that I had forgotten about. A tiny flicker of hope sparked inside me as I reached over and picked it up.

It was my only chance.

I picked up my cell phone and made the call.

I was lying on the bed with an arm slung across my eyes when Kimberlee came bursting through my wall.

"You can't do it!"

I just stared at her with my mouth agape.

"I know you have all these ideas about being noble and everything, but this is stupid and I won't let you do it!"

"Hello to you, too," I muttered sullenly.

She rushed over and sat beside me on the bed. "I'm serious," she said—and she looked it. "You can't turn yourself in. You don't *deserve* this."

"How did you know about that?"

She looked a little abashed. "I heard the other end of the conversation," she admitted.

"You've been spying on Sera?"

"Well, *you* wouldn't do it. And I *knew* there was something going on!"

I sighed.

"Won't you at least admit I was right?"

"I knew you were right!" I said. "I *knew* something was going on; it was obvious. The point isn't that there was or wasn't anything going on, but that I *trusted* Sera had a good reason, and I was right."

"She was spying for Hennigan! There's no good reason for that!"

I rose to my feet. "Yes, there is! You heard what Sera said, but were you *listening*? She did this to protect Khail. She loves Khail more than anyone else in the world and was willing

313

to do whatever it took to save him. That's not something to scorn; it's something to admire."

"Admire? She's siding with him instead of you!"

"He's her *brother*."

"And you're her boyfriend!"

"Until she finds out," I groaned, flopping back onto my bed.

She was quiet for a long time. "Why are you doing this? No one could blame you if you didn't."

I sat up and looked her in the eye. "Because it's the right thing to do, Kimberlee."

"Right according to who?" she asked, her tone plaintive rather than argumentative. "God? Fate? It's not fair. Khail got caught; let him take the fall. He won't tell anyone—I know he won't—so Sera will never know it was you. You *don't have to do this.*"

"Yes, I do!" I shouted, surprised at my own fervor. "Getting caught isn't what makes something wrong. Even if Sera never found out, *I* would know."

Kimberlee glared at me, almost as if she could use some new ghostly power to change my mind. Then her eyes widened. "But you have a plan, don't you?" she said quietly. "I mean, in the end this is all a setup. It's all just part of the plan, right?"

It was hard to look at her. She believed I really was some kind of master planner. I'd gotten lucky before, but really, that was all it was. Luck. And my luck had run out.

"No," I said. "I don't have a plan. I . . . I thought I did for a minute, but…" I shrugged and then my hands flopped helplessly at my sides. "It's not going to work."

"So you're seriously going to go over to that school tonight and turn yourself in because it's 'the right thing to do'?"

It did sound irrational the way she said it, but I knew I wouldn't be able to live with myself if I did anything else. I nodded.

Kimberlee looked at me with a mixture of sadness and pity on her face. Then she straightened up and her mask came back. "You're crazy," she said bitterly. "And stupid. I've never met anyone as stupid as you."

Then she turned and left, sliding through the wall and out of sight.

Thirty-Two

TERRIFIED IS THE LEAST OF what I was when I turned into the parking lot at six that night. I could see three cars against the curb near the front entrance and wondered who Hennigan had called for backup.

I pulled right up close and stalled for a few seconds, taking in the scene. Hennigan stood stiffly in front of the main entrance, eyeing my car, but I knew he couldn't see me through the tinted windows. He started to take a step forward, then stopped, pressed his lips together, and apparently decided to wait for me to make the first move.

Coward.

Beside him, looking a little embarrassed, was our assistant principal, Mrs. Bailey. I knew what she'd gotten back: a homemade frame made by her young son with a family picture inside. I'd be embarrassed to be there if I were her, too.

I did, however, almost laugh at the irony when I saw that the third member of the party—almost certainly summoned against his will—was Coach Creed. I knew from a brief discussion with Khail yesterday that the whole team would be leaving very early the next morning for State. I had no doubt Mr. Hennigan had blackmailed their coach into being here as "the muscle" by threatening his two-time state champion with expulsion if I got away, the same way he'd put pressure on Sera. Coach Creed's arms were flexed across his chest and, despite the fact that Kimberlee had never stolen anything from Creed, I would bet that given the choice he'd rather strangle Hennigan than me.

I shifted into park and Mr. Hennigan got a very strange mixture of excitement and fear on his face as the engine died. I had just unlatched my seat belt and reached for the door handle when light flashed across my eyes. Another car was pulling into the parking lot.

I couldn't help but feel nauseous when I saw the row of lights across the top of the black-and-white cruiser as the cop parked just behind Hennigan's car and stepped out.

I hoped I was doing the right thing.

There was nothing more I could do now. I slid out of my seat, stood, and swung my car door shut.

Hennigan blinked several times. "Mr. Clayson, what are you doing here?"

I reached into the pocket of my hoodie and grabbed what was left of the stickers. I tossed them down in front of me and then added the master key, which tinkled almost melodically. "I said I'd be here, and here I am."

For a long, tense moment, nobody moved or spoke.

"But . . . but . . ." Hennigan sputtered, "you just moved here." I could almost see him reviewing our interaction from Monday morning in his head—knowing he'd had the culprit in his grasp. "How could *you* have stolen everything?"

"I didn't," I said, my voice much steadier than my legs. But this would be my only chance to have my say and I was going to. "It was never about stealing. It was about giving things back. You were so focused on what you were sure I'd done wrong you didn't stop to see what I was trying to do right."

I knew my words wouldn't convince Hennigan, but I saw Mrs. Bailey and Coach Creed nodding. The cop didn't move from his spot beside his cruiser. He was so still I wondered if he was even breathing.

Hennigan's face was turning red as he realized his plan to catch a notorious thief was crumbling to dust in front of the cop, in front of his employees. But I knew he wouldn't give up so easily. He wiped the shock off his face and pointed a finger at me. "It doesn't matter. Your list of infractions is still plenty long. Destruction of school property, breaking into lockers, trespassing at *my home!*" he said, as if the personal offense was the greatest one of all. "If you really are this Red Rose Returner person"—he said the name like it was a bad word—"then you're guilty of all those."

I nodded. "And I take full responsibility."

Hennigan smiled as if he had caught me in some elaborate trap instead of asking a very straightforward question. "There!" he said, calling out to the police officer now. "He admitted it. Arrest him!"

The cop began to walk toward me. His eyes met mine for a second and then I turned, giving him my hands before he could ask. My breath was short as the cuffs clicked shut. In a matter of moments I'd been read my rights and the cop had set me in the back of his car and slammed the door.

It was over.

What the hell had I just done?

The cop went and talked with the adults for a few minutes, then got into the cruiser and closed his door.

"Officer—"

"Not here for small talk," he said, cutting off my words and flipping on the radio.

It was a surprisingly short drive to the police station. The cop pulled up to a well-lit side door and I got my first good look at him. He was tall and blond, and even though most of his bulk was the kind you get from cheeseburgers, I suspected he could rough me up without any trouble. Pleasant thoughts. His badge said BURKE. Jerk was more like it.

He grabbed the back of my hoodie and pushed me toward the side door, which opened automatically. I didn't know what to expect—I'd never been in a police station before—but I didn't actually expect bars. But that's where I ended up. Me and one guy who looked homeless and another who was totally drunk off his ass. The cop removed my cuffs and I was about to sigh in relief when he simply relocked them in front of me.

"Sit," Officer Burke said, pointing a meaty finger. What choice did I have? I sat and laid my head down on my fists, my elbows balanced on my knees. The longer I squeezed my eyes shut and drew my face back into my hood, the more I managed to convince myself I wasn't there at all. I imagined anywhere else in the world I'd rather be.

Sera's room, for one.

But mostly I imagined Phoenix. Everything in my life had blown to bits since I moved to Santa Monica. I'd avoided too much homesickness the last few months, but sitting in that holding cell, I let it wash over me.

Just as I started to feel tears burn behind my eyelids—for the first time in years—the jail phone rang. My head jerked up, and some irrational part of me hoped I would find myself in my own bedroom with my cordless ringing on my bedside table. But I was still in the drab cell with my reeking cellmates. Officer Burke answered the phone. I tucked my head back into my hood and squeezed my eyes shut again.

"Clayson!"

I straightened so fast I knocked my head against the bars

of the cell. *Ow.* "Yessir," I answered reflexively.

He glared at me. "Come on."

Hope leaped inside me. "Are my parents here?"

The cop snorted. "Hardly." Nothing else.

I clenched my jaw and the cop unlocked the door and held it open just enough to let me slip by. Then the firm hand returned to the back of my sweatshirt. We went through another door and it was like a different world. Desks, cubicles, offices.

My handcuffs felt heavy—like iron chains. We walked into a small room, empty except for a table and a couple of chairs. And one big mirror that was no doubt one of those two-ways you see on TV. Pointing to a metal folding chair, Burke said, "Someone'll be here soon."

And before I could actually get to the chair to sit down, he left and closed the door behind me.

Reflexively, I turned toward the sound. As I did, I caught my reflection in the mirror. I couldn't help but stare. A black hoodie pulled forward to shadow my face, baggy jeans and old Converse, cuffs binding my skinny wrists in front of me. My eyes were wide and scared, my expression tight; I looked more like a terrified twelve-year-old than the famed Red Rose Returner of Whitestone.

I turned away; I couldn't look at myself. It made me doubt that I was doing the right thing. And that was the one hope I couldn't let go of.

I sat in the chair and pulled my knees up to my chest, not caring who might be looking. I laid my head down and started counting slowly—a trick I'd learned when I was a kid and something scared me. Most things would be gone by the time I reached one hundred.

I doubted I'd be that lucky this time.

I was up to five hundred fifty-seven when the door handle clicked and a cop walked in.

"Hey, Jeff," Officer Herrera said.

"Officer Herrera," I said breathlessly. I don't know how you can feel like someone punched you in the stomach in a *good* way, but that's how I felt.

"Sorry I missed your call," he said.

I rubbed at my eyes. "When you didn't answer, I thought it was the end of the world; I almost didn't bother to leave a voice mail."

Officer Herrera chuckled. "Sorry for not calling back. I didn't know just how many strings I could pull for you and I had a lot of research to do before I could tug on *any* of them." He looked up at me. "I've been watching you, Jeff. I heard about the big drop-off at the homeless center. Someone mentioned weird stickers and I knew it had to be you. That was really generous. You could have sold that stuff for thousands of dollars. More, maybe. There was one bag of jewelry that was all genuine article. And when the school break-in was reported it didn't take long to link you to that, too." He shuffled through the files on the table and put the largest one on top. He looked up at me, his eyes suddenly serious. "Does the name Kimberlee Schaffer mean anything to you?"

I sputtered and choked.

"I'll take that as a yes." He flipped open the file, seemingly oblivious as I coughed up a lung. "There's not an officer in the place, except maybe a rookie or two, who doesn't know her name. We tried to make something stick to her for years."

I was so shocked I almost couldn't speak. "You—you caught her?"

"Not red-handed. But we had enough to prosecute. The problem was finding a willing prosecutor."

"Why?"

"Well, technically, everything we had on her was petty. I wish we'd caught her stealing some of that jewelry you left at the homeless shelter. That would have been something we could *work* with."

"I don't get it."

Officer Herrera let out a long breath. "For one thing, her father is about the most influential judge in Los Angeles County. For another, his family's got more money than God and he's not afraid to throw it around. We couldn't pick her up for stealing earrings or stuffed animals. Some fancy-pants lawyer would get her off with a judge who was in the Schaffers' pocket to begin with, and there'd be a big black mark on our station. Build up too many black marks and we'd see our funding get smaller and smaller. Not a nice guy, Judge Schaffer."

Kimberlee instantly made more sense to me.

"But we kept records and they match up with a lot of the stuff you've been returning. It wasn't too hard to put two and two together. And that's what gets you off on the theft charges."

Hope flooded through me. "Really?"

"And the codes get you off on B and E." He shook his head. "I tell you, I don't know how you got that key and those codes, but since you had Hennigan's personal code, he can't prove he didn't give them to you, and that implies permission to enter. It's a technicality, but I'll make it work."

I wanted to hug him. Really.

"The damage to the chem lab, however," Officer Herrera said soberly, "is a different story. There's a dollar amount associated with it, and unless you or your parents cough up the money, the school can sue you for it."

My stomach sank. Hadn't Hennigan said ten thousand dollars? Good kid or not, my parents believed in natural consequences; they'd expect me to pay the bill.

And there was only one thing I owned that would cover it.

"But none of our prosecutors are going to try their luck arguing criminal vandalism or malicious mischief to a sympathetic jury," Officer Herrera said, interrupting my dismal thoughts. "Which, under the circumstances, I have no doubt you'd get. I've spoken to some of my friends downtown and criminal charges are off the table. So it's just the restoration expenses and those are between you and the school."

I felt myself grow a little weak with relief and I sank down in my chair a little. "Really?"

"Yep."

It was all I could do to keep myself from bursting into hysterical laughter. I had to take several deep breaths to push it back. "So I'm fine? Everything's okay?"

"Well, almost. I can't fix much with your school. And Mr. Hennigan's not really the forgiving type."

I hate Mr. Hennigan. "What do you mean?"

"I've spent the better part of the last hour on the phone with him and, since it's a private school, the only people he really has to answer to are the board of directors. For starters, you're suspended all next week."

My heart sank at that, but it was a hell of a lot better than expulsion.

"I can't convince him you're anything but a hardened criminal, but I told him that keeping you in school is a vital part of rehabilitating you. That's when he went ahead and decided against expulsion. You can remain at Whitestone."

Lucky me.

"But he's going to watch you like a hawk for the rest of high school; there's just nothing I can do about that. This is the best I can do."

"Oh no, it's great," I said. "It's so much more than I expected. Thank you."

"You're welcome." He paused. "You're a good kid, Jeff. I mean it."

I didn't feel like a good kid at the moment, but I hoped he was right.

"Now, standard protocol at this point—even though you're being released without being charged—is to contact your parents and have them come pick you up. But we haven't been able to get a hold of them."

"They're on a weekend getaway thing. They won't be back till tomorrow." *Or so.*

"Okay. I'll vouch for you this time. And there better not be a next time." His face got as hard as stone. "Are you done, Jeff? Because if you're not, it's time to *give up* this project. I'm serious."

"I'm done," I said honestly. "As of last week everything was returned and . . . Kimberlee can rest in peace." Whatever that meant.

"Good. Because if I see you in here again, you're on your own, good motivation or not."

I nodded.

"Okay. Come on."

"Where are we going?"

"My shift's over. I'll drive you back to your car."

He stood and opened the door for me. As I got to my feet my handcuffs jingled.

Officer Herrera rolled his eyes. "Oh, for the love—" he muttered, digging into his pocket.

There has never been a sweeter moment in my life than the second when those cuffs clicked open and released my wrists. "Thanks," I said for what felt like the fiftieth time.

"Let's go," Officer Herrera said, pointing down the hallway.

Thirty-Three

FOR THE SECOND TIME IN as many weeks I slid into the passenger seat of Officer Hererra's cruiser. The sky was dark now and for the first few minutes we rode in silence. Then I cleared my throat. "Officer Herrera?"

"Yeah?"

"Thank you," I said. "Thank you so much." I ran my hands through my hair, the realization that everything had actually worked only beginning to sink in. My hands shook as the adrenaline of pure relief flowed through me.

"I wouldn't have done it if I didn't believe you were doing the right thing, Jeff. You earned this." Officer Herrera turned into the school parking lot—empty now except for Halle.

"I just wanted to make things right," I said.

He pulled his car beside mine and shifted into park. "And that's something I support. It's why I came to your rescue."

"Well, I'm glad," I said, cracking a grin. "Because I would have been so screwed if you hadn't shown up."

He hesitated for a few seconds before adding, "I have to call on Monday and tell your parents what happened. But I think *you* need to tell them first."

"I will," I said, although the thought made my stomach feel like I'd just swallowed a chunk of ice.

"I also feel you should know that the two other teachers who were at the school with Hennigan told Officer Burke that you're a good kid and that he should go easy on you. He thought it was a joke, but I'm telling you so you know that you'll have support at school." He laughed. "Hell, the kids'll probably all love you."

I hadn't thought that far ahead. He was right—by Monday, everyone would know that Jeff Clayson was the Red Rose Returner.

Sera would know.

I had to tell her before she heard it from someone else.

I didn't even know where to start.

As if he could read my thoughts, Officer Herrera patted my shoulder. "Get on home," he said gently. "You'll have your work cut out for you soon enough."

I nodded and got out of the car. Then I stood in the parking lot and waved as I watched Officer Herrera drive away. I unlocked my car and was about to get in when I looked over and saw the last of the stickers still sitting on the pavement, though Bailey's key was gone. I picked them up and put them in my pocket. Something to remember this by.

My house was dark except for a couple of security lights. I opened the fridge, but I didn't feel hungry; I felt *empty*. For weeks I'd wanted nothing more than to get Kimberlee out of my life. And now, it looked like maybe I had.

But not by helping her move on. I'd chased her away, and even when she came back to stop me from turning myself in, we'd just argued more. I felt like I'd failed her. And she didn't have a backup plan.

I hesitated as I pulled a quart of milk out of the fridge. Maybe she did. Maybe there *were* other people who could see her. She'd lied about everything else at least once; why not this? Maybe I was just the only one gullible enough to try and help her.

But a painful thudding in my chest told me it wasn't true. It was the same ache I'd felt when she'd cried on my bed—a smoldering, hollow sense of helplessness. I spit my mouthful of milk into the sink and turned off the kitchen light, my appetite completely gone.

I dragged my backpack up the stairs, enjoying the thud of my books on the steps. It made me feel better, though I couldn't say why. I walked through my open door and, just because no one was home, slammed it.

Damn, that feels good.

I opened it and slammed it again, harder. I started to

smile as I opened the door again.

"Please don't."

I froze, still holding onto the doorknob, and waited for her to speak again.

When she didn't, I flexed my arm against the door and started to swing.

"Jeff."

I let go of the door and turned to look. "Kimberlee?"

I almost didn't recognize her. Her blond hair was pulled back into a ponytail and there was no makeup on her face— no red lips, or thick black lines around her eyes. She was wearing a plain white T-shirt and jeans. She stood leaning against my headboard with a pair of light blue flip-flops on her feet. "You're back," she said softly. "I was worried."

She sounded serious, but I'd known her too long to believe it. "No thanks to you," I said darkly.

She looked down at her feet. "I should have come with you."

"Little late for that."

"It's a little late for a lot of things," she said, her voice shaky.

I glared at her, trying to figure out what the trick was. Finally my curiosity got the better of me. "You look different."

Kimberlee nodded but said nothing.

"Have you been able to do this the whole time?" I asked bitterly.

She shook her head. "No! I promise." She looked down at herself. "And I can't change back, either. Not that I'd want to," she added quietly.

That made me pause for a minute. I figured for sure she'd be mad about her plain appearance. "What happened?"

"After I left here . . . I was so pissed. I went to the mall and tried to steal things, spied on a bunch of couples making out in the movie theater—all the stuff I used to do. And I couldn't get you out of my head."

Boy, that sounded familiar. A little payback is always satisfying.

"You did something today that didn't benefit you at all. It was just for other people and your screwy sense of *the right thing to do.*"

I didn't bother to argue.

"And I realized that even though I don't feel like you do—I don't care about doing the right thing—I *wanted* to. I wanted to have something, anything, that I believed in that much. So I came back," she added after a long pause.

"You did?"

She nodded. "I was too late, though. I even went to the school, but everyone was gone. What happened?" she asked.

With a sigh I dropped my backpack on the floor and related the story. When I got to the part where Officer Herrera came into the interrogation room, Kimberlee started to smile.

"All that drama and I wasn't even around to see it." She

paused, then said, "You've gone through so much trouble for me."

"What else was I going to do on a girlfriendless Friday night?" I asked, forcing a smile.

We both laughed shakily for a moment before Kimber-lee's eyes filled with tears and she looked down at her feet. "I went to my parents' house. Inside, I mean; not just to the cave. I hadn't done that before."

"Seriously?" Home was the first place I would have gone if I'd woken up and discovered I was a ghost.

She sniffed and wiped a tear from her cheek. She laughed just a little, then sank down on my bed and flopped to her back. "Yeah, you'd think everyone would want to go home when they were dead. But I hated my parents, so I didn't. After a few months I thought maybe *they* would be able to see me. They're my parents, after all. But you know where I went?"

I hazarded a guess. "Their work?"

She sniffled and nodded. "Their work. I went to their jobs. Even as a ghost I wanted things my way and on my terms. I'm such a spoiled brat."

"No, you—"

"Don't lie."

So I didn't.

The room was still dark. I thought about turning on the light, but it seemed too harsh. Instead I flipped on the bathroom light and closed the door halfway so a soft glow illuminated the room. I sat beside her on the bed. After a while that felt funny, so I lay down instead, at an angle so our heads were almost touching.

"One year, four months, and four days. That's how long it took me to go home." She rolled over onto her elbow, our faces only a breath apart. "And you know what? They loved me. They weren't the greatest parents—I know that—but they loved me. Still do. They have my room just the same way it was, but with more pictures and old awards than I ever let them put out before. They have a huge painting of me in the entryway. It's little embarrassing, actually." Her voice was very quiet and serious. "My mom puts fresh roses in my room. Over a year later and she still puts fresh flowers in my room. I stood and stared at those roses for, like, an eternity," she said so quietly I strained to hear her. "They were so beautiful and I could *almost* smell them. I wanted to try to touch them but I couldn't stand to see my fingers pass through one more beautiful thing.

"Then I caught sight of the mirror on the wall and looked at myself . . . and I looked perfect. Just like always. When I was alive, I would have killed for makeup that never came off and hair that always fell just right." The tears shone in her eyes for a few seconds, but she blinked them away. "I lost it, Jeff. I didn't want to look like myself anymore. I wished so desperately that I could see whatever it was my parents saw."

She smiled now, and it was a different smile than I'd ever seen on her. There was no guile or trickery in it—it was the kind of smile I was used to seeing on other people's faces.

It was the way Sera smiled.

"That's when my clothes changed. And my hair and face. And for the first time I can remember, I looked in that mirror and I liked what I saw."

I smiled back. For real. "I'm glad. And for what it's worth, I think you look better now too." I didn't mean the clothes and makeup. The real change in her appearance was something else—something deeper. And I could *see* it.

"Thanks, Jeff. That means a lot to me—really." The tears fell onto her cheeks now, but she didn't really cry. Her shoulders didn't shake and there were no sobs. Just tears.

"Kim—"

"Don't. Don't try to convince me I was just some girl who made a few mistakes. Don't let me keep doing what I've done for the last year—the last five years. Don't let me hang on to the lies."

I couldn't speak as her wet, blue eyes bore into mine.

"I was a bad person, Jeff." The volume of her voice hadn't changed, but she spoke with intensity. "I was a bad person and it's about time I faced up to that. I had everything in the world, and it wasn't good enough. And you know what's worse? You were right; I hated *everyone*. Can you imagine hating everyone you know?"

I shook my head again and she laughed sharply. But when she spoke, her words were soft. "Of course not. You're too good. Too willing to see the best in people. Even me." She stared at the ceiling for a few seconds. "I don't know how to be a good person, Jeff. I don't naturally do the right thing, like you. But . . . I think I *want* to learn. And maybe I'm finally ready."

I nodded slowly. "Maybe you are."

"Could . . . could you teach me?"

I was silent for a long time as I contemplated this. "I don't know," I said honestly.

She looked disappointed, but nodded. "At least you didn't say no. I would have."

"So what now?" I asked.

She sat up and looked down at her hands in her lap. "Would you do me one last favor?" She peered up at me from under her lashes—but it wasn't the flirtatious look she'd often used to convince me to do something she wanted—it was a look that said she wasn't sure I'd say yes.

"I'll try."

"I need to return one more thing."

Thirty-Four

MY STOMACH WAS TWISTING ITSELF in knots as I rang the familiar doorbell. Sera's mother answered, her smile soft, but wary. "Jeff, I'm afraid we have company tonight."

"I know, Mrs. Hewitt, and I'm really sorry, but I just need to talk to Sera for two minutes. It's about school," I lied, holding up a shoe box.

She glanced in toward the dining room. "All right," she said, "I'll get her, but please make it quick."

Sera came around the corner a few seconds later with a big smile on her face. "Jeff, I can't believe Mom let me leave the table to come see you." She stopped long enough to press a kiss to my mouth. "She must be starting to like you."

I grinned. "I don't know if I'd go that far." But I sobered as I lifted the small shoe box I had brought—a box Kimberlee hadn't put in the cave but in its own little private hiding spot in the cove. Because, she had explained, it wasn't something she stole; it was something she *took*. I snuck a glance at Kimberlee, standing close to my shoulder, and she nodded encouragingly. "I brought you something," I said seriously. "And I need you to not ask questions about it. I'll tell you later, but there's just not time tonight." I shoved the box into her hands and she stared at me for several moments before lifting the lid.

Tears filled her eyes as she reached in and touched the long, thick braid of red hair tied with miniature blue-and-green pom-poms.

"Kimberlee's sorry. She wasn't before, but she is now." I glanced back one more time, but Kimberlee's gaze was fixed on Sera's face, her brows knit together in concentration. "She knows she has no right to ask, but she hopes that someday you can forgive her."

Sera tried to speak, but nothing came out. She looked up at me and I tried to show on my face that this wasn't—could never be—a joke.

She closed the lid again and looked at the sticker—one last sticker—that I'd affixed to the top. "It was *you*?"

I nodded.

Her hand came up to cover her mouth and she shook her head. "But . . . you just moved here. How could—?"

"I'll explain everything tomorrow," I said, hoping I'd still have the nerve when tomorrow arrived.

"I didn't know!" she insisted. "I didn't; I promise. I would never . . . I didn't . . ." She couldn't finish as tears filled her eyes.

"It's okay," I said, rubbing my hands up and down her arms. "Everything is *okay*. I'm not getting expelled."

"I'm so sorry."

"No, no," I said, squeezing her hand. "Don't be sorry. This is not your fault; this is Hennigan's fault. Don't blame yourself."

"I didn't want to," she said, clutching the box to her chest.

"I know. And I trusted you. I knew you had a good reason for whatever was going on and *I was right*. I'm proud of you for what you did. You saved Khail."

"But I could have taken your place and saved you both," she whispered.

I shook my head. "No, you couldn't have. We both know you tried. And if you knew it was me you probably would have lied worse, not better." She mustered up a teary smile at that. "I had someone else to save me. Khail needed you and I'm glad you did it."

"Really?"

"Yeah."

She nodded uncertainly.

"Oh," I said, remembering the last thing. I pulled a small scrap of paper from my pocket. "This is for Khail."

She took it and read my scrawly writing followed by a phone number. "Preston? Khail's friend who moved a couple years ago?"

I nodded, then held my breath.

"Should I tell Khail to . . . call him?" she asked, confused.

She doesn't know. Not even his sister. His best friend. "Just give it to him," I said, my voice wobbly. "He'll know what it's for."

"Okay," she said, her thumb idly stroking the sticker on the shoe box. She looked up at me; then her eyes flitted to something over my left shoulder.

To Kimberlee.

Sera blinked and shook her head before turning her puzzled expression back to me. "That was weird. For just a second I thought I saw . . ."

"We'll talk tomorrow, okay?" I said, squeezing her hand before she could try to finish her statement. I leaned a little closer and whispered, "I love you."

"I love you, too." Then the door closed between us.

I exhaled slowly, trying to calm my racing heart. I turned around and faced Kimberlee.

She was still staring at the door, but a hint of a smile lifted the corners of her mouth. "Thank you," she whispered. "Thank you so much."

Kimberlee and I lay on my bed, head-to-head, for a long time that night. Streetlights slanted through my blinds and laid stripes across her face. "How long have you had Preston's number?" I asked.

"Almost a year. When I realized how fast I could travel as a ghost I spent about a month tracking him down. Seriously took ages. His parents did *not* want those two together again. I hoped maybe doing that would help me move on. But then I couldn't tell anyone the number, so it was totally pointless."

"But it was a good thing to do. See, there is goodness in you somewhere," I said with a grin.

"Jerk," Kimberlee said, but she was smiling.

"That's me," I said, stretching my arms out to both sides.

"He still hates me," Kimberlee said after a moment.

I lifted my head and looked her in the eye. "Did you have *anything* to do with Preston's parents finding out about him?"

She met my eyes, her gaze steady. "No." She laughed bitterly. "It's the one thing I *didn't* do."

"Then it's not your problem."

"It feels like a problem."

"Oh, it is a problem—it's just not *your* problem. And after tonight, I think you've done what you can."

"Are you sure?"

I chuckled. "I'm not sure about anything." We both laughed quietly in the darkness until a comfortable silence settled over us. For several minutes neither of us spoke.

Then Kimberlee asked, "You don't believe in God, right?"

I shook my head.

"Why not?"

"Well, maybe there's a god; maybe there isn't. I just don't know. My parents didn't teach me to believe in God. Maybe if they had, I would."

"What *do* you believe in?"

"What do you mean?"

"Do you believe in karma, or reincarnation, or some greater good, or something?"

"I don't know. I guess I believe in karma to some degree. I believe that if you try to put something good into the world, the world will try to give something good back to you. I believe in balance."

"Balance." Kimberlee echoed the word almost mournfully.

"But I believe in learning to be better, too." I stared up at the dark ceiling. "I believe in family; I believe in relationships. I guess ultimately, I believe in people."

"People like me?"

"People like everyone."

"What about bad apples?"

"You're not a bad apple."

"Let's say Hitler."

I grinned. "Okay, he was a bad apple."

"So what was waiting for him when he died?"

I didn't have an answer for her. Until I met Kimberlee, I'd doubted there was an afterlife at all. I believed like my mom did—that you should live every moment of life to the fullest because when it was over, it was over. I chose my words carefully, trying to decide what I thought even as I said it. "Maybe it's like Newton's law: 'For every action there is an equal and opposite reaction.'"

"How do you mean?"

"Well, I think there have to be consequences. But that doesn't mean I believe in hell with fiery whips or anything. I think maybe sticking around as a ghost is your punishment." I rolled over to face her. "Maybe not even really a *punishment*, but a chance for you to learn without the distraction of being alive." I studied her face in the darkness. "You *have* learned something, haven't you?"

She smiled and nodded. "I have." But the smile slipped from her face almost as quickly as it had appeared. "I just worry that it isn't enough. Do you remember what you said to me on Tuesday?"

My lips pursed into a thin line. "I said a lot of things on Tuesday."

"Yeah, you did. And I'm glad. I needed to hear them." She flipped onto her back. "Before you left to screw Sera's brains out—"

"Hey!"

"Sorry, that wasn't the point. Before you went to make up with Sera, you told me I was still here because no one in the universe wanted me."

343

"I shouldn't have said that."

"No, you should have, because I think maybe you were right. I've learned a lot of things from you, Jeff, but the things I've learned—" Her voice cracked as tears leaked into her hair and her breath came in ragged gasps. "They hurt, Jeff. It's hard—so damn hard—to see myself for what I was. And I'm afraid—" She paused to take another breath before continuing in a quiet voice. "I'm afraid of how hard the next lesson is going to be."

Then I did something I'd been afraid to do since meeting her. I stretched an arm out and pushed it through her back—as if she were lying against my shoulder. My arm filled with a creepy tingle and I wanted to yank it back, but as she sighed and moved her head a little closer, I forced myself to hold still.

"I'm glad I met you," I said. And I wasn't actually sure whether or not it was a lie until I said it out loud.

"Me too."

We lay there in silence for what felt like hours.

I don't know when I finally got comfortable enough to close my eyes, but the next thing I remembered was my alarm screeching at me. I looked over, but Kimberlee had gone. I sat up and tried to stretch the kinks out of my arms. My whole spine was sore and the popping was audible as I turned this way and that.

I froze when my eyes settled on the blue flip-flops sitting

on the floor at the end of the bed. "Kim?" I whispered. I was waiting for her to pop out from the closet or something. "Kim?" I called a little louder. I stretched my foot out and hesitantly poked the nearest shoe with my toe.

And felt something solid.

I leaped onto my bed and curled my feet underneath me.

"That's not funny," I said once my breathing was under control.

I sat there for a full minute, staring at those shoes. Then carefully, I slipped off the bed and crouched beside them. I tentatively reached out a finger and touched one.

It was real.

I picked them up and studied them from every angle. Just a pair of slightly scuffed, pale blue flip-flops.

I never saw Kimberlee again.

Acknowledgments

This novel requires so much thanking. It's the book that almost wasn't and would continue to *not be* without the help of an embarrassingly large number of people and six and a half years. Thanks always go first and foremost to my editors and agent, Tara Weikum, Erica Sussman, and Jodi Reamer. This book is so different, so quirky, and I've never fought any of you so hard to keep it that way. Thank you for your never-ending patience with me.

Eternal thanks to Miss Snark, who gave me the encouragement I needed back in 2006 to go beyond chapter one. To my sister, Kara, with whom I nervously shared the first five chapters when I wasn't sure I was ready to share it at all, because it contained so much of me. The real me. To fellow (but much more veteran) author William Bernhardt, whose workshop I grudgingly went into only to come out a changed writer. Bill, thanks for helping me make this book grow a plot. And to Saundra, who reminded me that Jeff was supposed to be the good guy. But not exactly in those words.

And the biggest thank-you, always, to Kenny, who never stopped telling me this book was the best thing I'd ever written. If no one ever thinks the same except you, I'll still believe you're right.